BLOODBUSTERS

FRANCESCO VERSO

TRANSLATED BY SALLY MCCORRY

Luna Press

PUBLISHING

Text Copyright © 2020 Francesco Verso
Cover Design Guido Salto © 2020
First published in Italy by Urania-Mondadori, nr. 1624, November 2015
Translated by Sally McCorry
First published in English by Luna Press Publishing, Edinburgh, 2020

www.lunapresspublishing.com
ISBN-13: 978-1-911143-97-0

Acknowledgement

This novel owes much to the editing carried out together with Giammarco Raponi. It was made stronger by the observations of Davide Lisino. It has benefited from the advice of Francesco Mantovani, and received valuable help from Riccardo Grecco.

Contents

I'll say it now to stop any preconceived ideas before they take hold: this is not a story about blood. Blood comes into it, but not for the reasons you might imagine. In short, appearances are deceptive.

Blood evasion

Rule number one: The heart is an organ that pumps blood, not emotions.

I tighten the strap around my arm and it digs into the skin. I'm dripping sweat, bent in two on the sofa. I hit the muscle twice with my fist and open the nickel-plated box. Inside is my Pravaz, my beautiful shiny chrome hypodermic. I take it out and choose a medium-sized needle, I don't want to hit the same tired old vein that doesn't cooperate anymore.

I scrabble about amongst the gadgets strewn over the table looking for the iPod remote control and touch the PLAY button. The first song on the play list is The Specials with "A message to you, Rudy".

I like the way the rounded edges of the grip fit into my hand, it feels like an extension of my arm. In comparison all those single-use plastic syringes, including the latest silicon models with their Quick-Fit hook/unhook needle bayonet systems, are no more than toys, cheap disposable rubbish, a sign of our lazy and comfortable times.

Another scrabbling hunt, another remote found and I attempt to switch the air-conditioning on. Again and again. Nothing. I get up and thump it, but it wants to have nothing to do with cooling the thick hot air. It doesn't work and I've found out in the worst way possible, on a suffocatingly hot day, my back wet with sweat and beads of perspiration dripping into my eyes. I give up.

I grab a 450ml plastic bag from the coffee-table drawer. Liquid gold, so to speak. A guarantee of happiness, satisfaction in the safe.

I'm ready to stick the needle in. I'm ready to go.

I glance upwards to the living room ceiling and the poster of Mexico up there seems to be taking the piss. When we visited Tulum, Cecilia and I were a couple worthy of the term, but now we hardly even remember to send each other the odd text message.

I shake the syringe and flick the barrel twice. If I had Cecilia here with me now, I'd shoot with her, not the needle. Still, I'm not going to moan about how things went... We split up, I came to terms with it, and it was better that way. No fighting, no troubles, no regrets.

I drive the needle into my arm gently, the hole makes a reddish shadow on my skin which looks like a bruise, or better still, the type of bastard boil that occasionally appears where the sun don't shine... You get the picture. Don't tell me you don't know what I'm talking about.

It's funny how some ideas lead on one from the other and distract you. Years ago I used to stare at my arm while I drew blood, but now that it's all become one single automatic gesture, I prefer to concentrate on the barrel of the syringe. People with experience know that this is where the good stuff is going on.

Take my word for it: I'm an expert on puncture holes. Those that care about us call us *punchers*... Come to think of it, so do those who, deep down, envy us, hate us, and see us as a sign of how the system is degenerating.

Degenerating huh!... It's not our fault if things are going downhill, is it? I pull back the plunger slowly, watching the ridged end sliding up the glass cylinder. As soon as I finish withdrawing the first bagful I feel weak and drained like after running, like after a breakneck speed chase... Who needs to trip when you can have this end-of-the-world rush of ecstasy and excitement? Despite appearances what I'm doing is simply a precaution: certain sayings never go out of fashion "a syringe every thirtieth day, keeps the taxman at bay."

And anyway, I hardly feel the prick on my arm, anymore.

I throw myself against the backrest, but I already know that I'll have to suck out another bagful if I don't want to run any risks at the end of the year. The principle is simple: you give up something small every now and then to get something big back in exchange.

For me it's clear, but try explaining things like that to Cecilia... Despite all the blood I drained to help her meet her haematic rates to cover the plastic surgery procedures on her cheekbones, breast rejuvenation and thigh sculpting, she said she couldn't stand coming second place to my work.

She said there were lots of different types of betrayal and being a workaholic was one of them, she said it was just as bad as sleeping around. She couldn't think straight sometimes, but in the end she was right. Okay, she was too inflexible and I would never have let her get pregnant while things were like that, coming home (her home) to a scolding about what I *hadn't* done, and where I *hadn't* been. That wasn't my idea of family life. It just made me happier to go to work, even to a job like mine.

As soon as Ceci figured it out, I couldn't see her for dust. One morning while we were having breakfast at Tornatora's she dumped me; you know what some women are like, they suffer in silence until they can't stand it anymore and throw a new reality in your face, changed and transformed forever. Without hesitation, without remorse. One moment I was sipping a *macchiato*, the next her ring was balanced on the plate of croissants.

At least Ceci used her contacts in real estate to find me a place at the top of the Silos Aureliano building. She didn't come herself; she just gave me the heads-up.

I leave the needle in my vein while I change the bag.

The level of juice in the bag increases rapidly, I can feel it growing heavy in my hand; and it's like my energy is being transferred wholesale, leaving my body proportionately weaker.

I pull back the plunger again and fill up the barrel. Then I remove the needle and put my *Old Faithful* back in its box. The magic potion is ready to be sent off and kept safe in the blood bank in Viale XX Settembre. This is the sixth bag this year, a net weight of nearly three litres of blood. In absolute terms it might not count much, but it is safe blood, blood of my blood, and it can be subtracted from my yearly contribution.

In any case, not to put too fine a point on it, I like to put a bit of liquidity aside for a rainy day. The signs have been the same for a while now, like heavy clouds immobile and darkly glowering. I have never had much faith in insurance policies and even less in haematic prevention plans. If ever a door to door seller knocks at my door the first thing I do is show them my Haematax Collector's badge. That makes them step back and stops them in their tracks with their "possible complications with conformity to regulations for admitting patients to hospital" bullshit. It stops them worrying at it like a dog with a bone like they do with poor old Ilario because they know about his sister Mirna, pushing those diabolic yearly policies where the client is guaranteed a flow of sure blood and, if during the year they or a member of their family use a certain amount of blood, the company will reimburse the rate paid in.

They don't dare play stupid with me, but they know that Mirna is a haemophiliac.

I keep a tight hold on my blood.

While I'm drying my hands in the bathroom, a *haemergency* call makes my smartphone ring.

I curse anyone who works on Saturdays although I already know it can only be my two partners. "Hey, Alan? It's Ilario, you better get here quick..."

"What have you done this time?"

It's a video call and I can see him so I already have an idea. His face is a mess of half-dried blood sprays that are even dripping from his hair which is no longer blonde but more a kind of copper red.

"Listen, don't get angry but... this woman isn't *withdrawable*. Another drop and, she'll be dried out."

At this point, I'd better introduce myself: my name is Alan Costa and I run a team of blood collectors called BloodBusters, we are phlebotomists and scarifier for the Ematogen Company owned by Emory Szilagyi. Business is good in the sense that every month I can pay my mortgage without anyone coming to suck *my* blood.

"Shit, Ilario... Where are you?"

"We nicked her at her friend's house. *He* got away as soon as we got here, must have seen us coming from the window, but she couldn't move because *she* was still all tubed up. That motherfucker left her here alone... We're at Laurentino 38, that's 107 Via Ignazio Silone, on the tenth floor, above the social centre. Quick, Alan hurry... It's looking bad."

Right, 'cos I'm having the time of my life with three litres less blood in circulation. All I can do is make the best of a bad situation, so I take a double dose of Haematogen, relishing the revitalising bites of the bars. Milk flavoured. My favourites.

"Okay, I'm coming... but stop dawdling, you two. At least clean the room up a bit and for fuck's sake clean yourselves up too."

*

When I get to the blood withdrawal scene I find Ilario and that other shit brains Farid, both covered in blood and other liquids that I'd rather not mention, they look like two mosquitoes after a free meal.

"*As-salamu alaikum, yakhi.*"

Farid, wearing a black fez and a flowery waistcoat with his usual impeccable air of the bully, is leaning against the wall.

"Amen! How many times do I have to tell you not to wear that shit over your uniform. It looks wrong dammit..."

He snorts and from the headphones around his neck I can hear "Muhammad My Friend" by Tori Amos: while we're working he must listen to it at least twenty times a day.

Ilario is licking the cigarette he has just finished rolling.

"Ah, there you are... You look like you haven't slept..."

"Thanks to you. Come on, tell me, where is she is and what's her name?"

My colleague lights his roll up, wipes his filthy hands on his trousers and points to the room opposite. My nostrils flare and twitch with the buzz of the smell. It's hardly surprising seeing as it looks there's been a bullfight in here.

"Anissa Malesano, 37, and she's an illustrator."

I can smell the stink of blood and skin in the air. To be more precise I can smell skin riddled with holes. I slip on a pair of surgical rubber gloves, the type you'll have used yourself countless times, but I bet you've never had to make a forced blood withdrawal from someone who refuses to let you near them with a needle.

"She's calmed down now, but you should have seen her before... She's a tough one Alan."

Ilario's hair is weird, he has this blonde tuft that bobs over his forehead looking like a ridiculous hat. Farid's eyes are hooded under thick eyebrows; he is staying at a safe distance and cleaning his nails with a syringe needle.

Emory is always giving me these losers. They don't take anything seriously. Some are goofs who have no idea how to look after themselves. Fortunately, they're the ones who disappear first, who don't even last a month. Some of them leave after just three days of *haematax collecting*. Not Ilario though, he's good. He usually knows what he's doing, especially with men. Let's say he knows how to walk in their shoes.

It has only taken him six months to go from being a harmless level one *Mosquito* to behaving like a seasoned *Bloodsucker*. Whatever, in my eyes, he's still a "bloodfucker".

If you saw him in action, you'd be impressed by the countless ways he invents for distracting tax evaders He chats to them smoothly, a bit of a wink and a nudge, putting them off their guard with football stories or whatever shit it takes to make them pull their sleeves up.

He must have messed up with this Anissa though. What I can see of her from the bedroom doorway isn't a pretty sight, to be more honest she's in a right state. There are monstrous bloody marks all over the place. The floor is scattered with smashed phials, cotton wool pads, gauze soaked in disinfectant, coloured butterfly valves, half-bent single-use syringes, shattered graduated pipettes, finger-prick lancets, probes and Luer adaptors: all the components of a BloodBuster's kit in fact.

"What are you pulling that face for, Alan? Are you allergic to a bit of anaemic hotty?"

"Shut up, look at the mess you and that other syringe happy

maniac have made."

The girl is only semi-conscious, her palms facing upwards, eyelids flickering up and down. There are bandages hanging off her wrists, trailing right down to her feet, and the dark circles around her eyes are not makeup.

"And what do you know? Maybe that's how you act with the girls. First you play it hard, then you lose it 'cos you're scared they might end up taking the piss. I was saying before to Farid that sometimes it's better not to..."

"I told you to shut up... You're getting ahead of yourself and that's not what we do. We're blood hunters, not third-rate doctors."

Anissa has been thrown into an armchair with one leg over the armrest and the other askew. Her arms are wide open like a sacrificial virgin, her flesh has the same texture as rubber, and she is covered with finger marks left by Ilario and Farid.

"How much were you supposed to take?"

He acts all offended and throws the injunction in my face; then he points to the few remaining phials they managed to save from the fight.

"She's up for total tax evasion. She fought us...you'd have thought we were trying to rape her."

Her eyes are only open a slit but I can see they're full to overflowing with blood. She is wearing a green sleeveless tracksuit, her bare arms are covered in track marks, violet lines and blue circles, the decoration caused by self-inflicted haematic withdrawals.

"You two never get it right... I'm not asking much, but, I mean didn't you notice that she's a donor? Those aren't *our* holes. Shit, did you at least check the butterfly valves before starting?"

Farid sticks his head round the door. As far as he's concerned *butterflies* are things that fly away on the breeze. Fortunately, Ilario has realised the danger we're in.

In this job you learn to smell a failure a mile off. The worst kind are those who think they know it all. Farid, for instance, needs to be reminded of things so often that I've worn my tongue out. He's been heavy handed from his first day, he'd skin anyone and everyone at the drop of a syringe, and instead of learning by watching his more experienced colleagues he's going to end up driving away a good worker like Ilario.

Anissa isn't paying any attention, she has turned her head the other way, on purpose, as if she wants to ignore us.

"Idiots…what about her haematic contribution records? What d'you want to bet she's 0 RH negative?"

Ilario rummages through the documents in the file and says nothing. Maybe I was a bit hasty when I promoted him to the level of Bloodsucker so quickly. Farid, on the other hand, can't stop being a clever dick. He'll never be promoted to the same level, however good *he* thinks he is.

"What, do you think she's in with the Robin Blood lot?"

"Exactly, bloodfucker… Didn't you notice her pale face and straw-coloured blood? She *donates* blood, that's why she doesn't have any more for the Intravenous Revenue. Look here, three hospital admittances in a year. She nearly died twice. What's the point of having records if you don't bother to read them?"

I tear off the tape that my colleagues have stuck over her mouth to shut her up. Then I loosen the haemostatic band from around her neck. It sags like jelly.

It's as if bad circulation has hardened her character. This pin-up is rigid and angry. Her cubital and cephalic veins have collapsed due to lack of blood pressure and the veins in her wrists and feet are like an estuary in a drought. Anissa Malesano, who is now fully comatose, can still hear us and curls her lip, sardonically.

I glance towards the window. I can see the G.R.A. ring-road in the distance, and then something, like a hiss getting sharper all the time, tells me to watch out. This vague warning turns into a slap in the face and I realise I've got no choice.

"Get away from the window!"

I just manage to yell out before a huge 10 kilo snowball smashes through the window shattering the glass completely. What the fuck? Snow? In Rome? In June?

I put both hands on Ilario's chest and push him away. Then I fling myself out of the room as a shadow lands on the floor. Farid uses the mirror in the kit to find out what's going on.

"Give it to me!"

I grab it out of his hand and in the reflection I can see a figure in paramilitary clothes lifting Anissa up over its back and leaping out through the window. This is when I put my head round the door and wave the injunction about.

"Stop! You're aiding and abetting a tax evader, that's punishable by law with a forced withdrawal!"

"Fuck the Law! Withdraw this!"

The figure giving me the bird is a woman and she's built like a house, a sort of Scandinavian Brunhilda. Her hair is a mass of golden braids and her gaze is as *sharp* as a 20 gauge needle.

"Robin Blood sends its greetings..."

With that she throws a phial on the floor which releases a light-blue cloud that stinks worse than an ancient Roman urinal. It's poisonous blood, bad blood, tax evader's blood. Tears come to our eyes.

With a nail gun, Brunhilda shoots a mountaineering bolt into the building's outer wall and throws herself into the thirty metre void. As soon as I reach the windowsill I can see her playing out the webbing tied wound around her waist like a spool of thread. After spinning for a bit she lands with ease on the road, nearby a pick-up truck with "Ovindoli Magnola ski slopes" emblazoned in red along the side and a snowball shooter in the back is waiting for them with the side down.

The only thing missing are singing dwarves, elephants in carriages and trained falcons and the Robin Blood circus would be complete.

"Shit... It always ends up like this, ancient Italian culture in pieces and we get a show from the losers and hot-heads."

As if this humiliation weren't enough, it starts raining and the drops splashing off the windowsill start playing a squalid oriental karaoke tune. My bile starts rising like nobody's business...

"Bloody hell... Dead, dead cool, man. Did you see what that Wonder Woman did?

"Cool? It's totally embarrassing. Ilario, they just totally fucked us over. Come on; get a move on and clear up instead of standing around staring. I'm in no mood for putting up with the squeaking of those grey-uniformed rats.

"Do you think we give a fuck? Let's get out of here... The Robin Bloods made this mess, not us."

"A mess like this? Listen up, both of you, don't start fucking with me. Get it into your thick skulls we are BloodBusters not louts from Haemocalypse Now."

Farid won't move from the windowsill.

"The pick-up's turning onto the Laurentina."

Even he is a bit worked up, and the most he ever does is pick his nose or scratch wax from his ears to vent his anger.

"If we hurry we could catch them, couldn't we, boss?"

I give one of his jug ears a flick. Him, a promotion? Oh yeah, why not? When Cardinals volunteer to deposit blood at the Revenue offices...

The life of a BloodBuster isn't exactly a piece of cake.

"We've got her address. I'm going to pay that Anissa a little visit."

Life transfusion

Rule number two: Not everywhere there's blood, there's a corpse;
but where there's a corpse, there's blood.

"Oh crap!"

The outside car park of Silos Aureliano has become an open
air latrine. Hundreds of pigeons have taken turns to bombard the
whole area, and my taxbulance has not escaped the raid.

It takes me five minutes to get the door looking decent and
get in before another storm passes over. On board the taxbulance
I check the state of the week's withdrawals.

The refrigerated section is on and though the temperature
outside is 39°C, inside the van the blood bags are being kept
at a cool 4°C. All the sweat and stickiness of the night dries on
me within a few seconds. Despite all the installations, repairs
and urgent summer call-outs I've finally managed to fix an
appointment with the air conditioning people in the next
couple of weeks, if I last that long... I tried elsewhere, with other
companies, but if you haven't been their client for generations
you've got no chance.

At this point it'd be worth stretching out on the taxbulance
z-bed-chair instead of tossing and turning in my mini-apartment
at the top of Silos Aureliano: the few extra metres are costing me
160 monthly instalments of 900 Euros.

As well as blood the bags contain a concoction of citric acid,
sodium citrate, dextrose and monosodium phosphate, which act
as anticoagulants. Don't ask me if it's true, I just read the labels.
Whatever. In Emory I trust.

The bags are kept upright and must be handled with care
and not moved around too much, otherwise they start foaming,

developing air bubbles, or worse still they go into a state of haemolysis, and that's bad, it would mean throwing the whole lot, blood, plasma, and all the rest, away. With all these precautions the tax payers' blood keeps for up to 50 days, not like in my day when you risked dying on the battlefield for a simple cut. Some of my comrades, like old Marzio Poleni the "Gladiator" and Giancarlo "Jajo" Soldini, just to mention a couple of names, didn't half talk shit, they reckoned dying from blood loss was the best sort of death, because you lose consciousness and don't feel any more pain.

I don't know. They don't know either. I only know they stuck a needle in my vein just in time to stop me donating my blood to the Creator of all Worlds.

Leaving the Silos block I take the Aurelia ring road to Piazza Irnerio and then turn into the Olimpica, where the traffic jam starts, that eternal and unchanging colourful serpent, 2000 years in the making, a contender for any city-congestion competition in Italy and maybe the world over.

Nothing doing, in Rome you always travel at the same speed, whether you're carrying tourists in a horse-drawn carriage, showing off in a Ferrari or driving a taxbulance with the siren screaming. The traffic island is punctuated by hundreds of advertising billboards, but my attention is drawn to the poster of Lucio Sergio Catapano, MP for the PPRR (Popular Party of Responsible Reformists), who, for one reason or another, has been evading us for three years. People like him don't want to know about our rules and regulations. They come up with new ways of avoiding paying their haemataxes every day. They act as if their blood is better than ours... One of these days, sooner or later, we'll get an aspirator stuck in his vein and turn the suction on full. Emory has spent a fortune on these awareness raising campaigns against high ranking blood dodgers.

On the poster, Catapano is sucking on a cocktail with a straw by the side of a swimming pool and his huge, happy, haughty face has phosphorescent writing across it which is visible even at night:

DODGER, YOUR DAYS ARE NUMBERED!

The traffic is slow and restless and takes my thoughts back to when I had to crawl in a similar way, shuffling along to cover less than a kilometre. In those days I wore a uniform, but instead of *withdrawing* something I had to *deposit* mines in enemy territory. When I fixed my documents to add a few years to my age so I could trick the military personnel in Viale delle Milizie and enlist in the army, there was no way I could have known I would be assigned such a terrible job.

I had left the technical college a month before. I had no idea what I wanted to do and at the time there was no way of getting me behind a desk to study, but I wasn't allergic to hard work like the other students. Maybe I was just at a loose end. Whatever, in one sense all I did was bring forward the date when they would have called me up for military service.

I was a *miner* in the literal sense of the word; in the sense that I had to bury explosive pizzas under a layer of earth so that they were invisible. *They* were invisible, and *I* was expendable. It was not something that was generally known about, it was considered inhumane. We were supposed to be marking a perimeter, even though it wasn't our territory.

I used to feel like one of those cripples in the olden days that were thrown from the Tarpeian rock to see whether they would survive. There were probably people who bet on our dubious fates just to make a few Euros.

Four blokes had already gone before me and not returned to tell the tale over a meal in the canteen. Only Marzio, the *Gladiator*, had made it back, and he came back without his legs.

Instead of the coolness I now enjoy in the taxbulance, all I could do then was sweat; I sweated in the protective padding of my uniform, I sweated under my vest, I even sweated in my socks and underpants. Under the unbearable heat of the Middle-Eastern sun even my blood seemed to sweat in my veins.

To cut a long story short, when I got to the chosen location, I began to realise how thirsty I was. A raging thirst, dominating sense and reason. I hadn't had anything to drink since dawn, ten hours earlier. Thirst isn't something you can control, thirst is a bastard tax tormenting you more than hunger and you can't even pretend to ignore it because it devours your brain and drives you right down into delirium.

Imagine a case of notorious away-from home diarrhoea, add crawling across the ground from wall to wall, then the insufferable heat that had dried up my liquids and leached me of minerals, then you'll have an idea of the state I was in.

If I had made a wrong move while looking for water in the surrounding area, a shower of bullets would have rained down on me. Whichever way I turned my parched mouth there were shuddering shadows that looked like enemies.

Enemies everywhere, like those hangers-on who are driving right behind me now and pull up next to me at the traffic lights on the Gianicolense bypass with their armoured vehicles at half the length of a little finger away.

I blast these motorised lice, stuck to me closer than the shadow of my own arse, with the Stones, *Sympathy for the Devil*, just to remind them who they should have sympathy for and, as soon as they realise that I'm in a taxbulance, they start feigning nonchalance, tapping their fingers on the steering wheel, staring the other way and pretending to be intent on the beat...

When the lights turn green they don't dare overtake anymore, they've all become considerate drivers and good Samaritans.

Then I remember the Mosque steps, demolished by dozens of cluster explosives, and the transparent outline of a bottle. A light-blue plastic bottle that I had thought might just be a hallucination brought on by dehydration.

I checked the perimeter, even though my thirst wouldn't let me concentrate. The area scan was negative. At times like these and I know I'm not wrong, water is worth as much as blood. You can't do without either during a battle without suffering for it.

I was a *false* eighteen-year-old and if I had asked to jack in the mission because "I was dying for a drink", they would've given me a kicking and then I'd have been crossed off the list without so much as a second thought. If they had said "Yes", the best-case scenario was that Emory would have had me cleaning latrines for the rest of my sorry life. Not exactly good prospects for surviving in the army.

So, I crawled to the first of the Mosque steps like any other thirsty animal would draw near a watering hole. I reached out and took the bottle which someone must have left there by mistake. Unfortunately, that someone had just remembered about it when I started tipping the water down my throat.

A *thud* sounded on the sternum of my bullet-proof jacket. Then another *thud* exploded in my right leg.

I dropped the half empty bottle and it landed standing upright. I'd got my water, but now I was losing blood.

I didn't have time to ask myself if that bottle in full-view on the stairs had been a clever trap or a senseless trick of fate.

All I knew was that the gash on my thigh had reached the femoral artery and I had about three minutes at the most before I could kiss my life goodbye. If I had had my throat slit it would have been less than fifteen seconds. I know this because Emory has taught me well. He was the one who made me a BloodBuster.

Near Ponte Bianco, I head down the ramp leading to Via Portuense. The Ematogen depot was built in an abandoned wing of the San Camillo Hospital.

I park the taxbulance in an area full of other vehicles like mine and climb out with the blood transporter case in my hand. We use the MT67F model, a neat polyethylene container that only weighs 600g when empty and can store twenty-four 450 ml doses for over 120 hours.

The container is like a piece of Tupperware with four flaps on the lid that clip it shut with an airtight seal. The base is flexible and acts as a kind of shock absorber. The plastic is tough, resists cuts, and it appears to reseal light cuts and scratches. Another thing to remember is the fact that if you rip off the lid the MT67F turns into a kind of bloody hand grenade, and when it's empty it can be a shield against blades of all kinds.

Not even He-Ho-Fook, master of martial arts and a member of the West Rome squad led by Sawn-off, has ever managed to break or damage one. Nothing, not with his hands or feet. He-Ho-Fook is always saying this thing to make fun of us, he says, "every single part of my body is a weapon, your bodies are just bags full of organs." His body might well be a lethal weapon, but the MT67F beats him hands down, him and his hair that looks like it's been oiled with paper that used to be wrapped around a piece of pizza.

In the shade of a palm tree the Gladiator Marzio Poleni strokes his beard, eyes resting on my liquid treasure. He half smiles at me, giving me a flash of his metal teeth, another price he paid for surviving the front. The BloodBusters who report to him, Jajo, Swamp Bird and "Lazybones", the small bloke from Mazzara del Vallo, have no scruples about passing animal blood off as human and sticking their needles where they have no right to; thank fuck that when Emory catches them out you can hear his yells all the way to the Portuensi Hills.

Not that I really give a shit from a professional point of view, but as a customer you would notice if the blood wasn't human. You can add all the chemical additives you want, blood doesn't lie. Anyway when it comes down to it, we at the Withdrawals Agency have a small incentive on the total invoiced amount, an annual production premium on the collected sum, so I don't find it difficult to side with Emory on this.

As far as me and my team are concerned, we keep a strictly low profile and prefer to use patrols and spies, like the gypsies who scour the city areas, or the tramps who have their ears permanently open, for catching the juiciest tip-offs.

Standing out against the depot garage I can see the hunched figure of Emory Szilagyi welcoming me with open arms into the Ematogen Headquarters. Actually it is just the back of the Withdrawals Agency, where taxes are paid without fuss, in alphabetical order, by appointment and with a soft-drink in one hand and a magazine in the other.

He's wearing the same identical camouflage fatigues as when he was fighting in the Balkans and then later, with our lot in the Middle East, the difference is this war isn't military, it's commercial.

Another slice of memory surfaces in my mind. Nearly two agonising minutes had passed when some grains of dust and

16

sand started falling against my cheek. I felt terror rising up in my throat like a lump of saliva. What was left of my bodily salts were encrusted around my eyes, at the corners of my mouth and on my forehead. Then, the searing hot barrel of the rifle slid into my right nostril. My breath came in short sharp, fast gasps. To make things worse, the more my heart pumped blood, the more I left of it on the ground for free.

On the other end of the rifle was a kid girl, not more than ten or eleven at the most. She was wearing a transparent veil in front of her mouth, but she had no *chador*, *hejab* or other head covering. She tried a tentative half-smile, her two front teeth were missing. The tip of the barrel stank of wood, leather and goat. She must have used it for hundreds of other things over the course of the day. She was too small to be loaded down like that with a contraption almost as big as her.

In less than a second I was hyperventilating and starving for air. It's dead, dead common for us BloodBusters to see this during our work: technically it's called "respiratory alkalosis" and it's a symptom of fear which makes the carbon dioxide levels in your blood shoot up, transforming it from an acid to an alkaline solution. Chemistry lessons apart, it's no laughing matter...

She grabbed *her* bottle and out of modesty, turned away to lift up her veil and drink. She fell to the ground instantly, hit by a bullet between her shoulder blades.

The roaring of a Jeep's engine came closer and soon afterwards Emory's shadow fell over me, pulling me to safety. He was the area medic, but his job was not that of a normal doctor. In wartime soldiers are not treated so they can be healed, but so that they can be sent back into action as soon as possible. The last thing I remember before losing consciousness was hearing Pink Floyd's *Goodbye Blue Sky* floating from the Jeep's radio.

"How's this week gone, Alan?"

His curved cucumber nose makes him look like a gargoyle, one of those dirty, creepy monsters that enjoy scrutinising the world from above with their own sly reasons for existing, an opportunist in many senses. Opportunist because today, as in the past, his mission is not very orthodox, and that's putting it mildly.

I believe in the Bible, the BloodBusters Manual, made up of haematology lessons, a phlebotomy training course, principles of tax law, and then a sprinkling of political economics and by Emory's explicit request, a pinch of Eastern philosophy, but I have to admit that seen by an outsider it might easily seem a cynical and radical way to treat taxpayers.

Each drop of blood deposited is delivered to our dear old Emory who sits there waiting for it, eagerly rubbing his hands together. I, like the good blood collector I am his vassal and hand in the war booty, a rich tribute of blood and plasma, over the depot counter to pay one more mortgage instalment. The way things are going I'll soon have a CV that looks like a medieval warlord's.

"We collected 95% of the outstanding payments, but in one case we had problems."

"What problems?"

"Anissa Malesano, total tax evasion, no declaration made. A Robin Blood cell got her away from us. We only managed to withdraw 20% of what was due."

Emory stares at me in silence, a calculating silence. The stainless steel frames of his glasses are wrapped around his skull like a surgical instrument. I know that pitying look well, or rather that type of professional disappointment, the attitude of someone who doesn't know how to explain or come to terms with even the smallest of failures.

He shakes his head this way and that disparagingly. I swear I'm off now if he starts spouting nonsense about advanced withdrawal techniques, or starts waving even just one finger in my face and starts pontificating.

"Show me her haematic contribution records."

His voice grates like he's snoring even while he's awake.

"She's a compulsive donor. That's why the Robin Bloods took her. Maybe she's one of them too, she certainly had some strange marks on her."

I pass him the report and, after having given it a cursory look, Emory squeezes the bags and weighs one in his hand at random.

Then he checks carefully for clots, bubbles or other complications.

The pained expression in his eyes caused by the missing repayment is the same with which Emory watched me being wounded. He only stepped-in when the target came out of hiding. I've never asked him if he would have risked his life to save mine. I've never asked him what would have happened if the girl had stayed in her hiding place, and I have never dared ask him if he ever came to see exactly what a bloody fool I had been about that bottle of water. On the ground, flat out instead of me, lay the girl with the rifle around her neck. She is no longer there, long dead, long gone, but I go back there in my mind quite a lot, perhaps too much. It's time to feel guilty perhaps. But is the guilt mine or that stupid bottle's?

In the Jeep, Emory fixed me up with a unit of Arteriocyte 0 negative, an extremely expensive treatment that was still being tested. This was followed by five transfusions of natural blood a few hours later. Now, like then, he is still aiding my survival by paying me for every good delivery.

"Taxes, my dear Alan, are like God... Only when an evader is found and punished can he be saved. Ashes to ashes, blood to blood."

Opening one of the bags of blood, Emory dips his finger right in and tastes it. The taste of the blood melting in his mouth should be metallic, rich in haemoglobin. Think about it, gold is a metal and blood transports metal. Doesn't that say anything to you about the economic value of blood? On the other hand placebos and every other false transfusion liquid don't taste of anything. Artificial cells are the same as red blood cells in the sense that they function in the same way, but they are not real blood and they are no good for making Haematogen bars.

Anyway, you can't fool Emory, expert blood sommelier that he is; he can recognise any blood group by its flavour. Some people exaggerate and say that he can see even beyond that and into people's souls because blood is an alchemical liquid which contains other personal information. I'm not just talking about eating habits or illnesses that show up after analysing blood samples, I'm talking about all those activities behind closed doors, dangerous acts, or those illegal substances that if discovered can fry your future prospects to a crisp.

The lads in the laboratory, down in Riva Ostiense by the river, affectionately call him the *HaemoGoblin*.

"I get you; it's just that Anissa is a public donor, and that means my hands are tied. I'd need a court order to flush her out..."

"You'll have one. The Robin Bloods can't be seen to interfere in this business. Even a small, innocent tax violation, can blow up into a large-scale issue. If you break a window and you realise that no one comes to fix it, you will feel justified in breaking all the others."

During my convalescence in hospital Emory spent a long time by my sickbed and explained the details of his plan to me. At the time he already had some contacts high-up in the army so all he had to do was reach out from the Ministry of Defence to the Treasury.

He also told me that as a boy, to cure his iron deficiency, his mother Natasha, a Russian exile in East Germany, would buy him bars of Ferrohaematogen, a sweet medicinal candy made of the blood of slaughtered animals and sugary syrup.

In the Soviet Union it was used to cure anaemia. His mother had it smuggled in with the help of friends of hers who ran a leather-selling business between Istanbul, Dresden and Saratov.

For children there was also a liquid version, a kind of condensed milk syrup enriched with ascorbic acid and honey.

Emory loved it.

At the front his task was to recover the wounded, and in the midst of all that blood going to waste and only if you were lucky being put back into circulation, he realised how much it was worth. He also explained to me how in wartime, the State didn't think twice about requisitioning blood from the population seeing as no one ever died or suffered permanent damage so long as the blood was taken carefully and without exaggeration. The same argument was also used for mothers' milk and sperm if serious social welfare issues were at stake.

When the Treasury issued the first tender for granting blood collecting licences, Emory was at the front of the queue. He had partners, unspecified figures, who had declared their willingness to invest in the project. Artificial blood was too expensive to produce on a large scale, and its commercialisation was a huge financial risk. On the other hand the demand for blood derivatives was growing steadily: the average age of the population was rising and health service spending with it, especially for care of the older members of the population. The number of road accidents caused hospitals to need thousands of haemodoses every month, and plastic surgery operations also required plentiful quantities of fresh blood, not to mention organ transplants and cancer patients.

My father knows something about that and so do I by association. To be admitted to hospital, I mean just to accept him as a patient, the Sant'Andrea Hospital demanded that he provided the blood he would need for his operation, a simple cyst removal.

Like they say: no blood, no party.

Anyway, to cut a long story short, businesses began running ad campaigns in the papers and on the internet, discretely and anonymously, looking for fresh blood to buy (it couldn't be called donation) for a small monetary consideration.

Do you really need me to say the offers poured in?

Then spurred on by this move the State lost no time proposing a law to regulate the sector through the introduction of a "haematax" to avoid the inevitable price speculation on blood derivatives, the spread of infected blood, and any indemnification costs that would weigh heavily on public health spending, further dragging down a service afflicted by inefficiency, holes in the budget, and cutbacks.

Some people saw this proposal as a form of compensation for all they had suffered following political scandals, the tax evasion of sly businessmen, the exodus abroad of the capital of unpunished bankers, and the corruption at all levels that has always afflicted the nation.

The moment was ripe for an example to made. The majority of the population felt it had a common enemy, and nothing unites people like taking a stand against a haematax evader.

Even Catholic dogma has its champion elected by blood sacrifice in Jesus Christ, and even though the AVIS and its volunteers and the Red Cross weren't short of skeletons in the closet, they were totally in agreement with the parliamentary proposal, convinced that it would bring them the blood they had always been short of. How wrong they were. Poor bastards, the haematic sharing regulations assign them an even smaller portion of the blood than they used to collect.

Then there was the population. The familiar if ancient practice of leeching or blood-letting. Initially used as a way of removing an excess of unhealthy humours in the blood it became the "blood tribute" of wartime military conscription, and then mutated to become this haematorial tax, putting into action the old complaint of being "bled dry". Initially the people grumbled, they were cynical and irritated, then when it came to it they queued up at the various Withdrawals Agencies to fulfil their duty as citizens on the day that was renamed the Day of Blood.

In fact the Day of Blood is nothing other than the Tax Returns Day with an added separate section dedicated to haematic withdrawals calculated according to a subject's annual income and body weight.

A portion of the blood paid as tax (about 20% of that deposited) goes towards the PHA (Personal Haematic Allowance) which it is theoretically possible to claim against in the case of hospital admittance, or to donate to family friends for health needs. Another portion (about 30%) covers social obligations like transfusions and blood derivatives. Where the remaining portion (50%) goes is unclear. Some people say it goes to the NBR (National Blood Reserve) which goes towards helping "our lads" on peace missions around the world, other people are convinced it is used for commercial ends, important though less ethically sound, like the production of Haematogen.

It was no surprise then that in Rome as soon as the Withdrawals Agencies started operating, matters that hadn't mattered to ordinary tax collectors until then began to be chased up. On-site withdrawals were carried out on whoever was picked up jumping over the turnstiles at underground stations, aggressive beggars, or anyone caught pissing by the roadside or wiping a dirty chamois leather over a clean windscreen without the driver's consent.

In any case, most Romans were proud, to begin with at any rate, to pay their haemataxes and contribute to the city's health. Blood started flowing in, in quantities that had never been seen before, and that was just the start.

"Tax evaders have to pay the consequences", the most honest and enthusiastic citizens said to themselves. State employees were the strongest supporters of the new taxation measures, a sense of poorly veiled triumph animated their arguments. Private-sector employees, who had been lurching between thousands of taxes and a load of absurd deductions, finally saw some logical practical sense in this form of taxation. The employers, for once, kept their mouths shut and adapted.

Then, slowly, the fear of tax controls began to spread and with it the practice of paying in instalments took hold among the less well-off, while at the same time, amongst the wealthier citizens, there was an increase in the use of tax substitutes in order to avoid the larger withdrawals. Rome has always been a cauldron of cunning and so-what attitudes, of shabby tricks and improvisation. No one has ever tried to deny this. Put it how you want, tax evaders have always and will always exist here. That's why there are BloodBusters.

Emory pulls out his mobile phone, punches out a number and has a brief muttered conversation.

"Your injunction's on its way. Get busy."

You might or might not believe me when I say that there are still a load of people out there who shamelessly claim they are responsible for the care of anaemic people in order to be eligible for tax credits.

There are even people who are convinced that Bobby, Fuffy or Lalla, dogs cats and budgies, are haematax deductible.

Bloody Thursday

*Rule number three: If you have to collect on a debt,
do not think about the debtor.*

With the injunction in my hand I ring Anissa Malesano's doorbell. The files say she lives in Torrino, in a semi-detached, two-floor house.

From the stinky rubbish lying around the doorway I get the impression that she really does live here. Today is obviously not a cleaning day, nor the cleaner's day either. The remains of her breakfast have been left on the table under the pergola. Orange juice, dirty cups, and bars of Haematogen like there's no tomorrow. In the background I can see the outline of a shiny Ducati parked on the path in front of the garage accompanied by a group of garden gnomes.

I can't imagine what Anissa illustrates to have this much money. My mum always said that generally the richest people are the biggest thieves... Maybe that's why she brought me up to be so *mercenary*.

I sent Anissa a text yesterday notifying her of this official visit. She didn't answer so I'm authorised to enter the premises and check that the tax payer is effectively absent.

I climb over the gate and go through the garden. I swipe a plum, bite into it, and pocket a couple of bars of Haematogen as a pick-me-up.

I peep into the living room from the front window, then go around to the back of the house, but I can't see anyone. It breaks my heart but I'm going to have to force a window and break into the house. Okay, I'll admit it, I made up the bit about it breaking my heart. In the distance from the next door villa I can hear the bass riff of Queen's *Under Pressure*.

"Is there anybody there? I'm Alan Costa, from the Withdrawals Agency."

The ground floor is deserted. In the kitchen, the coffee pot is still warm, which tells me something's not right. My nasal mucous membranes are transmitting *that* smell to me, the smell of blood.... I am like a shark. The barbells of a shark can detect one part of blood per million of seawater, well, my nostrils can do that with fresh air.

I sniff my way along the corridor, right down to the end.

"I've got an injunction against Anissa Malesano, is anyone there?"

I go upstairs and open every door. This is the worst part of being a BloodBuster, as if it weren't bad enough intruding into people's veins. People are so unimaginative, all their houses look the same, the same furniture, same objects, sometimes even in the same positions. I feel like I know them all, my taxpayers, down to the smallest detail. It gets worse not better after a while; believe me, when you start seeing everyone as if they are nothing other than potential blood tax dodgers. You look at them under a different light, you look out for track marks on their skin, you check for veined contribution channels and their old haematax scar tissue... and when you find it, it's bad news for them. As a BloodBuster you can't let yourself be fooled by simple cuts, accidental injuries or the occasional wound. In the end this fixation can begin to get you down.

The question that starts nagging at you is always the same: which of your friends really do pay their taxes? Which of them, when it comes down to it, don't have even one haematax hole in their body? It gets to the point, believe me, when you can't sleep for thinking about it.

Every social relationship is coloured by this banal, if you like, but crucial question. Every relationship is sucked into a vortex of suppositions, a chorus of mentally torturous, sometimes even ethical, doubts.

Being the child of a dodger... Going out with friends who are dodgers... Having a mother who only does her blood withdrawals once a month, *that* time of the month... Loving a woman who never gives you a receipt... Being among colleagues who are stones that you'll never get a drop of blood out of... All "cash-in-hand" relationships which, at the very least leave you a bit jaded.

OK, no one is really convinced that this is a perfect tax system, but it is a widespread belief that to make it work all we need to do is believe in it. Taxes, democracy, liberty... Who can possibly doubt they aren't good causes?

Anyway, getting back to the point, I'd like to convince this Anissa to pay up without having to get heavy handed, but from what Ilario told me I'm pretty sure that she won't collaborate. Compulsive donors feel they have the right not to pay blood taxes, but this means their flow of blood is lost revenue for Ematogen.

When I walk into the last room I find Anissa. She is lying on the bed, her eyes are wide open and staring at the ceiling, there's a needle sticking out of her neck. Her cheekbones are even more prominent than the last time I saw her in Laurentino. They look razor-sharp.

Some wonderful, emotionally loaded illustrations are hanging on the walls: BloodBusters *being subjected* to forced withdrawals, and Robin Bloods, who, on the contrary, are carrying out mass blood donation rites. Urban myths. The fantasies of the gullible.

Anissa is as immobile as stone, almost completely exsanguinated. Instead of veins she has one-way roads all pointing out of her body. Her eyes have made her aware of my presence and they have moved almost imperceptibly, though they appear incapable of following my movements as I move closer to the bed. There is a photo of her in a nurse's uniform on her bedside table, she looks sexy.

I click my fingers in front of her face twice, her eyelids don't even flicker.

The blood bag at her side is full and the excess liquid is overflowing and running down her arm, forming a pool in the crook of her elbow, and dripping onto the rug where it is thickening. The parts of her body which should be white, or at least pink like her lips, look blue; her eyelids and knuckles are purple. In other points, she has scraped at her skin to make thick white liquid ooze out. This is a scarification technique that Farid knows well given his jail experience.

Because of the amount of blood she has lost Anissa is about to commit suicide in the name of a hypothetical transfusion patient in need of being saved.

Things are getting complicated. I would have liked to speak to her, but you know, not try it on with her. Well, maybe a just a bit. Someone like her, a follower of the Robin Bloods, could never ever fall in love with a BloodBuster. At most I might get her to want to change me, to make me stop chasing up blood taxes. This is the point though: those who believe in something are always determined to convert you to their cause.

It's time to get stuck in, literally. I open my bag of tricks and get ready for an emergency procedure. I want to play on the nursing instinct that drives her to donate compulsively, because everything about Anissa Malesano has a profound air of the willing martyr.

I pull the wrappings off a Little Prick, fix it to the Pravaz and stick it in my arm. I draw a 900ml dose of blood. Our blood groups are not compatible—she is 0 RH negative, I'm a B – but plasma can be transfused without problems to compensate the collapsed veins. Taking the portable centrifuge from my bag I spin two haemodoses to get enough plasma. If you have ever seen it you'll know that the process looks very similar to the fractionation of oil. The speed of this portable device means I need less than two minutes to separate the plasma from my blood.

Anissa's pulse is hardly perceptible; her pupils don't react to the light. Her time has almost run out and I am losing a taxpayer. As soon as the plasma is ready I put in the Pravaz reservoir and slide the needle into the radial vein in her elbow. I push down the plunger and wait.

Plasma is liquid dynamite.

After the first 250cc injection the vein is already looking better and after another 150cc Anissa starts breathing evenly again.

I've just finished cleaning the puncture mark as well as I can when I hear the sound of footsteps on the floor below and then coming up the stairs to the bedroom door.

"Mum, are you there?"

A kid of about thirteen or fourteen holding an iPod, earphones hidden under his long hair, drops his backpack on the floor.

I reach a hand out to block him and keep him from panicking. "Don't worry, everything's okay... I'm sorting it."

"And who are you?"

"Alan Costa, Withdrawals Agency. I had an appointment with your mother."

His face flushes red and angry.

"I told her it was too soon. She was too pale this morning. What, is she dying?"

He's on the verge of tears and leans against the door frame, wretched. I lift Anissa's legs and put a cushion under her feet so that her blood can get to where it's needed most.

"No, she's not going to die, she's just fainted. If you'll just let me re-animate her... you know, a dead dodger isn't any good to anyone..."

He's not listening to me anymore, but I still get the feeling that I've said the wrong thing. "Listen... Your mum didn't want to kill herself; she was just taking blood to donate it to someone else who needs it."

While I go and open a window to let some fresh air in, he keeps his head down and avoids looking at me as though he's already heard these altruistic lies. It's just that from a stranger they have a different effect than from his mother's mouth.

"She fainted because the amount of blood in her brain was too low, because she gives *too much* of herself to others."

The kid glares at me with a look that could kill and wipes his damp hands on his jeans.

"I want a bit of her too but she's always got a needle stuck in her somewhere. Those holes, those bloody holes, she calls them "happiness holes"".

I feel sorry for him, it can't be much fun having a mother like this, a mother who, as soon as the adrenaline rush from donating wears off is assailed by the anxiety that someone somewhere needs her blood.

I chivvy him along to stop him feeling more depressed than

necessary.

"Come on, get a move on... Bring me a glass of water with sugar in it and we'll wake her up."

*

"What did you say your name was?"

"Alan Costa."

Anissa is sitting next to me at WOK, a Sushi Bar in the EUR district of Rome. The only thing that's Japanese here is the furniture. There's a bit of everything on the menu from cous cous to goulash and uramaki to tortillas, all sorts of exotic dishes. The background music isn't plucked string instruments or relaxing honeyed harmonies like the muzak in dentists' waiting rooms or airports, instead there's an electric guitar, a drum, and a tambourine playing the Kinks' *Girl, you really got me going, you got me so I don't know what I'm doing.*

It's a connected and disconnected ambient. At sixes and sevens, a bit like Anissa with her intense but elusive gaze.

"Well... thanks for earlier Alan."

Anissa has two huge funeral bags under her eyes. With all that's been drained out of her, I appreciate the fact that she's accepted to come and talk about things in private, without her son.

"Think nothing of it, it's my job."

The game is simple, all I have to do is talk, whet her curiosity and pretend I don't care what she thinks. Deep down it's true anyway, and to make it work I just have to pretend I'm the sick one, the scab sticking to the rules; whatever, I have to pass for a nasty piece of work with wasted potential. Funny really, I only have to be myself, and I certainly don't smell of roses even when you get to know me better.

"No, I mean... Thanks for how you handled the situation with Nicola."

"Ah, that... The kid was scared, he was shaking like a leaf. He thought you'd snuffed it."

I am trying to lay the foundations of a relationship starting from a very long way down in her esteem. This will make it easier to create the illusion of change and transformation, showing potential for what I could become. The thing is to show her the symptoms of my disease first, and then convince her *she* can cure me.

"Nicola is a problem. He doesn't approve of what I do."

I don't approve of the Robin Bloods' indiscriminate donations either, even if my reasons are different: it's all revenue that goes into someone else's veins, untaxed and nothing for us.

"What you lot do is illegal. You deprive Rome of valuable resources, obstruct the collection of outstanding blood taxes, and risk spreading epidemics and infections. Like those *weresquito* bots you use for sucking the blood of innocent taxpayers in their sleep, those things are diabolical..."

"Don't you dare talk to me about unorthodox methods."

Anissa unbuttons her shirt, lifts her skirt up to her pale skinny thighs, and shows me the bruises left by the "Ilario – Farid" treatment.

I've seen more flesh on a bacon butty.

"They were only doing their job. You, on the other hand, were resisting a public officer. You know you could be sent to jail, right?"

She pulls a "Who gives a shit?" face. There's no denying her values clash with mine, and yet for some reason I imagine Anissa's heart has a similar look to my face, full of wounds, bruises and scars that won't heal. The similarities end there, though.

Mind you, the limit between a legal and illegal blood level is a thin line traced on a case-by—case basis by the Eternal City's Council. So, a blood level which can send you straight to jail in Rome, can leave you free as a bird, at your own risk, in the rest of southern Italy. The North, on the other hand... Well, after the introduction of haematic federalism it's best not to even go there. They say that in some cities people cudgel each other to steal their blood to pay in "blood cash" and save on paper liquidity. Some, following in the age-old entrepreneurial traditions of the north have set themselves up selling under the counter blood to the local Withdrawals Agencies, at the other end of the spectrum there are the loan sharks dealing in blood. In between are those who attempt to fabricate artificial blood and spread it like false bank notes.

Northerners always did have a business streak. Not that we lack the spirit of initiative in Rome either, but they're always a step ahead up there, more efficient, more professional.

"What kind of job is yours anyway? Have you ever asked yourself that?"

Getting her attention because I'm one of the *baddies* is better than not having it at all. It's no problem, hate turns into love much more easily than indifference does.

"I don't have enough money to ask those kind of questions."

I order a beer while she, it goes without saying, asks for a Bloody Mary to reintegrate the vitamins she has lost.

The barman winks at me knowingly, with that air somewhere between affability and eagerness to help that I come across wherever I park the taxbulance.

"This round's on the house..."

Don't think I haven't already taken advantage of the situation to meet vulnerable or *fiscally* delicate women. Don't think I haven't given the impression that I'll scratch someone else's back if they scratch mine... The inhabitants of Rome have always whimpered before the throne of the King and grovelled before the altar of the Pope.

In any case, everything can be improved with practice to reach a kind of "perfect naturalness".

Anissa looks at the barman as though he's just offered her the still warm blood of a lamb whose throat has been slit on the Tax altar. Then she looks at me with a sickened expression for having accepted without a murmur.

"Don't look at me like that, you're the one who doesn't respect the Law..."

"A pint of *blood* can save three people's lives."

My plan of deception picks up speed. The track that'll lead me to Anissa's pit-stop and beyond is full of useful lies. I decided on my course the very moment I saw her half-dead on the armchair in Laurentino.

"Tell me, Alan... How many people have you bled-dry?

How many dodgers have you sucked blood from till they lost consciousness? Don't you think the same thing could happen to you one of these days?"

Now she's talking rubbish, like she's a haemophiliac or something. She donates because she wants to, no one forces her to do it. If all these pale Robin Blood do-gooders had a decent shag a bit more often they'd be more generous towards the Intravenous Revenue and they wouldn't hide behind a thousand fads and imaginary illnesses.

I'd like to know how much Anissa really does earn...

"You're not in any position to talk about being *bled dry*. You give your blood away for free." Just a few more tricks and I'll be right up there with the Top *Vampires*.

"If blood is so important to this world, then you lot are just scabs and your bosses are pus." The words Anissa Malesano has just spat out of deathly pale lips sum up the philosophy of the Robin Blood movement and the message they have been trying to spread for years. She is sitting there bursting hostility from every pore and yet her sickly pallor is very sensual, it's a bit like staring Death in the face and allowing yourself to be wrapped in that air of someone who knows when the world is going to end. I'm not what you would call a *fussy* type.

OK, so Anissa is pleasing to the eye. She's not exactly well endowed with curves, but skinny suits her. It's not her fault if this is the type of challenge I am most drawn to.

As you can imagine, this is a crucial moment but I let myself be distracted. There's a triple-chinned, flaccid-armed fatty who's ordered a rare steak and is staring at me as though he's asking permission to gobble it up. His boobs are resting on the restaurant counter as though he's forgotten to wear his 38DD bra.

Fatty has guessed the danger he is in and is crapping himself. He is wondering, as am I, how much those overhanging rolls of flesh, well-fed with piles of euros, might be worth in Haematogen bars. Half a month's mortgage payment? A clear 4 weeks of work?

I don't expect you to really understand, but you're not allowed to have more than a certain amount of blood in circulation, those who do have to pay more taxes. That's why Haematogen loves large people. That's why wherever I lay my hat, everyone wants to pat me on the back, everyone wants to say "Hello" everyone wants to pass for an old friend.

Didn't we do military service together in Cuneo?

Didn't I have the changing room next to yours at the Circeo beach bar?

What, don't you remember the fun we had at the "Sunshine Valley Holiday Resort"?

Yeah, right... In a city like Rome, the length and breadth of which has been plundered for thousands of years, the people have learned every imaginable strategy for surviving. It's not unusual for birds to give you the eye, simper, and invent unlikely moral talents, while tight-fisted louts put their hopes of evasion into a filthy sense of comradeship which disgusts me, in an attempt to make me look the other way.

Still, I understand them, you never know who you'll end up needing in life.

"Listen, I'm not easily offended. As far as I'm concerned the only saying worth anything is: "It's never too late, if you've blood in your veins." I'll be back to collect as soon as you're on your feet again. It's against the BloodBuster rules to let anyone postpone payment, so don't try and be smart or make me regret my generosity. Your tax rating is the lowest there is so there's no point in even trying to escape me... at the third recall I am authorised to take you away."

I pull a finger-prick lancet out of my uniform pocket and motion her to open her hand for me. I grab it and prick the skin of her index finger and analyse the composition of her blood.

"In 7 days, when your blood count's back to normal. And try to drink as much red wine as you can, maybe some Cesanese. It'll do you good."

An invisible thread of psycho-sexual energy snakes out from my pupils and penetrates hers. You might find it hard to believe but as things stand now I'd like to turn into blood, splash around in Anissa's veins and inundate her heart. I'd like to be her boast, her greatest triumph for her Robin Blood comrades. I want to make her feel important, I want her to think she has had the power to melt the heart of a BloodBuster and transform him into a half-traitor. It's just that a stroll under this Arc de Triomphe will demand its own levy, that is, she'll pay with herself. They say all is fair in love and war, and right now the situation could go either way. A war against evasion waged in the name of love...

"You don't know what you're doing... I'm a Mother Donor."

I sigh and add a snort for good measure; then I hand her a bar of Haematogen.

"Listen babe, why don't you get off your high horse and down some iron. Ah, another thing, adding some beetroots and carrots to your diet won't hurt either..."

Anissa stares at me: who knows what's going through her head. It's hard to tell if she's trying to make me feel pathetic or burn me to a crisp. It's a shame she is so run-down she only succeeds in making me feel sorry for her. She's running a serious risk, I wish she could understand that on her own, I've no intention of brainwashing her with loony ideas, like the civic responsibility of taxpayers for the greater good, haematic honesty, social justice... I bet she knows the official bollocks by heart anyway.

For a couple of seconds, we play at who'll look away first. She loses and starts up again with the same old regurgitated clichés...

"Think of all the haemophiliacs, anaemics, and people waiting for organ transplants, babies who need heart surgery..."

The way things are going, a good measure of cruelty won't hurt. Ask me if I give a shit. That's for other people to deal with.

"Talking about kids, if you hide from me, the injunction is valid for Nicola."

At these words she crumples. If she was feeling down before she's turned to jelly now. Her ability to stand up to me has gone belly up, substituted by stroppy exhaustion.

"What's it got to do with him? Keep him out of it."

Then a hot-wash of tears fills her eyes and wets her face. Anissa does nothing to hide it. Just as she doesn't donate blood for personal reasons, she's crying for Nicola, not the taxes she has to pay.

"Oh, I was forgetting..., what blood group is the kid?"

Anissa gets up, wipes her face wet with tears, and slaps me.

Then she rushes out, her face blotched red from the broken capillaries around her eyes.

Nothing like a job well done. Now she hates me and I'm safely tucked away in the darkest most contemptible corner of her sad little heart.

I massage my cheek where a deep red droplet has formed. If you've ever argued with a girl and her ring, you'll know that you only need a styptic match to stop the bleeding.

I throw back the last drop of beer before signing off.

Blood wars

Rule number four: If you can't get blood out of a stone, grind it to dust.

Next day at the Headquarters in Via Portuense my colleagues are searching the Internet and Withdrawals Agency database for news and information. I drain a cup of coffee from the machine while they bring me up-to-date on the area's virtual gossip.

"Get this one, Alan... "If you make a donation to the Catholic Church, you'll be helping a young patient at Bambino Gesù Hospital."

"The shits... They don't even pay one drop to the State but they ask the people to hand over their hard earned cash, just like that. Have you ever heard of a banker being excommunicated? Have you ever heard of a swindling politician being criticised by the Church? That's enough for me to see how things work round the Vatican's way"

Farid stretches and crosses his arms behind his head.

"I got no problem with priests. They're elegant and they work with people. They live well. When I've paid up enough blood to gain Italian citizenship, I reckon that's what I'm gonna do."

"Wait what, you want to be a priest?"

Farid looks like one of those monsters on a spring that jump out at you unexpectedly. He bends down under the desk to where his portable mini-bar is, and pulls out a box of kefir, a type of goat's milk, top of the list of *halal* food. Farid is always knocking it back.

"What's wrong with that?"

I kick the back of his chair. Up until last year he was a new recruit in the midst of those delinquents that I send to Infernetto, the part of town where you learn to harden up or die trying. On-the-job training that's worth more than a thousand lectures and useless training days. I let them try and raise a drop of blood there before building themselves up and expecting stuff that would make a crow laugh. If they're no good, I send them straight back to prison like faulty goods.

Ilario takes out his palmtop.

"Now that I come think of it, I've got a mate in Gemelli who owes me a big favour..."

He scrolls through the agenda hardly able to contain himself.

"What is he, a repentant priest?"

"No, no... Even better, he's an anaesthetist. Here he is. Saverio Fusco, the Scroogeface. We studied medicine together. The first two years anyway but then I got bored."

"Yeah, I know, history of psychiatry. So?"

Ilario clicks on the mouse and sticks a flag on the Surgery ward of the Gemelli hospital on Google Maps.

"What do you mean, "so"? I mean there are a load of priests there, Alan. Virgin priests..." Ilario is visibly excited as he calls Scroogeface.

A thousand points to him.

*

Half an hour later, the three of us in our scarlet BloodBuster uniforms make our way into the Gemelli hospital, each with a *transfusion* bag in hand.

"We need to deliver these bags to Surgery right away."

The nun at Reception verifies our request signed by Scroogeface in person. Whether out of fear, honour, or for money, it's never too hard to find someone in Rome willing to falsify a document.

Behind the nun there is a hospital light blue wall, its aim is to spread serenity. They are normally plain white, a symbol of hygiene and cleanliness, but in this case the light blue suits the spiritual vocation of the patients better. Some of them are fighting for their lives, or in a Christian sense, flying close to the criteria for becoming saints. To me it smacks of marketing, whatever kind.

"Dr Di Stefano is busy at present with an operation, but Dr Fusco is starting to prepare the patient. They're for Cardinal Pezzi, right?"

I wink at her.

"Guessed right, sister, like it says on the form. Let's hurry it up there's a soul to be saved." She shows us to the lift without hesitation.

With Ilario and Farid as my wingmen we take the lift and fly up to the fourth floor.

Just to stretch our legs and have a bit of fun, we crawl past under the Surgery ward window.

Farid slides along on his belly in assault mode, like a Navy Seal. Actually the fewer people who see us the better, especially if they are gossipy nurses. Then the loudspeaker announces:

ATTENTION PLEASE: DR DI STEFANO IS REQUIRED IN
OPERATING THEATRE 4 FOR THE OPERATION ON ALBERTI

We slip stealthily into Room 7 and Scroogeface lifts his gaze from his Sudoku. He's wearing headphones monitoring the mad "beep-beep-beep" of the Cardinal's heartbeat. He snatches them off and comes to meet us in one bound. Ilario pre-empts him putting one large warning hand on his arm, and lays down the law straight away.

"Hey, Savè!... Howzit goin'? Here we are, we got here as soon as we could, like you said. Is this the Cardinal? What a piece of luck, a fresh one to be milked..."

"Shhh... Shut it will you. Yes, it's him, but it's the first and last time, got it? You should see the amount of priests, prelates, cardinals, bishops and monsignors that we get. He'd better not notice anything has happened either, right?"

"Otherwise, otherwise. Always the same old story with you. Remind me, weren't you the one wallowing in blood taken from bodies in the morgue? And did I ever open my gob?"

"Right, exactly."

Another turn of the haemostatic lace by Ilario makes

Scroogeface grimace. "Right, exactly. Now it's your turn to button it."

Ilario brushes him aside with his arm and I step forward and take the icy hand of the Cardinal between my grubby collector's fingers. His veins are all standing out, like the marquetry of the door of Saint Peter's.

I make the sign of the cross on his chest.

"You preach one thing and do another, my dear old Cardinal... Whatever, I'm doing this for you. In the eyes of God, there are no tax borders."

Farid hands me the syringe and the needle selection. I choose a special one for the occasion. A Yellow, what we BloodBusters call a "Quickie" and use when we have little *transfusional* time.

In the case of a senior member of the Church like Cardinal Pezzi it can take up to sixty seconds before the *liqueur* reaches the barrel of the syringe.

The Quickie is a 30 gauge article with a conical point that wouldn't make a baby squeak. The hole it makes, not counting the redness, is almost invisible: 0.3mm.

The classic mistake beginners make when using small needles is that when they don't see the blood appearing straight away they think the point must be in the wrong place. They try again, making another hole and risk causing a multiple puncture headache.

I fix the Quickie to the syringe and twist the point until it is the right way round, with the hole pointing up.

The Vatican is the largest hotbed of tax evaders that I know of, a nest of barterers who fill their mouths with the blood of Christ but won't hand over a drop of their own for others. Others, meaning us of course, good Christians working away without ever complaining. So it gives me twice the usual pleasure to stick this needle into the arm of a false fellow citizen who plays the foreigner when it suits him.

Question: how much should I take?

Judging by his work-shy mass and applying the sliding tax rate, I should divide the sum (haematically speaking) in half giving me around three litres or thereabouts... When he wakes up, Saint Pezzi will feel much lighter, as though he's woken up in someone else's shoes. Isn't that the sort of stuff making up the sermons he preaches to the pews every Sunday? Is not confessing to tax evasion the same as unloading one's sins? I finish filling the first bag and signal Ilario to give me another.

ATTENTION PLEASE: DR DI STEFANO IS REQUIRED IN OPERATING THEATRE 7 FOR THE OPERATION ON PEZZI.

Scroogeface is starting to get edgy. If they find us here with the needle still stuck in the Cardinal's veins it could spark an international scandal. I can just see the headlines in the Vatican newspaper.

SCANDAL AT THE GEMELLI HOSPITAL. CARDINAL PEZZI EXSANGUINATED. POLICE HUNT FOR THE PERPETRATORS

Or:

THE POPE HAS ASKED FOR A FORMAL BRIEFING BY THE TREASURY OVER THIS REGRETTABLE MISUSE OF FISCAL POWER.

It's time to calm Scroogeface down a bit. I put my hand on his chest and hold him at a safe distance.

"Wait, I've nearly finished."

My grandfather, just to give you an idea of his point of view, used to say: "Where there are church doors, there are whores." Not to put too fine a point on it, with all the terrible things that priests have done and continue to do to little boys, the wrath of the Gods should be brought down on some people. Don't you think all the minor Gods out there should get together and explain a thing or two to the one-and-only Lord God above? Whatever, we are upholders of the Law of man and this is our territory.

From all the hand waving and gesticulating going on

Scroogeface seems to be getting upset. Ilario takes him to one side and gives him a telling off. He's getting wound up because he's worried they won't let him do his Sudoku anymore, or listen to the sound of a rickety heart.

My colleague turns on me, but without much enthusiasm.

"Come on, Alan... Get a move on. They can't be far away now."

Now the blood bag's full I pass it to Farid who puts it safely in the container.

"Look at this delight Mr Africa... D'you have any idea how happy Emory'll be with this bonus?"

He gives the sack a squeeze and the blood-red sauce bubbles.

"What d'you reckon, this lot's probably worth two days' work?"

Ever more panic stricken, Scroogeface starts pushing us towards the exit.

"You've finished. Get out of here."

I back off, putting the needle cover back on the Pravaz.

"Your friend Pezzi there suffers from liquorrea. You should put a cork in him or you'll lose him before five minutes are up."

He's about to lose it and quickly opens a drawer for some cotton wool and starts dabbing at the withdrawal hole.

"Just go. We're even now."

Ilario approaches him, cups his ear and whispers something with a sneer.

"The corpses down in the morgue... More than just blood, know what I mean? Keep shtum and no one need ever know."

*

We climb back into the taxbulance and drive along the Pineta Sacchetti. We follow the flow of traffic that guarantees the slow survival of the Eternal City day after day carrying car cells and human anti-bodies to the shops and offices.

Circulating is human, obstructing the flow is diabolical.

Think of the devil and the display on the dashboard comes on and Emory's ugly mug invades the screen.

"What's new and exciting? Any blood out there for us?"

"You guessed it... Right here by the Agency in the Ponte Bianco area, the police have just notified us of a head-on crash between a lorry and a sports car."

"How much are we talking about?"

"Not much, but you're the closest... You've got about five minutes advantage on our cousins. If Google Sat has got it right the car and tram traffic in Viale Trastevere is going to keep them busy for a while."

Farid huffs. He hates shifting his arse for less than ten litres of juice.

"Alright, consider it ours."

I pull out the siren from the glove compartment and slap it on the roof. Ilario leers as he pushes his foot down on the accelerator. A crowd of old guys sitting on benches in search of a little fresh air and a horde of grannies toiling across the pedestrian crossings curse us as we zoom by.

"What am I always saying to you Alan? The early bird catches the worm."

Sometimes I wish I could have his enthusiasm.

At the far end of the Gianicolense area the road is blocked and when we get to Ponte Bianco, we find the circulation has been brought to a standstill by the umpteenth thrombosis of cancer-ridden vehicles: a truck has jumped carriage ways and smashed into a station wagon.

We climb out to offer some first aid and maybe, if we can, drain off a few bags from any victims on the brink of death before they become useless, cold meat. We can already hear the sirens leaving from the nearby San Camillo hospital.

A sports car has also been involved in the accident, leaving tyre tracks up ahead.

The lorry driver has jumped down from his cabin and is running at full speed towards the car. He's yelling like a demon and waving a jack in the air. A sausage about to burst out of his own skin.

"Son of a bitch! Get outta the car if you've got the balls." The doors of the Lamborghini Gallardo go into lockdown. "Get out and look what you've fucking done."

The engine starts up.

"No you don't. Where the fuck d'you think you're going?"

He lifts the jack and the windscreen shatters. The lorry driver sticks his arm through the window, pulls up the latch, and flings open the door to drag the driver out by the neck. He finds himself face to face with a top model dressed up to the nines with stiletto heels and a belt for a skirt, a sight worthy of a short prayer on bended knee.

This is when I intervene and block the redneck, stopping him from carrying out his own form of justice: red in the face, short and thickset, his hair is gingery and he's wearing boots with buckles, he has the air of being easy to irritate. Even if he's shaved his single-eyebrow and waxed his chest, his flashy sunglasses and the snakeskin decoration on his shirt scream out for all to see where he's from, and I don't mean his mammoth lorry, I mean right down south in the land of rednecks and sharecroppers. Pass me the highbrow quote.

"Cool down, mate... Tell us how it happened. That's how things are done around here."

"This shit-for-brains was going full tilt. She overtook on a solid white line and to avoid hitting her, I swerved, and then to avoid the bridge I swerved again and ended up here..."

He turns towards the crushed car where Ilario and Farid are pulling out the remains of two blood soaked bodies.

"Well miss, is that what happened?"

"Wait what? Just because she's a doll with a Lamborghini that don't make me a liar and her a saint."

Despite the hundred years he's been living in Rome he hasn't lost his country bumpkin accent, that doesn't make him wrong though.

What's worse is that this Barbie doll won't deign to open that lipstick covered pout to talk to two lurid bastards like us. Dressed in her best for a classy cocktail party, she reeks of perfume and keeps her gaze down on the tarmac, looking at the skid marks left by the shiny brand new Lamborghini. Not that I particularly want to side with the redneck but birds who act like their shit don't stink get on my nerves.

"The less you say the worse it'll get..."

Farid whistles to get my attention.

"Nothin' doin'. Stone dead, both of them."

"...much, much worse, sweetheart."

Farid comes over and leans through the other door of the Lamborghini. I hardly have time to blink and I see his eyes are popping out of his head.

"Oh, shit. It's Aurelio Mazza!"

Whoever he is, Aurelio Mazza realises he's been caught, jumps into the driver's seat and puts the car in gear. The car door slams against Farid's back. He moves back and out just in time.

"Will someone tell me who the fuck Aurelio Mazza is?"

Ilario is already back in the taxbulance and screeches to a stop practically on my toes. From the window he gives me a signal to get in. Led Zeppelin's *Kashmir* is blasting out of the stereo so Ilario has to shout what he knows about Aurelio Mazza to get me up to speed.

"He's a shitty ex-Rome football player who owes the Intravenous Revenue something like one hundred times his own weight in blood. Come on, get a move on..."

Farid and me shoot another quick glance in the direction of the snooty bitch before we move off. The lorry driver has no intention of taking his hands off her before the boys in blue arrive and check her over, very thoroughly.

Our uniformed cousins aren't as chatty as we are. They have a more hands on approach, so to speak.

In the taxbulance and on the road again. New destination, new target. A mobile one this time, an arrow flying along the fast lane of Ponte Bianco.

This is our trench war, our front line: the joy of piercing a vein, chasing after a dodger, hunting down the bastard who thinks he's above all and any bloody haematax demands, to say nothing of the satisfaction of throwing him into jail and seeing him cooling off behind bars. This is when you get the desire to rough them up a bit and give them the thrashing they deserve, just to off-load the tension; call it a "liberating beating" if you prefer.

In this sense the boys in blue, grey, and us in scarlet are made of

the same meat. Fuck me, blood taxes really are a great invention!
Isn't life a wonderful thing?

Farid keeps one shoulder hunched up towards me and tells me some more about our fugitive. "Mazza lived on a yacht outside our territorial waters. He's one of the highest ranking dodgers. He was in Corsica and then Montecarlo... We've been hounding him for months and months."

Mazza takes advantage of a green light and heads straight down Via Grimaldi.

"Come on, Ilario... let's have a laugh. Turn down onto Via Oderisi and we'll cut him off..."

"No! It's full of traffic lights..."

Ilario looks from one to the other for a millisecond.

"Well then? What the fuck am I supposed to do?"

"Don't listen to him. I'm in charge here."

So we take in the line of red lights along Via Oderisi da Gubbio, foot down on the accelerator without even touching the brakes once all the way down to the Piazza Meucci roundabout.

The taxbulance blares out its frightening shriek, a battle cry going WAWAWAWA and the cars shift out of the way, scared. We burn up the road like nobody's business and join the straight stretch of Lungotevere degli Inventori.

"What if Mazza heads back towards the centre of town?"

I unfasten my seat belt and open the glove compartment to get the traffic-light scanner, then I sit with my arse on the window leaning out as far as I dare.

"He's already been into the centre of town and can't be exactly dying to go back. He wants to make a clean get away on his yacht."

Farid gives me an ugly look. I point the scanner as if I were sounding the charge and transform the green light a hundred metres away into a permanent red.

Mazza's Lamborghini can be heard honking away in the distance. He's jumped the centre strip and is heading the wrong way down Viale Marconi to avoid the queue at the traffic lights. You can add this to the list of infractions he has to pay for as soon as we manage to get a needle in his vein.

Our model tax evader appears to think he's driving around a formula one circuit or playing one of those videogames, *Nascar Whatever* or *Grand Fucking Prix*, he's just missing the vehicles that don't have time to get out of the way of his suicidal trajectory.

The junction at Ponte Marconi is a sort of black hole where you can't say what direction you'll end up going: you might turn left onto Via Ostiense towards Garbatella, then go straight on towards the EUR district or turn left for the DogTrack near the Model Ship Basin.

"Overtake him! Overtake him and get the bastard!"

"Keep your gob shut, Farid. Don't overtake, Ilario, just pull alongside him."

Ilario makes the handbrake growl and the taxbulance does a perfect 90 degree turn with only a slight wobble. We're now racing side-by-side in parallel lanes.

"Look at that, we're a hair's-breadth away from him now! Nice one, Ilario! Let's see if he can worm his way out of this one, the bastard..."

Mazza seems to think he's a stunt driver, and he's not letting up; he tries to overtake us to get back into the right lane, but we knock him out again, back onto the wrong side of the road where he decides to stay.

I can see his fury as he just misses two other cars and then makes the mistake of asking too much of his Lamborghini: he tries a clean spin, straight out of the book, but he only manages three or four swerves before crashing into the Bridge's railings.

"Time to get satisfaction."

We cut across the lane and park the van in the middle of the road. Farid climbs out first and sticks some red and white tape around the scene marking this section of the road as ours.

This time Aurelio Mazza climbs out of the contorted wreckage of his own free will. Crying and snuffling in a continuous whine, it's hard to say if the cause is the wrecked car, the lost top model, or who knows what else.

Ilario gets hold of him by his Prada jacket and pulls his sleeve up to the elbow.

"Keep it quiet, Mazza... I'd never have thought a footballer like you would be such a cry-baby. Y'know what, I used to envy you, strong, rich and famous, and look at you now... I'd really hate to be in your shoes."

The first curious onlookers are elbowing each other out of the way for a place in the front row. They still haven't quite caught on to who it is we've got hold of. Thinking about it, our work is a bit like a game of football: the game plans, the formation on the playing field and the strategies aren't important, what counts is *scoring* the goal and our goal is made up of a network of tax dodgers' veins.

"Tell the truth, you wanted to score, didn't you? You let the doll drive, let her get a taste of squeezing the Lambo's engine under that pretty arse... Hoping it wasn't the only thing she was going to squeeze..."

The fight's about to kick off. Mazza chunters something under his moustache.

"Shopping... If it weren't for her damned shopping none of this would have happened."

A crowd has formed on Ponte Marconi and these spectators are shouting, egging us on now that they have recognised who we're grilling.

"TEAR THE BASTARD'S LIVER OUT!"

"WITH ALL THE MONEY HE'S STOLEN, LEAVE HIM WITH NOTHING BUT HIS UNDERWEAR."

"GIVE HIM A GOOD HIDING AND THEN SYRINGE HIM!"

"So, what about it, Mazza? I can't hear what your excuses are with all the commotion your friends here are making. What do you say, d'you want to answer to me or to them?"

Someone's throwing lighters at us and Farid has to growl a bit to calm them down and let us do our job. Mazza gets the hint and stops whining.

"It was her, she made me come off at Ostia because of shopping."

"In Viale Marconi?"

"No, we were on our way back from Prati."

When I hear this I can't help but giggle. I almost burst out laughing and in the end everyone is sniggering, including our growing audience. With his head down, Mazza withstands the abuse.

We give our body and soul to our job. We rarely miss a target. We are great experts in finding sly evaders with false track-marks.

"AH MAZZA, WHEN IT'S YOUR TURN, IT'S YOUR TURN!"

Then Farid's face turns harsh. He rummages about in the container and the clatter of needles sends Mazza into a panic.

With a straight face I ask Farid to pass me the blood detector, then I say the words of our famous magic formula clearly.

"Well then, to-pay-or-not-to-pay?"

"I... I'm... not an Italian resident."

Ilario butts in and I can see he's barely managing to contain a head of anger.

"Pull the other one. We've heard that one more times than you've had hot dinners."

From the way he's clutching his family jewels, you can see Mazza is losing it. I wouldn't like to end up with the wrong kind of *liqueur*.

"It's all in the hands of my lawyers. He manages things with the Withdrawals Agency."

This is when, as punctual as a Swiss watch, Ilario loses it. Up until a few years ago he had a season ticket for Rome matches. He often took a day off work to go to see his team playing their mid-week away matches. He totally hated it when that sad and unsporting phenomenon of "split football" started, with matches broadcast at the weirdest times of day and odd days of the week. It meant he couldn't follow the championships as much as he used to, he couldn't keep up with what was going on as much as he wanted to. How can you blame him if he is letting his resentment out now, even if he is venting it on Mazza, who at least from this perspective is as much a victim of the system as Ilario?

The answers his ex-golden boy is giving are evasive to say the least. They're almost irritating enough to make it worth taking him up Monte Mario and flinging him off the top.

Incited by a furious crowd, you can't help getting brutal.

"Do you think we give a shit about your lawyers? The only thing I know is that you don't come to see us anymore, Aurelio Mazzolato, and a hell of a long time has passed since you were last seen near the Agency. You fluffed that goal, Aure'... Rome-Inter 2-2, we could have won but you disappeared into nothing."

There goes the first slap.

"They wanted to kill me! That's the reason, you've got to believe me..."

Believe him? Ilario has never believed in him, and now he can't see passed his anger either. In an attempt to keep calm and resist the urge to stick a suction-pump into his aorta, Ilario starts pacing up and down in front of our dear pale-faced dodger.

Farid and I keep watch over the area, worried this might be the spark that sets off this powder keg of disadvantaged youths, unemployed passers-by, and disillusioned housewives who can't wait to wash their hands in the blood of a tax dodger. To even things up a little.

While they're running up and down a football pitch behind a ball they're gods. As soon as they swap their footie boots for flip-flops they turn into criminals.

"Oh yes...yeah, I believe that. It's all the fault of the usual trouble making fans yeah? It's always their fault isn't it? The hooligans in the Curva Sud.

He nods his head.

"You're more stubborn than I thought, Aure'. That's how you always got the ball in, head, dribbling, or a whammy...any technique so long as it hit the back of the net."

He shakes his head. Ilario lets fly with another backhander.

"GIVE HIM THE SUCTION PUMP!" "GIVE HIM A WHIPPING!"

"Come on now Mazza... Look, it's only a little prick."

Ilario opens the MT67F and pulls out a huge icing-syringe, one of the pump-loading type. Then taps the empty cylinder a couple of times.

It's all for the effect. We use this type occasionally on people who act like they're Rambo or something. Like that time in Piazza di Spagna underground station when to stop a train an evader was getting away from us on, Ilario pretended his head was caught in the sliding doors. An idiotic move that worked...

"Who knows how many steroids you've shot up in your time, I mean look at those thighs, and now you're afraid of a little pinprick? Well, fuck you..."

He's still shaking his head, no-no-no, anymore of this and he'll hypnotise himself. The onlookers can't take it anymore. The drip, drip, drip of it is almost offensive. They just don't get the joy of our job. From the corner of my eye I can see some of them picking up pieces of glass and stones, ready to throw them.

"Stop! Stop everyone, no one throw the first stone, unless you're sure of getting him full-on." They laugh out loud. The tension loosens a little, but I don't know how long it will last. Mazza can't stand the pressure anymore, he half-closes his eyes and his fear pushes him into an extreme act. He frees himself from Farid's grip, launches himself at the railings and looks for unlikely salvation by throwing himself off the Ponte Marconi bridge into the river.

The crowd roars and breaks through the symbolic fencing of striped-tape. They want to see where Mazza has gone.

"Shit, you should have got it over with straight away!" says Farid.

I glare daggers at him. A hard wet thud comes from the Tiber below.

"Are you looking at me?" I say. "You're the one who let him out of his hands, shit brains."

"You wanted to have some fun with him, didn't you, eh? And now, what are we going to do?"

"Don't even try that holier than thou stuff with me..."

We run to the opposite side of the Bridge followed by a crowd of curious bystanders. Mazza is already in the distance, fifty metres away and floating like the turd he was. Stone dead in the midst of his own blood.

"WHO THE FUCK DID YOU THINK YOU WERE, MISTER OK, DIVING IN THE RIVER AT NEW YEAR?"

"BACK OFF TO THE SEA THEN, MAZZA."

Farid gives me a funny look as we get back into the taxbulance.

Some of the kids have made off with bits and pieces of our equipment, the spray protector masks have gone along with the spare haemodetector and Ilarios's jacket which he'd left on the seat. You can be sure they'll wear every piece of clothing as if it were a trophy, or for showing off to the girls at school.

I call Emory to tell him about the fiasco.

The crowd slowly disperses. A few of the stragglers, let down by the way events have gone give us dirty looks. Never mind bad apples, I can't help asking myself if there are any good apples left in the Eternal City.

When it comes down to it, even though we're working for the well-being of the community, we're not making many friends.

Homo homini lupus

Rule number five: If we respected all the rules,
breaking them would stop being fun.

Five days to go before the appointment with Anissa. Not that there's anything exciting about tax assessments, but I never have liked things being served to me on a silver plate.

I could lie in wait for her by the office where she works part-time in Via Trionfale.

I could light a fire under her and watch what happens, but someone who gives herself airs like she does might react badly. I wouldn't be surprised if she turns out to have some friends in high places, a lawyer who works in the Magistrates Court, or even a proper Judge that she went to school with from nursery to senior school, ready to defend her with the Revenue law book in one hand and the Civil law book in the other.

In any case, I don't reckon I'm one of those thick meat-heads driven by primordial instincts. I've read Sun Tzu and Von Clausewitz, I know how to transform an apparently courteous and correct tax check-up into a perfect bloodbath. Sometimes not having a good reputation is an advantage: it immediately puts your adversary into a state of uneasiness.

It's early and I'm the only one in our office. Farid isn't answering his mobile and Ilario will be one day behind schedule as usual. So it's a surprise when I hear him running up the spiral staircase to the second floor of the Withdrawals Agency. I'm busy shaking the dried blood that has accumulated over the last few days off my jacket when he appears in front of me.

"Oh, Alan... Have you heard the latest?"

His voice comes out in a wheeze. He's out of breath and has

that scheming look in his eyes that can only mean one thing: black clouds on the horizon.

"What have you done now? Have you split a blood bag again? You'll have to answer to Emory on your own this time..."

If you want to know a trick for getting rid of congealed blood from a leather jacket, just sprinkle some flour, or talc, or powdered milk on it. Leave it to dry and then brush it off vigorously.

"It's not me this time, it's Farid, he's left the team... He said he's sick of being a Bloodsucker and that 50 withdrawals are too many to make the Bat grade."

That explains why "kebab head" isn't answering the 'phone... Courage isn't a substance that's found in great quantities in blood; maybe it's somewhere in our DNA, but I'll believe it when I see it.

"What? I don't believe it. We're the ones that got him back on the straight and narrow, we pretty much weaned him ourselves. We taught him the basics, everything he needed to know. I've been trying to ring him for two days..."

"I bet. He's turned his mobile off. I heard from Sawn-off who lives down there near Corviale like him."

Sawn-off is the head of the West Rome team and he manages those nutters He-Ho-Fook and Scrondo. They call him Sawn-off because he has a brother who looks exactly the same as him, but taller. One day his older brother went in through the front door and a second later Sawn-off came out looking exactly the same but with twenty centimetres "sawn-off". Poor sod, it's made him a butt of shorty jokes all his life. To make up for his physical disadvantage he always wears ridiculous platforms shoes with heels.

"Well Sawn-off isn't exactly the most reliable person around."

"He's right this time, though. I didn't think Farid was being serious. All he ever did was pick his nose and clean his ears..."

If there's something I can't stand, it's having dirty hands. So, if you want to get rid of traces of blood or any other residues left under your nails, stick your fingers in half a lemon. Then wash them in warm water.

"What a half-baked bloodfucker! I knew he wasn't cut out for this job."

"No, you don't get it... Farid hasn't stopped working, he's gone into business on his own. He says he considers himself a full-blown Bat and doesn't need Emory or anyone else to dig out dodgers."

"Yeah, right. He's turned into a full-blown Twat. So, from now on, he'll be working against us."

"Dead right... Who's going to tell Emory?"

In the good old days, tax collectors weren't dirty mercenaries. Sure, some were hired on short-term contracts and used as reinforcements for controls during special campaigns or during peak-times just after the annual tax returns, but people saw them as helping the community, not as a plague of vampires. What's more, through franchising Emory Szilagiy has got something like 70 Vampires working on a regional basis and around 900 Bats, as well as more than 5000 Bloodsuckers and Mosquitoes doing unpaid trial periods.

"I get the feeling that we'll have to nip down to Corviale. Just to let our little friend know how much we're gonna miss him."

Ilario shrugs.

"I've got things to do today. My sister, Mirna, you know how it is with her anaemia, she needs lots of blood at the moment. I need to visit Emory down in Riva Ostiense to ask for some. You understand, don't you?"

Ilario would do anything for his sister. His is real feeling, I bet he even keeps a photo of her in his wallet. Every fifteen to twenty days, if she doesn't get the right transfusions, she risks her blood becoming toxic. None of the pharmaceuticals on the market, the intravenous painkillers like Droxia or Hydrea work for her. They lower the pain but they don't get rid of it. Mirna has already had one operation when they took out her spleen. There's not a lot else that can be done. Only a bone marrow transplant can eliminate Sickle cell anaemia but bone marrow costs, it costs more than all the blood Ilario could ever contribute over two lifetimes.

"You're not scared, are you?"

He makes himself a rollie. Drum, no filter.

"No. Scared of what anyway? I used to hang around with

people like the Corviale lot. Sawn-off, Swamp Bird, I know people like them. It's like I said...I'm worried about my sister. Look, I've got to run or I'll be late."

Then he disappears. Just like the clots of blood on my jacket and smears of dirt on my hands. Bit strange how he came here so fast just to tell me about Farid and rushed off again just as quickly.

Streaks of pinky red clouds cross the sky above the "Serpentone" in layers, like lots of strips of bloody cloth. To me they look like globular bags hanging in the air. It's as if they're waiting for me, as if they want to invite me up or, even worse, as though they want to provoke me. If I pulled them down, if I could only find a way of extracting blood from clouds... Bingo. I would be rich. But there's no simple way out. I have to confront Farid, at his house, in Corviale.

I leave the taxbulance parked in full view opposite the Arvalia Public Library. As soon as I put my foot onto the softened tarmac I am hit by a wave of heat from one side. The air waves and trembles as though the whole area has been built in the slipstream of a jet ready for take-off. A few metres away, a group of bad boys are watching me. They are pissing, like a pack of wolves, through rusty railings onto the wing of a yellow Porsche and a metallic-grey Mercedes, both guilty of being left on double-yellow lines in their territory. Some people call these acts "barbarian" or "envious vandalism", but they're good kids really who are bored and have fun pretending to be the area's sheriffs. In the long term the effects of repeatedly parking where you shouldn't has worse consequences than a bit of smelly piss. It depends on perspective. For all I know, their alternatives are throwing stones off a motorway bridge, smashing windows, or slashing tyres. That would be real damage. That's what usually happens in other places. In the end what we're dealing with here is a joke because everyone knows everyone else. On the other hand, in other more closed enclaves the inhabitants are much less likely to tolerate strangers passing through. They put a security guard in a cubicle and a bar across the street to shut it off to non-residents. Simple.

In my day, we left cars *sans* wheels standing on four bricks.

That way the chassis didn't get ruined. Whatever, they need to know who I am and what I'm here for. That's why I put the taxbulance where it will be noted immediately: I want them to know I'm here, I want my presence to be obvious a mile away.

I climb the stairs to the ninth floor of the monstrous Corviale building and walk along hundreds of metres of walkway before reaching the western-most corner. A bloke walking quickly in the opposite direction passes me and slips into a stairwell then disappears into a doorway. The stairs stink of dust and stale urine. Some parents should check up on their sheriffs a bit more... I hold my breath until I reach the top floor.

From up here, I can see the fields on the outskirts of Rome spreading across from Casal Lumbroso to Ponte Galeria, and from Casal Bernocchi to Dragoncello and Vitinia. You can see burned fields and expanses of land that have been purified by the stubble burning fire.

The Tiber, which isn't far, is so drained of water that you can almost see the bottom. On the horizon strips of hot grey tarmac look like non-stop foundries, belts capable of melting the tyres of the queuing cars. Below me, stray dogs and cats look for shelter in the lee of walls, in the shade of courtyards and inside the entrance halls of semi-abandoned blocks of flats. We are all panting, with our tongues hanging out, human and animals alike.

I get to where I'm going and ring number 1290, an anonymous doorbell that no one answers. I lean back and a bright light pierces my eyes. On the roof, in the midst of a swarm of crooked aerials and satellite discs pointing who-knows-where, someone – at a wild guess I'd say Farid—has erected a two-metre pole with a sparkling golden Crescent-moon on the top. Next to it, there is a pair of speakers for broadcasting the *adhan* to all his fellow Muslims in "Quranway", as the area has been re-named. I turn my attention back to the door and taking a medium-sized needle from my bag, the 17 gauge deep pink one, known as the Little Slayer, I slide the protective sheath off the Pravaz.

A quick look left and right to make sure the coast is clear, and I start tinkering with the old Yale lock. Rusty and half broken with no reinforcing bolts it presents few problems and I have the door open in a flash, but I stay cautiously in the doorway.

If Farid were at home he would already have given me a special kind of welcome. This is my chance to discover what kind underhand business he's involved in.

On the floor I notice five take-away pizza boxes from the Five Brothers take-out left lying on top of some prayer mats. Him and his flatmates must have only just finished eating.

The sky outside the front window shows up the filth in the room. Hanging on the walls there are some gigantic posters of unknown Middle-Eastern musical groups and manifestoes written in unreadable characters.

Another sign of the strong faith pervading the flat are the *ayat* from the Quran hanging on the wall. Our Muslim friends recite these, taking turns to lead their daily prayers.

I wander around brushing aside bits of paper and rummaging inside drawers. My efforts are fruitless.

I go back down the stairs and quite cautiously get ready to question some of the local inhabitants. They all know who I am and that Farid works with me. Or maybe I should say worked with me. In these parts, people keep their mouths shut and their eyes open; ears are only switched on if it's worth their while. A couple of young women in traditional dress pass by me. The ghost of the dead girl haunts me, she is all around me, even if in varying forms. The same hungry for life eyes, the same rigid, desperate movements.

Anyway, the down-and-outs who walk the streets of Corviale are full of strange stories and tales: useless, often misleading gossip that can sometimes however prove to be worthwhile listening. By the edge of the graffiti-riddled amphitheatre there is a bloke who looks like he's worth approaching. He's got that classic look of a spineless suspect and, fortunately, I know him.

"Hello, Laxo..."

Obviously he doesn't answer. They call him Laxo because he can disappear at the drop of a senna pod as though a laxative has been injected into his carotid artery. Mostly though he gets left alone because he's deaf and dumb, and that's why, for the last two years, he's been one of my informants. When I tap him on the shoulder he resists the urge to flee and acts all vague. He's afraid, but on the other hand he knows there are goodies in the pipeline if he collaborates.

"I'm looking for Farid. You haven't seen him around here have you?"

I drop two euros in his offering plate. I have to act like a client to get anything out of him. He slides his hand into his pocket, takes out some paper and a pen, concentrates for a moment and then starts to write. Officially Laxo earns a living thanks to the haikus he writes. He writes them for people who make him a generous enough offering. It is an excellent way of passing me information without getting noticed. When he has finished his composition he holds it out to me on the palm of his hand.

HE'S BEEN GONE FOR DAYS MUST BE SOMETHING BIG HE'S GOT IN HIS DIRTY PAWS.

"What?"

He hesitates, and glances around suspiciously. But, it's me that's not got it. Laxo wants to know how much this is going to earn him. That's how things work with people like him, we cast the hook and they hide the line. So, depending on the fish we want to catch, they change the bait and put the right one on. I donate four bars of nice fresh Tiramisu-flavoured Haematogen to the poetic cause, new on the summer catalogue at fifteen Euros each. This gets me a second haiku:

MUSHROOM HUNTING ON
BY THE SHORES OF THE LAKE THERE
IS NO BLOOD TO SEE

"You're kidding me?"

He smiles and gets all sly. Bending down to the plate he picks up the bars and unwraps one. Then he shakes his head.

I know I can trust him; for years Laxo worked for the boys in grey before being caught fencing. No one around here knows this juicy little fact otherwise they wouldn't let him hang about by the amphitheatre, the trafficking crossroads of Corviale.

Thinking about it, the indications he's just given me are actually very precise. I take my leave, get back into the taxbulance, and head off in the direction of the EUR district.

*

In the car park of the Mushroom Restaurant there's already a crowd of people and cars with their engines still running, enjoying the scene of a capture. If Farid has decided to go about taxing every rich bastard in the district it means he has lost what little sense he still had. From above I can hear people shouting for help: they are clearly panic-stricken and completely terrorised, overt signs of the fear that's running through their veins.

I go inside. From the ground floor of the Mushroom Restaurant I press the lift button, but unsurprisingly it's not working; someone must be blocking it further up. I run up the stairs three at a time till I get to the top. Then I stop and lurk behind a corner.

I put the MT67F on the ground, silently click open the safety catch, open the lid as gently as possible and take out the mirror from the kit. Around the corner, less than a metre away, a Chinese bloke is keeping watch by the door to the Scenic Room. My gut feeling is that behind him there is plenty of other stuff going on, people trying to get away, people chasing them.

This is undoubtedly the work of the scum scraped together by Farid to make him feel like the leader of a team. I put the mirror back and load up a disposable hypodermic needle. I'm not going to use my Pravaz for this kind of shitty work.

I draw out a small dose of blood from my arm and when WonTon turns round to watch the madness of his colleagues behind him, I spray it right in his face. This obviously distracts him for long enough for me to jump him.

"Fuckin' shithead!"

Half blinded with blood, WonTon can't work out where I am.

"Shut up or I'll get nasty. It's not even infected blood... Take it as an incentive for your personal hygiene."

I knock him out with a whiff of chloroform, tie him up with the tourniquet, and drag him by his feet into the men's toilet. I stick his head down the pan, lower the seat onto his neck and seal the area off with six or seven rounds of red and white tape.

There might be a lot of them, but if you take them out one by one, they collapse like pick-up sticks. Back in the corridor, I put my head around the door of the Scenic Room and get a nasty shock. What the...! Alissa Malesano, Brunhilda and another one of the Robin Blood gang are surrounded by a handful of shabby ninjas led by Farid the Mad Syringer.

"Don't be shy, hand over all the blood you've collected."

As well as betraying the South Rome team my ex-colleague is also making himself look good with my taxpayers.

Compared to last week Anissa has more colour in her cheeks, she almost looks back on form. She's wearing a short tight black skirt and little boots, also black, with red laces. Whatever, a bat has more fat on its ears than she has on her body... In the midst of the confusion I hear her yell.

"This is not... taxable blood! These are voluntary female donations... menstrual donations." She has a feeble, shrill voice which contrasts with her hard bitch image.

I can't help liking her more and more: not only does she know exactly what she wants, she knows where her desires are leading her, and you know what? She doesn't give a shit.

In some ways, if you put the *taxfusion* issues to one side, you have to admire her obstinacy in not wanting to accept the fact that things are turning, not just iffy, but downright dangerous.

The female diners are lined up along the scenic window, they are not exactly being held hostage but they are really worried that things might degenerate and turn out worse than how they started. They are afraid it might end up as a mass-withdrawal by the Robin Bloods using a catheter during that period, that is, today. This lot are obsessed, they track the flows in ladies' toilets before planning them a courtesy visit. They construct statistical models and, even if there is a certain margin of error, they can forecast the quantity of blood available, week by week.

The men are grouped together on the other side of the room,

along the bar, and Farid's Chinese followers are scanning them with a certain amount of skill, using their blood-detectors to uncover anyone indulging in a little crafty tax evasion.

Farid is furious. He has put together this circus of trained apes and now he wants to show he can keep it under control like a skilled trainer.

"Give it to me anyway! I'm not asking your permission."

Brunhilda tries to wriggle out of the cords that these Chinese gentlemen, experts in the ancient art of *shibari*, have tied around her proud breasts. In the end, beaten, she growls dejectedly.

"Fuck you. We don't make deals with BloodBusters so we certainly won't with you. Can't you get it through your thick head this isn't marketable blood!"

I had of course heard the urban legend that the Robin Bloods would even extract menstrual blood for a good cause, as mass donations, and I'd also heard that they take care of cleaning it up with some strange device. In the end, you can even make wine out of grape juice, as they say.

Now I have proof that these rumours are true, but with this system the Robin Bloods are contributing to lowering the female taxpaying capacity. That's no good at all because when the Withdrawals Agency tax inspectors carry out their blood inspections they find these women don't have as much blood as they should and are forced to fine them on the spot.

I call Marzio. I need to scrape together a team of reinforcements. However, as soon the number rings, something absurd happens. Farid notices my call. His mobile starts buzzing with a Middle-Eastern ringtone, and when he looks at the display showing the caller's number, he makes a satisfied grimace. The shitbag has been keeping us under surveillance, now I know how to really get one over on the bastard.

After a few rings, Marzio finally answers.

"Hello, Alan... How's it goin'? Are you feeling lonely?"

Moving away from the Scenic Room, I lower my voice to almost a whisper. All I have to do is lie about my present position in the hope that Mr Suck-it-all-up will take the bait.

"Yeah, I miss you lots, so listen. I'm nearly at the Mushroom

Restaurant, there's some weird shit going down there. I've asked around a bit and it seems there's an unscheduled Robin Bloods meeting going on. Where are you lot? Can you help me out here?"

"At the 'Shroom? Yeah, we'll get there as soon as we can, but it'll take at least half an hour I should think. We're at the Racecourse in Capannelle."

"You lot are always messing around with animal blood. Right, in the meantime I'll have a look upstairs and see how the blood's circulating."

Right, let's see how Farid manages under pressure. Let's see if he comes to roll the red carpet out for me at the entrance. If he tries, I'll squeeze him like a lemon. Farid sends the cavalry to reconnoitre, two spring rolls who even before they've stepped over the doorstep get a door slammed in their faces and hit the floor, deadweight. That's when he realises there's no time to stand around twiddling his thumbs.

"Get them out of here. If they're gonna act shitty, so are we."

His Chinese blokes form a cordon around the three Robin Bloods: Anissa, Brunhilda and a third little chump. Being male he is on the receiving end of most of the punches flying from our Chinese friends who respect a certain criminal code.

Farid tags onto the end of the cordon and grabs Anissa by one hand, picking up the link that was broken only a few days ago.

"Let's see if you act so hard when you're in Regina Coeli prison."

I sneak into the Ladies toilet until the platoon has passed and then, since they have chosen to go down the stairs to avoid any unwelcome surprises on the way down, I slip into the unattended lift. The lift plummets to the ground floor and I use the fraction of a second advantage it has given me to find a place to hide.

I can hear the bar manager swearing and snuffling behind the counter with two waitresses whose hair clips are just visible over the top. Outside the 'Shroom I can see a horde of Sunday reporters and eager web-journalists gathering, ready to upload their videos of the situation at the drop of a hat. Behind them another group, made up of worried friends and relatives of the victims, throngs in the courtyard. Some have climbed up onto the bonnets of their cars and others are on their friends' shoulders to see better.

Uncontrollable rumours are becoming rife, strong terms, exaggerated accusations: kidnapping, blood ransom, slaughter of innocents.

I don't have time to think over the best strategy so, when Farid's group of Chinese helpers gets to the bottom of the stairs and overtakes me, I jump out from under a table, grab Anissa by the arm and find myself not only face-to-face with her but also with Farid who's sticking to her like a professional groper on a bus.

"She's mine."

As soon as he realises it's me, Farid growls, then starts laughing, showing his pointed yellow teeth.

"We've been waiting for you Alan! She belongs to the State!"

This shithead of a man who goes by the name of Farid Sedef has no shame.

"The State!? You don't even have the shadow of an injunction for what you're doing."

"Oh, yeah? We'll see whether they want her or not down at the jail, then, shall we?"

Anissa's hands are sweaty. I told her to behave and here she is in the thick of it, in full anti-haematax warfare. Every time I see her it becomes clearer that this woman is made of highly dangerous stuff, an ideal candidate for the loony bin. Another reason why she needs help.

"Alan, tell this bastard about the extension you granted me..."

Not even four days have passed and I'm already at the point I wanted to reach: I've got my result, she is begging me to save her. She's pleading for help. After this she cannot but be grateful.

Anissa is officially under my spell; bewitched by a haematax agent, Alan Costa the Top Vampire.

At the exact moment I close her in my grasp it's like I'm throwing a seed into her blood, one that will bloom inside her fast. But it's only a moment, it passes when Farid pulls her away fiercely without losing his balance even a little. He points a syringe against my chest, eyes bright with tears. I can't work out whether he's intimidated or excited.

This competition is going to prove unsustainable. You can't trust anyone these days, not even your colleagues, or those you thought of as colleagues. I lurch forward, trying to get past him. He leans towards me and strikes. Just missing my neck he grazes me along my jawline. As far as I know the syringe in Farid's grip could be infected or contain who-knows-what, any dirty contagious shit. I lose my concentration and instead of chasing after Anissa I stop and start thinking about the needle he has just cut me with; I start thinking about the poison which could be about to enter my circulation at any moment; I start thinking about bleeding out again like in the Middle East; I start thinking about everything except the right thing to do. In my moment of uncertainty the Chinese heavies pass Anissa along the cordon and load her into a large rickety Jeep.

Farid goes back on the defensive and I pay a high price for my indecision: one by one his henchmen go into the van and all squashed in together wait for their boss to join them.

"I swear you'll pay for this, Farid..."

"You never listened to me. Not even once."

"Why should I have? Shit, look at you, you're a Bloodsucking traitor. Why should I even ever have thought of listening to someone like you?"

Luckily, the blood detector tells me that the cut isn't infected.

"Well, fuck you too. *Mash'Allah.*"

Farid moves away and, walking backwards, he makes sure that I don't do anything silly. The only thing I can do is swab the cut the shithead has sliced my face with. It's worse than that though isn't it, he's taken away any chance I might have had of extricating Anissa.

In the end it is absurd that even though Farid is the villain of the piece, the bloke who betrayed his team to further his own ends, I am the one with a sliced face.

Bad blood

Rule number six: Man cannot live without blood,
but blood is a weight to be borne.

After letting the phone ring six times, Ilario finally deigns to pick up.

"Oh, Alan, I've just finished dealing with Emory. He's promised my sister blood for at least six months."

He's beside himself with joy. Good for him because now he's going to go through the worst five minutes in a long time. I let him enjoy a few more moments of this passing happiness.

"He treated me like a son. A haemodose every two weeks for six months, plus a crate of Haematogen bars to build up her iron. Basically, Mirna is sorted for half a year, which means I am too. It's just that now I have to run. Come on Alan, tell me where you are, I'll be there as fast as I can..."

I don't want to believe that Ilario cleared off because he was afraid of Farid, it's not like him to leave me in the lurch. But, if he had come to the Mushroom with me things wouldn't have turned out the way they did.

"It's over now. There was some trouble with Farid..."

"What happened? Did you find him?"

"Yes, I found him... And not only has the little shit set up his own band of bloodletters like you said, but for a first try-out mission they fucked over our Robin Bloods from the other week. Switch the telly on, it's on every channel."

"I haven't got one, I'm just leaving Riva Ostiense, tell me what happened."

While I explain, I start patching myself up with a needle and thread. I'm the type of bloke who can stand any kind of pain except for bullshit, then I'm like a bear with a sore head...

"What happened is that Farid and his handful of Chinese losers routed out a Robin Bloods cell and now he's standing in front of the television cameras in Via della Lungara, opposite the Regina Coeli jail, showing off. He's all puffed up with pride like those priests that help junkies living on the streets recover. You know the ones I mean? Those martyrs of the confessional booth, half pained half thrilled, who are convinced they can save the world by saving the people who live on it. He's just the same... Tax Office Hero, my arse."

"Slimy, arselicker!"

From the direction of the Sports Centre, a familiar sound finally reaches my ears: the BloodBusters siren is hot stuff compared to those sad distress signals of the boys in blue and the whimpering bleat the ambulance service have. Two taxbulances, covered with multi-coloured 3D stickers from Ematogen to show their allegiance, cut across the junction and slam on their brakes in the car park.

When Marzio and his boys meet me under the Mushroom they're not hiding how much they dislike the change of programme. They are also not particularly bothered about hiding the fact that they find my situation amusing, they are this close to openly taking the piss. One by one they walk past me, Jajo, Lazybones, Swamp Bird and Marzio.

"Did we miss something? You'll have to excuse us Alan, those horses took ages coming in..."

"Nothing to apologise for, the usual spurts of blood, that's all. Just this time it was menstrual. Oh yeah, and there's been a mutiny."

At which point their enthusiasm dissolves. Lazybones pulls an eloquent face.

"What's it got to do with us? That's women's stuff..."

Out of all of them, Marzio is the most interested in what happened. It's strange, it's almost as if he knows something I don't, but at the same time he's visibly worried that something like this could happen to him and his team. Things used to be different. In the eyes of the youngsters and the stragglers who grew up on the outskirts of town or in council flats in the rough parts of Rome, the profession of blood tax collector was a job like any other, dignified work which could guarantee, if not a good reputation, at least some power in the eyes of other people; and though wealth guarantees a certain amount of freedom, it's usually a person's job that gives him the most power: that of withdrawing and bestowing life, in the form of blood taxes or a one-foot-in-the-grave amnesty. That's why working as a BloodBuster has always been an excellent way of demonstrating that you serve the community, by punishing the dodgers and helping the poor gain justice.

At least, that is the theory, that is what was set down at the dawning of our Guild. Then as time passed, on the streets and in the main squares of Rome the Eternal City, the highest paying withdrawal points were fought over, knives flashing to settle matters, and the area around Piazza del Popolo became a theatre of syringe-armed nocturnal bands. Down the backstreets of Rione Monti and behind the Coliseum shopping Arena, naive tourists are the favourite targets, the choicest victims of the random *withdrawals* of bands of hoodlums who make ends meet by this abusive use of portable haemodetectors.

"Hold the line a sec' Ilario, Marzio's just got here."

Old Glad gives me a hug then turns my face towards him and tuts with his mouth all screwed up in a show of sympathy. His puffed out cheeks show the glimmer of a supportive smile, the brotherly sentiment that has united us since we were on the front-line together.

"Would you do me a favour? I'm talking to Ilario and I don't feel like explaining things to those blue uniformed idiots. You couldn't speak to them for me, could you?"

He walks away without adding anything else. Marzio never opens his mouth without thinking. The exoskeleton he wears to support the legs blown to pieces by the landmine speaks on his behalf with a clanking of light-weight metal alloys courtesy of the RF—Restore Functions—laboratories issued by the Department of Health and Social Security which enable him to continue to walk through the Eternal City instead of rolling across it. These legs provided by the caring state are shaped like a pair of brackets though, making his appearance unfortunately comic.

Glad sets out his men in a semi-circle formation, groups the victims together on one side and the witnesses on the other and waits. The fact is, that in our line, in contrast with the Fuzz, there's not much cause for waiting around and working things out. We have quotas to respect and precise levels of blood that we have to deposit with the Council. If we don't meet the Council quotas they'll take away our licence and the system will collapse, to use a related euphemism. So we have to act, track down tax evaders and their blood, clean it and sell it on. However, we are also the ones who defend the Law from the crafty men in collar and tie and those other walking-evasions: industrialists, resident for tax purposes in lost paradises where blood never flows, politicians with their backsides glued to thrones of power who dump their haematorial obligations on their underlings and stingy businessmen whose arms are so short not only can they not reach their wallets, they're too short to even roll up their sleeves.

Marzio isn't laughing as he points at me from a distance: the boys in blue have arrived in their own good time from Viale dell'Umanesimo with their sirens switched off. They've still got crumbs from their sandwiches stuck to their uniforms. He went to explain the situation to them; who, having arrived last as usual, were acting like they owned the place.

Glad doesn't need to know everything that's gone on to put together the details. He only needs to tell the Fuzz a smattering of facts, an apparent crime, a suggestion of which article of Criminal Law to use in compiling a shining report before going back to patrolling the old-people's Bingo hideaways, the Srilankan gambling dens with their video-poker machines, the slot-machines of our rowdy Chinese friends and all the recently inaugurated Mosques that have been closed during the last month in compliance with the law on religious equality. What's more, to tell the truth, Marzio is like a father-figure to nearly all of us.

"Here I am... Right then, have you seen the mess here, Ilario? Kebab-head has robbed us of a withdrawal. Done-and-dusted."

I put the phone onto speaker-phone and start sewing myself

up. In the taxbulance rear-view mirror I can see that the wound stretches for eight-to-ten centimetres from my jaw almost to my right ear.

"Hold it, Alan, wait... Are you talking about Anissa Malesano's group?"

"Bingo! Yes her group. The freaks were at the Mushroom ladling up menstrual blood."

"What, surely not?"

"They stop at nothing."

Take a city like Rome, full to bursting with highly-withdrawable shitbags. Then give me some sandpaper and a few syringe-happy mosquitoes and within a few months there'll be lakes of blood around. Guaranteed.

More blood for everyone. Call it the "Costa Treatment", if you like. Whatever, the withdrawal symptoms of Rome's population can be cured with Haematogen bars. It's a fact that demand for blood never drops, in fact, the more we put on the market, the quicker it disappears.

"Look Alan, I did some checking up and that Anissa is the Mother Donor of a band that sells blood under the counter to hospitals and National Health Service clinics. There's enough dodgy dealings down there to keep us occupied for a century or more..."

On the bar's big screen the news footage of Ms muscles-and-plaits Brunhilda and Anissa's group being arrested is making the rounds of the news programmes. Surrounded by microphones, Farid is puffed like a peacock in all his finery. He's standing straight as a die with his arms crossed opposite an array of television cameras and smartphones, flanked by his Chinese side-kicks as crooked as bamboo sticks and doing his best to get as much as he can from this unhoped-for triumph. Hard and self-satisfied my ex-BloodBuster colleague explains in his stilted Italian the wheres and hows of his bulldog parataxman antics. From the way the media-vultures are wetting themselves with excitement, jostling and fighting to get closer to him, you can see that as far as they're concerned it's all good news; the same old story of exaggerating scandals, stirring up fear and other rubbish blown up beyond all reason, any expedient to raise viewing figures which no longer have anything to do with the concept of being liked. at the end of the day, *blood doesn't stink.*

"Here, listen!"

I put my smartphone close to the big screen's speakers. In the meantime I haven't been idle, I've been sliding the needle back and forth through my skin, piercing the thin layer of platelets that are having a party on my jaw coagulating blood and plasma.

"... after days and days of long, exhausting stake-outs, Farid Sedef has managed to uncover the location of a criminal organisation's recent secret meetings. In a TFZ—Tax Free Zone—area near the Magliana flyover, where the Robin Bloods have been carrying out their unhealthy public donation rituals, without the least respect for the most basic hygiene and tax laws..."

The more I see him, the more I feel swindled and buggered. I'd like nothing better than to give him a good kicking... and I could kick myself too, for having let him get away with it.

"Listen, it's not over yet. Only the fireworks are missing."

"... furthermore, Mr. Sedef claims that the band, headed by a top member of this new type of crime Anissa Malesano, has been making use of thousands of electronic gnats and mosquitoes to withdraw considerable quantities of blood from unwitting taxpayers as they sleep. This dangerous method is responsible for spreading highly infectious diseases such as malaria, Tauopathies and sleeping sickness..."

I knew that someone like Farid had to be kept on a tight rein right from the start. With people like him you need to keep your shoulders against the wall so they don't get a chance to stab you in the back.

"I even had that bloody Anissa in my grip. She was in my power and then that bastard... Would you believe he even had the nerve to slash my face? He attacked me with a syringe, I'm bloody lucky it was clean."

"Why the fuck did you go on your own. Couldn't you wait for someone to go with you?"

Once again I can only hope that Ilario is being sincere. Anyway I'm not one to kid myself. I don't give a fuck about his not being available, good reason or no good reason.

"Yeah right, someone... Who gives a fuck about numbers, numbers have never been a problem. Farid had a whole reserve team of Chinese helpers behind him that not even Catapano in the good-old-days could have dreamt of. Ah, but if I get my hands on him, Ilario... I swear I'll humiliate him in front of everyone! I'll make a withdrawal from his butt cheeks and you... You can film the scene and stick it on YouTube."

"What, have you gone raving mad? With things as they are at the moment it's just stuff that can happen, fuck knows how many have slipped through the net. No, really, why should we give a shit about him?"

I tie an improvised knot in the thread. Then I glance at myself in the mirror and make a roll-up to ease the tension. I'll show that syringe-happy maniac *how* to do business; I'll re-order his important things-to-do list and it will take just seconds before I have him on his knees screaming for mercy. Mercy which I will of course never grant him. Obviously. What do you take me for?

"Do you study to be this thick headed? I was following that Anissa and he did everything in secret, sneaky bastard. It's a question of principles."

"Principles? Since when have you been interested in principles. It's not like you... you haven't got a crush on this *An-aem-issa*, have you? I wouldn't even have dreamed of bringing home some of the crazy bitches you've been with, limp dick hunters and fiscal beggars... But when it came down to it, at least they were healthy, this top model though, I mean her skin, what was it like, eh? You get fewer holes in a mosquito net."

"Come on Ilario, you're not going to feed me the usual shit, are you? You know whose side I'm on. It's just you have no control over some things. I am what I am."

I'm getting irritated. Talking to Ilario sometimes leaves me feeling emptier than after I've done a self-withdrawal. I start walking around the Mushroom.

"You are what you are... What sort of answer is that? And what precisely are you, if you don't mind telling me?"

"Listen, I need to know how to get her out of Regina Coeli.

Do you know any of our cousins down there?"

I grind my fag end out on the bodywork of the taxbulance.

"Let's not even go there. As the saying goes, *There's no blood for mosquitoes there*. Don't drag me into it. Just leave it, Alan. I mean you know what I'm saying, can you imagine it? In jail, they'll already have attached her to a drip to keep her metabolism at a minimum. With the standard Compulsory Tax Treatment she'll be there for who knows how long with the amount of tax evasion she's done, that holier-than-thou girl..."

"Fuck you too, Ilario! Is that all the thanks I get? Remember when I helped you out when you were in deep shit? What about when you lost 12 haemodoses in that illegal gambling den and so as not to look bad in front of Emory you wanted permission to suck blood from the first loser we came across? Hey, Ilario, forgotten about that already have you?"

"I get it, I get it... You've turned into one of those scabby Vampires who only help a colleague so they can call in the debt later. How do you managers put it? You scratch my back and I'll scratch yours? Alright then, cheers Alan Crust, you've convinced me. Let me know what I can do for you. Are you happy now?"

"Fuck you!"

We both slam down our videophones.

The bloody louse! I'll see him and his foul world drown in a bucket of blood! Him and his "I'm all right Jack" attitude.

When did obedience and respect stop being considered values? Sometimes Ilario behaves just like a snobbish show-off, just like a spoilt brat. Brat? I could kick myself... What's going to happen to Anissa's son? If I hadn't let her have those extra fifteen days, maybe Farid wouldn't have moved in with such arrogance. Is it my fault that Anissa has ended up in jail?

Marzio has got rid of the boys in blue without them even doing an inspection of the restaurant above the Mushroom. Don't take it as sloppiness or negligence; it's what is known as "collaboration between the Forces of Law and Order".

With his false legs twisting this way and that, Glad comes up and starts in on me.

"So, Alan, when are you going to learn your lesson? Are you

really so set on creating bad blood?"

"That's rich coming from you... If the State had given me what it gave you, I wouldn't be here chasing my own men around."

"Don't starting insinuating stuff you don't know about. I paid for my house with these legs of mine."

He punches the exoskeleton, it bends but doesn't break.

"Sorry, I didn't mean to insinuate anything. But it's not my fault if gunshot wounds weren't enough to get me an invalidity pension. You know better than I do that neither of us was granted the right to privileged treatment, I mean, not even a special mention or a promotion, special leave or permission for a few days of recreational drinking."

Glad raises his gaze to look at the sky.

"If they had, it would have looked like an admission of guilt, like acknowledging an error. They were supposed to look like "brilliant recovery operations", perfect from a strategic point of view."

Then he shakes his head and his venous pressure shoots up a bit. His neck swells, but he maintains an apparent calm.

"Don't you see, you're a soldier for the Intravenous Revenue? And even though a soldier has the power of life and death, he is still someone who will always take orders, a puppet who does what he's told."

"What's that got to do with anything, Marzio?"

"Everything. Does Emory know what you're doing?"

Looking at things this way, he's right. Looking at things this way, I'm behaving no better than that shitbag Farid. That's not the impression I want to give Glad or, more importantly, Emory.

"No, he doesn't know. Not yet... But I did it for him too. For the good name of the BloodBusters."

"You're reading things into it Alan, and that's not right. Soldiers don't choose their own targets, they don't plan anything, and you know what? They don't give a shit because soldiers, at the end of every mission, can forget about the consequences of their actions. You're only one of the arms that carries out the dirty work and don't you forget it..."

I want to put a stop to this military warfaresophy. Marzio

is a friend, a friend I care about, as long as he doesn't behave like a loser with a gong. When he does, especially when I've got something gnawing away inside me, I don't look up to him at all. I already have to deal with Emory rewriting every step of my miserable life in the style of a Roman epic.

"Yes, yes, wait while I write down these pearls of wisdom."

"I'm telling you... and I'm telling you as a friend, don't overdo it."

Bullshit. Think of someone like Julius Caesar, for instance. He didn't get where he did by obeying the orders of the Roman Senate, on the contrary, everything he did was a practical demonstration of how to make the interests of the State match his own.

Holding my cheek, I get back into the taxbulance and before leaving the Mushroom car park, I give a nod in the direction of the East Rome team: Jajo, Swamp Bird, that dissolute Lazybones, and Marzio. I switch the MP3 player on in shuffle mode and by chance *Who Killed Bambi?* by the Sex Pistols comes on. It would be a bad joke, but too many stupid things are happening and all at the same time.

Even if Anissa isn't dead, once she's inside Regina Coeli, she might as well be.

Thoroughbred

Rule number seven: it is only through the sale of Haematogen bars that levels of blood worthy of a civilised country can be made available without running into counterproductive unrest.

Nicola is walking hand in hand with a girl with fluorescent dummies tied in her hair. The pavement is crowded with school kids and these two are munching at Haematogen bars as if it is the coolest experience in the whole wide world.

Via di Vigna Murata is full of groups of school kids making their way home, the youngest on foot and the others are either in disorderly lines of careering sticker-laden cars, or on swarms of noisy buzzing mopeds.

An hour before the bell, I parked the taxbulance at Fabrizio's kiosk in the Garbatella quarter and drank two beers in honour of the whole mess. Thinking back on how things have gone fills me with an enormous rage. I made a right cock-up with Farid and now I'm paying for it, there's little else to say.

Every sip was made sour by my thoughts.

In the meantime, messing about with my smartphone on a social network I discovered that Nicola is a first year at the Armellini Technical High School. Section B. 27 students. 15 girls, 12 boys. Specialising in IT and so on.

So I drank another two beers without Fabrizio commenting either on my appearance (I was covered in sticking plasters), or my mood, half-way between glowering and sulky. Thinking about my dodgy temper and knowing the sort of *blades* I normally deal with in my job helped him come up with the great idea of offering me another beer, with a side shot of gin, on the house. And so it was five. A round number, I suppose.

We need more people like Fabrizio in this city, high-class neighbourhood psychologists.

At coming out time I set off towards Armellini again and as soon as I recognised Nicola's outline, I raised the volume on *Hey Boy, Hey Girl* by the Chemical Brothers.

I take the taxbulance alongside the couple and lean out of the passenger side.

"Ciao Nicola, do you want a lift home?"

He recognises me at once and his eyes light up. Then he stretches his arms, sticks his chest out and runs his fingers through his hair to impress his sweetheart, whose eyes are as bright as diamonds.

"Yeah, but can we take Lucy home first?"

"Lucy? No worries, as long as she doesn't live in the sky... Come on, climb in."

They are so young they don't catch the double meaning and continue taking bites out of their blood soaked candies.

"I live in Via Grottaperfetta, number 503."

As soon as we turn into Via Laurentina the traffic is a complete nightmare, an absurd phenomenon which appears unexpectedly, like a summer hurricane or a sand storm, because in the Eternal City there are always people ready to do anything to gain an inch on those that are behind, to the side, or in front of them. In Rome, this attitude often verges on car blackmail. Cars spread across the road with a naturally savage attitude, or rather, selectively, so as to block the day's victim: an elderly person, a Sunday driver, someone who simply never could get the hang of it. Someone who without fail, is forced to slow down, stop and give way, which is the most highly prized currency on the road.

"You couldn't put the siren on, could you?"

Lucy has very good taste, in sounds as well as flavours. She's realised straight away that if road Darwinism rules in this city, I'm the King of the Traffic.

"Shall we have some fun?"

Nicola looks at me, full of excitement. He's basking in reflected glory from me and this is a spoonful of pure sugar that I'll be able to use when the time comes to help him swallow some bitter medicine.

Lucy moves closer to Nicola and giggles.

"Yerrsss come on... I've always loved the noise you Buckmakers make."

It's not our fault if that's what the kids call us. They were born with high finance in their veins.

"Okay, hold on. I don't want to find you in the boot."

I switch on the scarecars and push the accelerator to the floor, just to shake the two of them up a bit like it shakes up the river of cars, making it divide into two banks leaving us to zig-zag down the middle, which is a real pleasure. At Piazzale Ardigò I cut across in the direction of Tor Marancia and then head up Via Grottaperfetta until the sat-nav starts beeping.

"This is my stop, I live here."

As soon as I switch off the siren, Nicola gets out of the taxbulance and his girl gives him a loud kiss on the lips. He finishes saying "Goodbye" to Lucy at the garden gate, then he and I head back off towards Torrino.

We go past rows of pine trees and squared columns and then a line of church domes and endless dried out palm trees whose pulpy pith has been sucked out by hordes of ravenous red weevils.

"Listen Nicola, something happened today."

He visibly deflates, he's not thick and he's guessed that my presence isn't about to bring him anything good.

"It's mum, isn't it? What, is she ill again?"

I don't know how to tell him. At least not without hurting him. Nicola might be used to dealing with Anissa's "happiness holes", but this is a completely different kettle of fish. Trust me to go and get myself involved in a mess like this. If Ilario gets to know about this, I bet he'll laugh till he cries.

"Your mum is going to be away for a good while, Nico..."

"So it's serious, then. Has she been taken into hospital somewhere? Can we go and see her there?"

Instead of heading towards Torrino, I continue on to the northbound Ring Road. Nicola is jumpy and unwraps another bar of Haematogen with plasma. I feel bad about having to tell him so abruptly but there's no point beating about the bush "the blood is cast", that's for sure.

"This bastard I know has had her locked up. I gave her 15 days to get ready and fit for the blood-tax withdrawal, but this creep didn't wait for your mum to produce the amount of blood that... Look, basically, Anissa's in Regina Coeli jail."

This time Nicola doesn't cry, he's too surprised for tears or maybe he doesn't really know how to react to news like this. How am I supposed to know, I've never had anything to do with kids of his age before.

"Listen, is there anyone you can stay with for the next few days? A relative, a neighbour, a friend of the family, something like that? I'm sorry, but I have to ask... Do you know where your father is?"

He thinks about it and then with a sigh he scrolls through the agenda on his smartphone as though finding somewhere to stay is a problem he deals with every other day.

"There's this friend of mum's, she lives in Santa Marinella, it's just that..."

Nicola closes his phone and takes a large bite of his bar, chewing to gain time.

"...if she sees someone like you, y'know a BloodBuster, I don't know how she'll take it."

"I get it, she's in with the Robin Bloods too then, is she?"

He nods his head and scratches a couple of spots on his chin.

"I don't know anything about my father. Mum hardly ever talks about him and when she does, she ends up crying or she starts throwing plates against the wall."

Perfect, I'm going to have to look after him myself.

I don't even know how long this babysitting service is going to go on for. At his age, I hardly ever saw my parents, they were only around occasionally. Not that I didn't care about them or they didn't care about me, it was just that our daily routines stopped overlapping. My father worked as an audio mixer, he still does, for a local TV channel, while my mum was a journalist for a free newspaper, one of those papers distributed in the trains and on the underground.

"It doesn't matter, it just means you'll be staying with me for a few days. Then we'll see if we can find a better solution for both of us."

"Why?"

"Because you can't stay on your own, can you? How old are you anyway?"

"No, I mean why are you letting me stay with you?"

On the other side of the taxbulance's windscreen the sun is setting behind Fiumicino airport.

A searing hot ball of fire like the one I saw going down every day during my stint in the Middle East. My old thigh wound itches. I can still see the girl soldier with the rifle slung around her neck and then here, now, next to me, this other kid also running the risk of losing his mother.

"We can't have you staying with those Robin Blood loons."

"Why not?"

The kid doesn't want to give in. Just like his mum.

"Because if you spend too much time with losers, you end up becoming one of them. That's why..."

There aren't that many people I know who I could ask to look after Nicola. My mother, between murder stories and editorials about events and crimes in the Eternal City, works from morning to night. When they call, she runs. She's worse than me.

At eighteen, when I left home, she must have breathed a sigh of relief. She never actually said it directly, but I think she was happy to have one less thing to worry about, in fact, to tell the truth, it was one less hole to be bled dry from.

My father, after the divorce, moved to somewhere near Naples; during the day he enjoys the sun and the sea, by night he plays with the coloured cursors of his mixers. We don't hate each other or anything, it's just distance and time seem to stop us meeting up a lot.

Maybe I'm wrong. Whatever, I choose a name from my mobile and dial a number which if you were to say was a surprise call, you'd be making an understatement.

"Ceci... It's Alan, how are you?"

"Yes, Alan, hello, I can see by the number... You don't have to introduce yourself. What's up, everything okay?"

"Sure, everything's okay. It's just I wanted to ask you a small favour."

"It's not work, is it? Because you know what my answer will be, don't you?"

Of course, I know. Her usual wariness.

"Work? No, it's got nothing to do with work."

I wonder if Nicola can be considered as "work". I wonder if he falls within the limits of my sense of duty. I wonder if this kid is simply something I haven't yet had the time to give a precise definition to.

"I know a boy... I mean a young lad, called Nicola, who needs somewhere to stay for a few days. I was wondering if you would be kind enough to put him up for a while."

"And who is he, this boy, he's not your son is he?"

"No, what, my son? Why would you say that Ceci?"

"You wouldn't even talk about having children with me and now you're going about with other people's kids. What's going on, eh?"

"Listen, nothing's going on. I'm not going about with anyone, what about it even if I was? I only said that I need a favour, one bloody favour for a few days. I have to go to wor-" I bite my tongue.

"You see! That's what it always is, Alan. Even when you're trying you can't manage a decent lie. You're a piece of shit, do you know that? Shall I spell it out for you S-H-I-T."

Here we go, as punctual as a tax demand! Insults spelled out letter by letter. This woman is a real pain. I'm the stupid one, thinking things might change.

"Okay, forget I asked you anything. Sorry for bothering you."

"I knew it would end up like this. You father a son with another woman and now you're calling me for help? You made your bed, now you'll bloody well have to lie in it!"

I put the phone down before I have to listen to any more of this rubbish. Then I slow down and brake sharply.

"Oh, Nico, I'm a bit thirsty... Do you want a Coke?"

Nicola nods, as the taxbulance screeches over the motorway service station tarmac.

Speaking of kids... We get out of the van and I take the portable blood-detector with me. I want to check something, which if I'm right would be absurd, but with someone as mad as Anissa isn't out of the question.

When we are sitting down at the table in Fast Blood munching Red Haematogen washed down with Coke, I take out the finger-pricker. Nicola stiffens.

"I don't punch holes in myself, you know. I'm not like her."

Poor sod, I'm going to have to butter him up a bit to convince him.

"There's nothing to be afraid of... I don't want to take your blood, I just need one drop."

To soften him up, I fix the insulin needle onto my Pravaz, the tiny little one that wouldn't hurt a fly.

"Look, I swear you won't feel a thing, not even inside the vein. Bet you a Coke?"

He accepts despite himself and I can see his unease. He offers me a timid finger and I spike it with extreme class, a real hit and run.

When I read the results of the analysis, depression hits me. I try not to show him, even if, quite rightly, he wants to know what I've seen in his blood. What I've seen is that his father is 0 RH-negative.

Just as two there are no two people exactly alike, the blood of any two given individuals is always different. Anissa though must have been so obsessed with the altruism of donating that she went and chose a partner with the same blood group as hers to be sure that when Nicola grew up he would also be a Universal Donor.

"Everything's fine, Nico. You're as sound as a Haematogen bar. I'll get you another Coke and then we can go straight to mine. I live at the top of Silos Aureliano, do you know where it is?"

He doesn't.

"Oh, well. What kind of films do you like?"

Infected blood

Rule number eight: Injustice is the best of all teachers.
Learn from its many lessons.

Just beyond Valle Aurelia, is the area that used to be called Hell's Valley because it was full of chimneys belching out fumes and heat from the furnaces of the old tin and iron works. It has kept its name because clusters of air conditioners continue to make the area's temperature a good 3 degrees higher than elsewhere. We can see the isolated outline of Silos Aureliano from here. Home sweet home.

The wide open spaces that used to spread all around here, the cultivated fields I used to race across on my motor scooter when I was younger, have been invaded by freshly painted prefabricated houses, building sites, and the silhouettes of new and soon-to-be-completed 3-family homes.

My apartment is a corner of the Silos building's fortieth floor overlooking the Montespaccato beehive, well, it'll be mine when I've finished paying the remaining 160 mortgage instalments. It is brand new but you can already feel the lack of a woman about the place. You can even feel it from a certain distance, as soon as you come out of the lift for instance. Ceci has never been here, not even out of curiosity, and Concita's visits won't do much good if she doesn't come more often. It's not that I want to impress Nicola, I couldn't care less about the unmade bed (what's the point in making it if I'm just going to mess it up again?), the pile of greasy dirty plates, (I might as well wait until I've used the last clean one before washing up) the DVDs of Rocco (without his brothers), it's just that I'm embarrassed about the smell that hangs around on the landing. Rubbish rots quicker in the summer. Leaving it outside the door only moves the problem around.

Just inside my house, a shadow slips away from the kitchen wall with the Van Gogh poster on it towards the terrace. Nicola notices and jumps when he hears a noise something like a breeze.

"There's somebody in here!"

I put my Ematogen bag down in the lounge on the edge of the dining table. That is, once I've moved the breakfast things, the croissant wrapper and the jars of honey, blackberry jam, and Nutella.

Have you ever tasted blood? I have, and mine is sickly sweet.

"No, don't worry... It's just Tino. He gets too hot outside and comes in every now and then to cool down."

"Tino? Who's Tino? Why does he live on the balcony?"

I get the giggles as I put away the empty bottles of beer and limoncello. As a last touch I sweep up the Haematogen wrappers with my hands.

"Come and have a look who Tino is..."

I lead Nicola onto the balcony and show him the "bat box" which I installed two years ago after a summer of unending torment. I was so desperate to find an effective way of stopping the hordes of mosquitoes that I ended up looking at the University of Florence website which explained, step by step, how to make your own bat box. It didn't take long and when the bat word was out about there being a den going for free Tino took possession straight away, not even a day later, drawn by the chance to set up home in an area full of mosquitoes. Considering the number of mosquitoes you can hear buzzing around everywhere at all hours of the day and night, Tino could become the supreme bat patriarch.

"What, is it really a bat? You really keep a little monster on the balcony?"

I shrug and lower the blind. Tino can sleep for up to five months a year and when he wakes up he spends most of the day hiding from the sun, but at night he goes out hunting in the surrounding area. A life on the edge of society, poor little creature.

"So? What's wrong with that, I need company, too... Someone or something to welcome me home. I chose Tino because he's discrete, and, most importantly, he helps keep the mosquitoes at bay."

Nicola looks at me sideways and then stretches towards the wooden box. The little beast is using its claws to turn round and climb down to the edge of the entrance, it points its ears forwards and tunes in to our presence. If you ask me he understands what we're saying too.

"He's amazing... If I let him out at night, he's capable of hoovering up hundreds of mozzies."

"Isn't he dangerous?"

"Not at all, he's almost scared of his own shadow. And shy, as soon as he hears an owl hooting nearby he hides safely inside the bat-box for a whole day. Come in and I'll make you something to eat. Are you hungry?"

I switch on the TV and sit Nicola down on the sofa to help get him used to his new temporary residence as quickly as possible. Then I go into the bathroom to powder my nose. Tearing off the plaster I search through the medicine cabinet until I find some antibiotic powder. I dose the cut with a cloud of the stuff to accelerate the process of healing and regeneration.

"Gimme two minutes and I'll be with you. In the meantime, make yourself at home."

The slash on my jaw has started to heal even though the skin around it is as red as a volcanic fault. The edges of the wound are red and swollen and form a light-coloured oblong which is filling up with transparent liquid. From tomorrow, until the stitches fall off, let's say about a week, the skin will pull and be uncomfortable. But the circumstances of the fuck-up I brought on myself to get it will stay with me much longer, and mark me much deeper down than the wound on my cheek.

I go into my room to change my sauce splattered clothes and notice I have left my outline traced in salt on the bed, a shroud measuring my every turn inside this perimeter of summer torture and suffering.

I need to get the air conditioner fixed. No fan that I know of has ever been able to get between me and the mattress.

I slip on a grey ribbed vest and green beach shorts with wedding tackle netting included. Who knows, we might go for a swim in the apartment block pool; while we were coming upstairs, I noticed with great surprise that the block manager had finally got round to putting some water in it. Just a couple of inches, no more, eh?! Water is blue gold these days, costs almost as much as the red stuff.

I pop back into the living room.

"So, what are you watching?"

I quickly slip past the sofa, and open the fridge. The contents leave me dumbstruck. There's a food morgue inside worthy of a panic attack. One plate holds the nibbled remains of the chicken with peppers I ordered last night from the take-away on the corner of Via Castel di Guido. It might still be alright to feed someone with an empty stomach.

"Nothing really... just channel hopping."

He should be *hopping* something else, he and his haemo generation. At least I try and survive. These limp kids, on the other hand, would rather eat bread and watch mini-series on TV.

The mozzarella is about to go off but I grab that and a couple of oblong tomatoes which are only still edible because of all the chemical shit that's been grafted onto their genes. Then I start slicing everything very thinly.

"Alan, come and have a look. I've got a feeling this'll interest you..."

Even with the sound down, the scene on the TV is blazingly obvious. Two Withdrawals Agency tanker lorries have been attacked by a Robin Blood cell near Monteverde Vecchio. They must be the daily deliveries heading for the Montemartini Depot in Riva Ostiense.

I turn the sound up and from the initial reconstruction of the scene carried out by the boys in grey it would seem that it's some kind of reprisal for Anissa's arrest and the EUR round-up.

The blokes at the Ematogen Distribution and Logistics Dept. have come up with some really stunning subterfuges in the past to make sure their loads get to where they're headed perfectly safe and sound: they camouflage the vehicles with fake sponsor's logos, they cover the ministerial badges with banal, anonymous crests, decorate the trucks in all sorts of ways, but it's never enough. 10% of withdrawn blood is lost from takings through the collection of fraudulent juices, sly watering-down by traitorous drivers and indiscriminate attacks on tanker lorries, like the one we're watching on the news.

"This is going to end badly, I can see it. I didn't realise your friends had so many resources."

Hundreds of litres of blood are spurting from the slashed tanker, commercial value gone: an enormous outpouring of arterial blood corpuscles flowing from the tanker onto the cobbles of Via dei Quattro Venti. What a waste. It's disgusting.

"Look they aren't my friends. Friends of my mum, maybe..."

I give him a sidelong glance. Experience has taught me one thing, the people who scare me most are the people who are scared themselves. Nico has shown me a couple of times already that he isn't afraid of saying what he thinks.

"Sorry, Nico, it's true, you don't punch holes in yourself, but you do know them, I mean, who knows how many times they've been to your house and how many secret meetings Anissa took you to when you were little."

He lowers his gaze. I must have guessed right. It looks like Nicola hates those meetings and all the participants. Those meetings, week after week, took his mother from him a bit at a time and when they went to them together, when he was smaller and couldn't put up any resistance or complain, he must have felt as though he didn't count for anything, as though he had to disappear and step to one side for the Robin Blood mission.

While Nicola is watching the scene on TV, it doesn't take much insight to understand what he thinks of them. I imagine him in his playpen and later crawling in a locked room full of cuddly toys and games, and finally scampering about in a garden watched over by a kindly guard dog. It might be a complete fantasy, but I bet it was more or less like that.

"I don't give a damn about them."

He says it as icily as a frozen dinner. Dinner, yeah right.

I heat up the chicken and peppers and slide them onto a plate. Then I drizzle a drop of olive oil over it, add a pinch of salt to the other plate and hand it all to Nicola: one day old free-range chicken, and a tomato and mozzarella salad fresh from the fridge.

"I know, that's how it goes. There's no point in getting angry about it. Listen, there was no basil, so I put some oregano on it."

"No probs. I could eat a horse..."

The report on TV ends and the whereabouts of the third tanker lorry is a still a mystery. The driver claims to have been thrown out of the vehicle and left in the middle of the road while the Robin Bloods took the truck and its contents away.

"They've really overstepped the mark this time. They've swallowed up a whole tanker."

I open a beer. Who knows who those haemodoses belonged to. Who knows who'll be swearing this month besides Emory. Monteverde belongs to the Rome Central team, Pino Goodman, Tinribs and Nibble II.

While Nicola is chewing the emotional storm that hit him dies down in a second. He turns towards me, looks at my bare arms and lingers on the valves for my monthly withdrawals.

"You do it too then?"

I wish I was as naive as him. I wish I was thirteen again, with no holes in my virgin skin. "Yes, but not like your mother. She gives her blood away, I keep mine."

Taxes leave terrible scars, a purplish sore that taxpayers wear like a label from school-leaving age till death. Those track marks around their arm or some other piece of skin is a kind of magic symbol, a badge of initiation. A sign of being part of the group, of joining society.

"When you're eighteen you'll get your very own haematax hole too... Even if it's not as subtle as the Robin Blood ones."

He pulls a face, half shocked.

"I'll tell you one more time, I never have and never will be full of holes."

"Ah, here we are, another blood objector..."

"I don't give a shit about the Robin Bloods or you BloodBusters either, don't you get that?"

"Yeah, but you don't say no to the odd bar of Haematogen, do you?"

He chews in my face.

"I've had it up to here with all this talk about blood! All of it... the fucking lot of it."

Nicola is going as red as a tomato. He drops his fork onto his plate in annoyance, gets up and goes out onto the balcony.

Moody little bugger, seems a bit too easy to get under his skin. I leave him to calm down while I down another beer. After things have settled a bit maybe we'll be able to put up with each for a week or so. Then I'm going to have to work something out. A couple of minutes later he comes back and sits on the sofa looking like he's pulled himself together, but he's clenching his fists so hard his knuckles have turned white.

"Do you want to know where that other tanker lorry is?"

"Why, do you know?"

Nicola nods. He comes back to the table and in a couple of mouthfuls his mozzarella salad disappears.

"I'll take you there later. As soon as it gets dark, 'cos there won't be anything to see before then."

*

As darkness falls, around 10pm, Silos Aureliano is gasping for air, a situation that won't change for a while yet.

The enormous ring shaped building made up of eight interconnected blocks, with a droplet-shaped swimming pool, a three-metre high diving board and a children's slide in its centre, is deserted. There are a few benches scattered around the tower block's gardens but they are only used in the mornings, occupied by dozens of old people desperately hoping for at least a small breath of cool air: old people between eighty and ninety who've finally reached their retirement, eating breakfast together like children, taking turns to read the paper and gossiping as their only ways of killing the time weighing heavy on their hands. I've got a feeling they really are killing time. On the upper floors, at this time of night, only a few Filipinos are looking out of the windows, apart from the sweet old lady who everybody likes intent on cleaning the satellite dishes on the balconies. Down below, the water is rippling in the pool and almost seems to be simmering after being exposed to the sun for hours.

On the hill opposite, as well as the repeated honking of cars, I can hear a Rome-style Harley rider go past, a roaring dandy rigged out in fluttering jacket and tie, heading off down town to meet up with others like him even though it's a Monday night, a tour for real roadster die-hards, between aperitifs, restaurants, shots and mojitos.

Not that I want to come over all judgemental, or anything, but I just don't get some people's idea of a good time.

Only the Bongiorno family somewhere at the top of the building keep Silos awake with their world-famous non-stop domestics over idiotic disagreements. While Nicola and I walk around the edge of the pool, I hear Mr He getting mad at Mrs She.

"Eh! Can't you smell that stink of piss? It's like living in the cattery in Torre Argentina!"

"Well then, clean the litter tray more often.... Instead of moaning all the time, do somefing."

"Ha! I'll tell you what... I'll really do *somefing* this time. I've just about had it up to here of being a slave to this bloody cat!"

"Really? What are you doin'? 'Ave you gone mad?"

Silence. Then a cat starts yowling like an eagle. And just like an eagle, it can be seen flying out of a window. A twelve-floor drop. A black arc against a backdrop of halogen light. The only difference being that unlike an eagle, the cat can't flap its wings, instead it flips over a couple of times and ends up straight in the pool. Fortunately for us and it, instead of blood, we are splashed by the equivalent of a bucketful of water.

"Fluffy! Are you alright?"

Mrs She leans out. We check out quite how wet we are.

From down here, she looks a bit on the heavy side. She's wearing a pink dressing gown, which reaches her knees, and two tiger-striped slippers, the horror! Mrs She doesn't say sorry or even seem embarrassed about her awful outfit, she's that worried about her kitty.

"Idiot! You're stark staring mad."

She looks threateningly at Mr He and goes back inside. First I hear the insults flying and then the kitchenware. Plates, glasses and cutlery, it all crashes across the room. I don't want to know how it's going to end up, but don't want to read about it in the crime section of the local news website either.

Fluffy pulls itself out of the pool half-senseless and looking like a drowned rat. It shakes off the water and then looks straight up. After that terrifying experience it doesn't seem to have the slightest inclination to head back to the Bongiorno abode. It lies down in the corner thinking fuck knows what...

This is the first time I have seen a smile on Nicola's face since I met him.

Back in the taxbulance, I decide not to call for reinforcements. This time I'm going in civvies. Me, my vest and my Bermuda shorts.

Nicola doesn't let out a peep during the trip. Fifteen minutes of silence that I fill with *Seven Nation Army* by the White Stripes and *Baba O'Riley* by The Who.

At night, the Villa Pamphili grounds need to be walked through with caution. Especially the darker less well-known areas running along the east side. "Here we are then."

Nicola gets out while I park the taxbulance hard up against the wall. On foot and in the dark we head along Via della Nocetta.

After just a few steps, he stops. Nicola knows a secret passage, a wall of bricks that can be removed one at a time and put back as they were afterwards. A sort of mosaic doorway. A good thought considering all the gates to the Villa are CCTV-controlled.

After five minutes of pulling apart and putting back together again we're in Villa Pamphili. I really want to know how the Robin Bloods have managed to get an entire tanker lorry in here. Not even Nicola knows that.

We make sure our phones are switched off and walk through the dark along barely visible paths beaten out by who knows who, Nicola briskly leading the way, and me following in silence. The grass being crushed makes a slight sound, but the crickets chirping out their protest against the hot night air are brilliant cover. In the pools of light made by the moon we can just make out the lopsided outlines of a few bats swooping down to drink from a fountain.

After a good mile Nicola breaks his vow of silence and opens his mouth. His eyelids blinking and fluttering even in this half-light.

"How long d'you think my mum is gonna be in there?"

He signals me with his hand to hold still. There's a rustle in the distance that's nothing to do with the wind. Footsteps, and lots of them. We slip behind the remains of a tree trunk, emptied and stripped clean by termites. We want to be sure these nocturnal walkers don't creep up on us.

I whisper. He squeezes up close to me.

"A long time Nicola... I'm trying to think of a way of getting her out of there, but it's complicated. You can't mess about with the prisons if you don't have the right connections, and I don't."

We move on, up and down a series of small slopes. I don't know this part of Villa Pamphili; we're in the centre of Rome, in the rotten lung of the Eternal City, and even so I feel lost and I can't get my head round it. Nicola points to something, a light-coloured area in the middle of the thicket. Half-hidden between the branches and the thorns I can just see the camouflaged profile of a large lorry.

"Can you see it?"

"Yes, it's *our* stolen load."

"You'll be able to see the Robin Bloods soon too... It's their fault if my mother is in prison. It's Sergio's fault."

He makes as if to move forward but I grab his arm. In the tangle of shrubs and trunks brought down by the summer storms I can see sweet wrappings and plastic cups and cutlery. Just beyond, I can see the blurred, poorly lit red, yellow, and green of some tents.

"Wait... Who is this Sergio? Tell me."

"He's the founder of the Robin Bloods. My mum used to be a nurse. He was a doctor at the Umberto I Transfusion Centre. It was Sergio who first spoke to her about free blood and mass donations. It's just that by handling so much of other people's blood he got Hepatitis C..."

Speaking of the Umberto I hospital reminds me of the infected blood scandal, 1400 dead and around 80,000 infected throughout Italy. "The long silent massacre" they called it in the papers at the time, including my mother in her free press paragraphs. After a few years legal action was started, one of the first *class action* cases in Italy which, once it started, like so many other things here, didn't come to anything.

"Did the doctor really get hepatitis?"

"Yes really. During a meeting Sergio said he had found a bag of blood that had been kept half-forgotten in the basement of the Courthouse. He said it was the blood of an Unknown donor. Blood that came from who knows where and was being kept there waiting to be analysed by some Judge who had forgotten all about it or would let it rot. Sergio said that the risk of infection was much lower than the probability of saving the lives of ill-people."

The tanker's engine starts up. A couple of Robin Bloods get out and put two medical kits on the ground.

"Another time they found some sacks that were from abroad. Stuff for the poorest of patients. "Powdered blood" my mum called it. It wasn't clean blood. In the 1990s, checks weren't as tight as they are now. When Sergio got sick, everything changed. They didn't have the time to start the family they wanted..."

Nicola hesitates. Sergio isn't his father. His father came after, in an attempt to right the double tragedy: Anissa not getting pregnant and the death of Sergio, the man who would never father her child.

"My mother told me that just before Sergio died he was taking 25-30 different medicines a day to fight the infection, but they compromised his immune system. He died within six months..."

This kid with his long fringe is speaking of death as if he were a war veteran. You can come across scars in the most unexpected places, deep wounds, even if they aren't visible to the naked eye, wounds with unknown incubation periods and even callouses, rough, painful callouses that remind you of their presence when you are least expecting it. He might not realise it but Nicola appears to have the full range.

The strange thing, at least as far as I can make out, is that Anissa believes that a scar is a symbol of healing and a "happiness hole" represents yet another success against a blood disease, a dark but positive kind of magic.

From this point of view, she thinks she is blessed, that as a Universal Donor she should be untouchable to the Intravenous Revenue regime.

"You mean your mother didn't manage to save Sergio and so she couldn't think of anything better to do than to carry on with his absurd crusade?"

"More or less... She resigned from the hospital and she started up as a part-time illustrator so that she'd have more free time. When she was young, before she became a nurse she wanted to be a painter. She was one of the few people who received the 600 Euros of damages before the statute of limitations expired. My granddad gave us some other money. Then he died himself and with her inheritance mum started organising pickets, strikes, petitions and protest marches. Everything and anything. At least in south Rome."

Anissa's obsession is clear. As transparent as plasma: she couldn't save Sergio, so she is trying to save as many people with blood diseases as she can.

I feel something damp on my leg. I can see a brown worm slithering along my calf. It's an earthworm and must be about twenty centimetres long. Here, in the Villa Pamphili woods I can imagine that Anissa has a similar kind of worm inside her, a hungry internalised worm, a sort of emotional tapeworm which can only be appeased with dangerous donations.

I keep this nauseating thought to myself. It's not something I'm about to share with the kid. I don't want him to get a worse idea of Anissa than he has already. If I'd ever had the chance to start a family with Cecilia, I'm not saying that I'd want my child to love me, but he or she should at least have some respect for me. That would be enough.

I don't know, seeing my parents and other people's parents,

I think fathers and mothers go wrong when they teach their children what *they* consider to be important and not what really is. They teach them what they ought to know and not what they need to know to live. Still, it's also true that parents, whatever their vices and qualities, are there for this, to give their children an idea of what the world is about.

My idea of the world is that it doesn't matter if the glass is half full or half empty, what matters is what you put inside it.

"Listen Nicola, I appreciate what you're doing for me, for Rome and for the State in general... but don't be too pissed off with your mother. She's the sort of person who has to go against the flow, she has to take life on in all senses... I don't know if I'm making any sense, but y'know even if that's the only reason, you have to have respect for her."

He isn't even listening to me. He's looking straight ahead. It's almost midnight and lots of things are starting to move around in the shadows.

Villa Pamphili by night

*Rule number nine: Just because you can't see them
doesn't mean tax evaders don't exist.*

What we are watching is a scene verging on the supernatural,
a mass donation ritual. It is a glaring contrast to the individual
empty experiences we have to go through again and again every
day, every month, and every year: I'm talking about expenses,
bills, taxes, and then what's needed for cleaners, medical check-
ups, holidays, and I'll stop here before I bore your socks off just
making you think about it.

A silent unspeaking crowd is emerging from every side of
the clearing where the stolen tanker has been hidden. Rapt and
lost in concentration, almost as if they are taking part in some
kind of procession, numerous patients are coming into sight in
a constant trickle. They look like the crowd in a painting of a
historical scene.

They don't gather together in groups, they stand alone,
isolated one from the other, or at the most in twos, arms crossed,
suspicious, watchful, but at the same time trusting.

The moon creates a line of shadows with the leaves and
branches moving in the wind. The only sound in the dark is
the tinkling of the bells attached to the spokes of the Robin
Bloods' bikes, a hypnotic relaxing melody. I can smell resin and
vegetable secretions in the air. It is a disturbing scene: a hundred,
a hundred and twenty people arranged in a half-circle waiting
for the tanker's pumps to be opened and start distributing blood.

A man with the air of someone who knows what he is doing
climbs on top of the Ematogen truck and explains the evening's
programme. He is wearing a black t-shirt with red lettering that

was all the rage a few years ago amongst the hard core Rome supporters, the CUCS (Commando Ultrà Curva Sud), and taken up by the combative rhetoric of the Robin Bloods. IF YOU FIGHT YOU MIGHT LOSE, IF YOU DON'T FIGHT YOU'LL NEVER WIN.

Ilario has one exactly the same. He usually wears it after Rome have lost a match, to cheer himself up a bit.

"Welcome, there are more of you than we expected. The donation will start soon."

Below him a couple of Robin Bloods are fixing special filters to the tanker's two huge reservoirs.

"We'd like to ask you for just a little more patience. The blood purification kits take about 15 minutes to do their job...You have waited so long that a few more minutes won't make much difference."

I look more carefully. These aren't even evaders. They are people who are right outside the intravenous revenue circuit. The poor, living below the withdrawal threshold.

There a large assortment of people taking part in the ritual: tall pale blokes who look like they might be homosexual, elegant paraplegics in shiny reinforced wheelchairs, smartly dressed blokes with tight bodies nervously smoking stinky cigars, terribly young and middle-aged woman in skimpy tops and mini-skirts; there are also adolescents all drawn faces with goatee beards and weird hair-styles, babies in prams pushed by haggard parents, all of them, to varying degrees, are visibly agitated and impatient to get their dose of blood for transfusion. They are willing to wait there, for hours even, for a relief ration of blood.

I am studying the queue from end to end when Nicola pulls me by the arm.

"Now watch this." My mum calls this bit "the magic".

The coarse blood from the tanker is slowly poured into a small device, a metal sieve about twenty-thirty centimetres in diameter, suddenly it comes to life, buzzing like a mosquito killer lamp, purifying the blood by capturing any infectious agents in it.

I have heard about these things, they're manufactured on a Chinese patent. You're always hearing about shit like this. As far as I know they could be simple air or water filters filched from the Magliana or Monte Cucco water pumping stations and modified with some kind of reactive formula.

At this point the people on the mountain bikes painted with the Robin Blood colours open their side saddle bags and pull out tins that they shake and empty by throwing the contents into the air. Almost immediately there is a new disturbing noise. An increasingly intense high-pitched buzzing, the same noise that torments me every night, multiplied by fuck knows how much.

A cloud mass composed of swarms of weresquito bots dives down and spreads through the crowd of men, women and children who actually welcome the insects with an unexpected almost resigned calmness.

The weresquitoes must have been set to TEST because they aren't sucking to fill themselves up; they prick, suck up a small haemodose, and buzz-off back to the bikers where the attendants have set up some equipment to test the patients' haematic compatibility themselves rather than relying on what the blood beggars have said.

Then the people are called, not by name, but in the order they arrived.

We stay crouching hidden in the dark shadows. The Robin Bloods are handing out for free what on the black market has reached a price of 90 euros per litre.

It might be a bad thing to say, but in Rome this system is so old, so well-rooted and part of most of the population's way of life that it is far more efficient, and in some ways more human, than the legal economy. It's hardly surprising the Eternal City doesn't feel the claws of the economic and financial crises that elsewhere end in drama and social tragedy at regular intervals.

It is common to hear everyone complaining, with those who are best-off making the most noise.

"My mum used to do the injections too at first. Then she became a section leader."

The blood beggars have their disposable syringes ready to be filled and whoever can't face injecting themselves asks for help from one of the Robin Blood attendants. So, four queues form, one for each blood group. One queue is made up of haemophiliacs and people with Von Willibrand disease who need plasma transfusions and therefore don't have compatibility problems.

"Then she started to organise meetings at home for the ill people of the EUR district. She encouraged the younger people and volunteers to do the injections to help them learn. I've seen scenes like this a thousand times over."

As soon as the liquid starts flowing so does the excitement. The blood beggars lose it at the sight of available blood. The first in line move forward in the same way as the first rows in a stadium do when the rockstar comes on stage, or at the football pitch when the teams come on. In this case though, it has nothing to do with the desire to get closer to an idol, but a kind of *haemomagnetism*: it is the blood circulating in your veins that feels the call of more blood.

Whatever, some of them are scared. The haemodoses they are about to receive are like money passing from hand to hand: it isn't easy to establish exactly whose veins it was in before being taken by the Intravenous Revenue. OK, they must have been healthy donors, but the exact provenance and above all the exact owners remain in doubt. OK, it has been cleaned so no worries, but what if I told you it came from a jailed but repentant murderer? Or a hairdresser, for who the height of happiness, no offence meant, is to file her nails? Or a reality programme contestant with a plastic smile on the look-out for their "big chance". Personally, I would be a bit worried.

"Your mum never stopped with the needles. To begin with, she used them on these guys, then she turned them on herself, and now someone else is using them on her."

I realise too late that it would have been better not to say anything. Nicola frowns and his face looks troubled.

"What does that mean? Are you talking about in jail?"

"Yes, sorry. Forget about it. I should have kept quiet."

He leaves it. He's got other things on his mind.

"How do you catch evaders, if it's supposed to be so hard?"

"With a strange thing called empathy. I'm just the same as them. Part of me hates the law. But they pay me to uphold it so that's what I do."

"Empathy..."

"Think of a fly. Have you ever noticed how they behave around other flies?"

Nicola makes an effort to follow my train of thought. He shakes his head.

"Well I have. It flies around, getting into every nook and cranny, it buzzes around where ever it wants to, it does this and that and doesn't answer to anyone, it knows its fly friends, it knows that when it's your time it's your time, no one really counts for anything and to gets its mouth around what it wants it will crawl over any kind of shit."

"I get it...What are you going to do now? Aren't you going to arrest this lot? They're evaders too."

"What's got into you Nico? Can't you see I'm on my own?"

From the right-hand edge of the clearing the lad who until a moment ago was acting as lookout keeping check on the avenue sprints to the truck.

"Anyway, I think someone is already on the job."

The lookout is talking with the Robin Bloods and opening his arms wide in a gesture of defeat. Without wasting a moments' time the officiator clambers back on to the top of the truck and warns everyone of the unexpected, but from my point of view entirely expected, goings on.

"I have just been told we've got company...The Carabinieri are on their way. We've got about four or five minutes at the most. Anyone who has problem injecting must ask for help. We have to get rid of everything as quickly as possible."

Then he slides into the driver's cabin, starts the lorry and drives off. To get a vehicle that size out of here the Robin Bloods must have some expert in the art of CCTV dodging.

The haemodoses are now being injected at a faster rate. Everyone is seeing red and accelerating the mass donation procedures. The sound of syringes being unwrapped accompanies every injection and within a few minutes the stolen blood has all disappeared into the blood beggars' veins.

As they finish injecting, the receivers dab at their reddened entry valves and fall, happy, to the ground. As soon as the men in black uniforms get there with their three big Jeeps to clear the area and arrest anyone caught in the act, the Robin Bloods have disappeared, like the stolen goods: the original load has been completely distributed.

The Carabinieri walking through the people are perplexed, they kick at the people lying down at random to make sure they're not faking. They try moving some of the bodies lying there completely immobile and take this ridiculous performance to be some kind of mass act of passive resistance, something to do with demonstrating pacifists, or political protesters. So yes, they all have holes in their arms and their bodies show visible signs of having been bitten by the weresquito bots, but it's difficult to prove in anyway that these crazies haven't simply exchanged blood or taken part in some other kind haematic weirdness.

The people lying there, with their new blood, are laughing like idiots and are in the happy clouds, stoned and hyper because they got their blood.

What a scene! It almost deserves to be called a miracle. It is so true Rome wasn't built in a day, and still it never ceases to amaze.

"So your dad was one of that lot, right?"

"Who d'you mean by that lot?"

"The blood beggars..."

There's not much left to see in the clearing apart from the uniformed boys' bad habit of bullying people who aren't doing anything wrong. A few more blows here and there with their truncheons and they get back in the Jeeps.

I motion to Nicola that we should be getting back to the exit.

"So? What do you care about him... You've asked me twice now."

My turn to leave it and shut up. It is delicate subject. Anyway judging by Nicola's impulsive reaction the relationship between Anissa and Mr 0 can't have lasted very long.

Outside Villa Pamphili and back in the taxbulance I turn my smartphone back on and find a missed call from Ilario. My colleague still deserves my attention even if he's been behaving badly. I call him back.

"Hi Alan, sorry about calling so late... Sorry for earlier too."

"No problem. You know me, I'm not one to hold a grudge."

"Yeah, I know. But I don't know what got into me. Perhaps Mirna has that effect on me. Try to understand what I'm going through trying to help her... It's only now that Emory has begun to notice me, that I've been able to ask him for a blood loan."

"Fine, really, water under the bridge. Talking of which, how much is that shark squeezing out of you?"

"450ml in self-withdrawals every two months. He swipes 15% of the total haemopoietic production. But, he includes the compatibility test."

"Is that all?... The Robin Bloods would give you a better deal."

"D'you reckon?"

"I reckon. I'll say goodbye now. I need to sleep."

"G'night, bro."

I close the call. Nicola can hardly keep his eyes open and has stretched out on the back seat. "Are we going home?"

I think he means my house. I leave his question unanswered and drive off. Turning on the MP3 player as his eyes close I choose a Jimi Hendrix track, and quietly listen to *Third Stone from the Sun*.

Blood Pacts

Rule number ten: the things hiding behind tax evasion and avoidance are often very bad, if not terrible.

I wake up with the beginnings of a migraine, the intensity of the pain is stronger than if my head was being assaulted by a storm of needles: a vortex of pins, nails, and spikes are getting off on plunging into my brain and torturing it. I've suffered with these since I was a kid, that's all there is to it.

Then I realise my mistake. This discomfort is the result of being turned into a target. I have been attacked all over, face shoulders and back, by a furious cloud of hungry mosquitoes typical of the Eternal City. Only my legs and feet have escaped, protected by the trousers and boots I forgot to take off when I threw myself on the sofa.

I look outside towards the bat-box. Tino is there hanging upside down deep asleep instead of circling like a guard bat. What the fuck is he up to, is it his night off or something?

I get up and when I look more closely at the holes in my skin, I have to stop being annoyed with him. I can tell by the marks, red outlines with a central bite mark, that they were made by weresquito bots, those bloody insects the Robin Bloods use and this time for me had set to SUCK.

The mosquito coils don't keep them away, sprays have no effect on them, nor do creams, and the electric bug lamps just tickle them. All because I let Nico sleep in the room with the reinforced mozzie screens and I fell asleep in the living room. While I was sleeping I became an unwitting donor to the Robin Blood cause, a supporting member of that band of crazies.

I slide out of my boxers and use them to wipe the sweat from my back, throw them into the washing machine and pull on another not quite so grubby pair.

When the doorbell rings I pray for it to be the Red Cross but it's Concita, she must have read the text I sent her yesterday.

"Hola guapo, ¿cómo estás?"

She looks amazing. Skin taut and glowing. Chrome nails. Perfectly rounded curves. Oh, and when it's hot around here, let's say six-seven months of the year, she shows off her bodywork like a cabriolet with the top down.

"Hola, Conci. Well just look at you..."

Pulling a couple of body builder poses I show her the game of battleships the weresquito bots have played over my skin. I stay standing sideways so I can keep the cut on my face for last.

"They put me through torture last night. My skin is pulling a little here, and my nerves aren't too happy either. Apart from that everything sucks."

Conci lays her delicate hands on my skin, gently and delightfully massaging my flesh. Anymore and I'd embarrass myself immediately there on the spot.

"I've had an evader snatched from under my nose, a colleague stick a knife in my back, and to top it all, there's a young kid asleep in my bed and he's not even a relative..."

Then I turn my face and earn a few extra caresses with my ripped cheek.

I know my neighbours get excited when they see Concita coming. The youngsters peer at her through the door peep holes. The older people give her dark looks and it's hard to tell whether they are expressing disapproval or enjoyment.

She makes her entrance on high heels swaying her hips like a catwalk model, almost. She hasn't lost her vice, street walking, trawling Via Cristoforo Colombo. The secret of her success lies with her derrière and the way its hypnotic swaying creates an immediate distraction.

"¿Dónde está el niño?"

For over a year now Concita and me have had an agreement.

"In here. He's still asleep. We were up into the early hours watching five hours of science fiction films."

When she came for her first tax returns as an Italian citizen, I lost my head over her a bit. I was delivering the annual accounts to the office on the sunny side of the Withdrawals Agency when I found her standing in front of me in all her sexed up and magnificent glory. The beautiful thing about Concita is that she has a completely exotic air with no hint of anything humdrum.

She asked for directions and I did more than answer her, I took her where she wanted to go. She said she was scared of needles. I made some stupid joke like your usual wiseboy would. She liked laughing, and a laugh from those lips would leave anyone standing with their mouth hanging open.

Pardon my French but her "high-class hooker pull" is hard to resist for any man still in his virile years. More powerful men than me, much higher up on the social ladder have lost their jobs if not everything they have, over less.

"Usted y la ciencia ficción... Recuerdo, que hizo lo mismo conmigo."

"It's not the same thing. You and me watched Star Balls, that's more of an exercise in sex-fantasy."

We went out together for a few months; we threw away a load of money on salsa dances, merengue festivals and in sex-shops. But then I had to put a stop to things: I had to get a hold of myself and get my head in order, I didn't want to end up as slave to a hot doll who goes on heat ten to twenty times a day for work.

Don't get me wrong, I've got nothing against what she does. I mean, people say it's the oldest profession in the world, it's just that after a bit I got tired of hearing her moans of pleasure all the time, of hearing her "calienti" phone calls with "horny" clients, of seeing her acting at home as if we were living on a porn film set amidst rows of electric dildos, vaginal lubricant, stimulating oils, retardant cream, military uniforms, chamber maid aprons, carnival masks, theatrical costumes and a whole load of cockeyed devices including gynaecological, cooking, religious, and sports paraphernalia, and a bunch of other gadgets I'm not even going to mention...

I lead Concita by the hand into the bedroom. "Ahi que lindo que es, como él duerme bien..."

Despite everything Concita and me have stayed friends, good friends. Every now and then she comes by to give me a "once over" in exchange for me looking the other way once in a while. She says she's worried about my health, she says I can't live in a pigsty as if I were no better than a solitary *sucio*. She says it's her pleasure. And with what Filipino help costs and me not wanting to open my house up to a horde of Chinese cleaners... Not that I'm racist, it's an aesthetic preference: I'd rather enjoy watching a curvaceous Venezuelan, who to occasionally wash my windows climbs up and down a stool, than a short Chinese girl with bandy legs. No disrespect meant but there's no comparison. I don't give a shit what other people think, why should I? No one gives a shit about me anyway...

"Listen, I have to run. Let him sleep until he wakes up on his own. We were up really late last night. Then when he gets up put the telly or PlayStation on for him, y'know let him have fun."

She winks, eyes full of mischief.

"No debe ir a la escuela?"

I cut her short.

"No not today. But listen, he's only thirteen. No funny business or strange games like playing doctors, understand?"

She plants her hands on her rounded hips in a provocative pose.

"Estúpido, me encantan los niños."

I ape her movements and tone of voice.

"With the mother he's got he hasn't been a *niño* for years."

Then I lean over to give her a pat on the arse and a kiss on the cheek.

"Ahi, como agujeros, Alan..."

"Sorry about the stubble."

She likes having a joke. If my flesh is weak you should see the state of my willpower.

The wall display tells me it is two o'clock. Late. Very late. I set off for the car park hoping that at least for today the pigeons are as constipated as I am.

As the day comes to a close, after the usual stuff at work, loads of juices in the right place and not many wasted needles,

I go to see Emory on the day when instead of coordinating the BloodBuster teams from the depot in Portuense he is in Riva Ostiense personally checking production progress. This is on Tuesdays usually.

The Tiber flows by slowly, almost at a standstill, a ribbon of purple ink. Above the scaffold covered cylinder of the gasometer the sky looks like a computer wallpaper image. There are clouds moving across the sky in the hazy fake looking light like something out of a dramatic film. These are the best bits of living in a city like Rome.

With a sigh I pull my gaze back down to the Eternal City and the loop of the river known as Riva Ostiense where the Montemartini power station used to be. This is now the entrance to the Cloaca Nova where a portion of taxpayers' blood goes to be turned into vitamin bars. You know the saying "all roads lead to Rome"? Well it should be changed to "all veins lead to the heart". I'm not exaggerating, the underground river flowing beneath Rome is made up of blood and dirty money.

The blinding glare of the sun has been persecuting me since the morning, torturing my eyes. It has burned a hole in the atmosphere and been bouncing from window to window of the houses flats and car windscreens and into my eyes all day. It's worse than the thumbs-in-your-eyes Chinese torture that's all the vogue down in the waste ground of the Casilino and Tiburtino districts. Use what you've got, as they say around there... Anything's better than in Esquilino I reply, where blades flash and sometimes even lead flies.

I can't wait for a hint of dusk to give my poor eyes a rest and cool my brain a little.

In the basement the smell of hot electronic devices hits my nose membranes with force. The cloying smell of blood makes my head spin; it feels like being a shark let loose in a fishmonger's.

This, down here, in the maze of sewers, gas conduits and depots adapted to the industrial demands of Ematogen, is Emory's sprawling Blood Empire: a not so secret fortress, an underground ruin full of the sounds of never ceasing machinery, long caverns echoing with the footsteps of specialised haematologists and fuck knows what traps. This is where the books are balanced every three months and promotions and redundancies are decided.

Just like in ancient Rome when, in addition to the Romans, there was a whole population sculpted in marble, a plethora of statues and mythological figures, today as well as the Eternal City there is another city, just as powerful and money hungry, that takes its substance from blood revenue and solidifies in juicy vitamin bars.

At a certain point it became obvious that investing in Ematogen was decidedly more profitable than investing in research and healthcare products. Selling candy has always been easier than selling medicine. People can say what they want, but if we look more closely at the figures, and if we lump together "voluntary" spending, we find that people of every age group are more willing to open their wallets in the name of pleasure than pain.

Emory talked my ears off with his "consumerism bateconomy" and "idiotology of desires". Money is only a means, not even a particularly efficient one, of transferring value, and if value is subjective, what does that tell us about money?

Just to add to my sense of disorientation I find myself looking at a fifty metre long row of Ematogen ad posters hanging on the wall. There are images of characters with superhuman powers, the gyrations of dancing starlets and muscle-bound footballers; the adventures of people boasting divine descent and fantastical origins, all sold and reduced to become a simple economic transaction.

I don't understand much about marketing, but to be honest, I think it's a bit over the top to use models with legendary abilities, great university results and grandiose business successes in the ads.

Candy bars, OK, health, OK, but the rest is just window dressing.

Whatever, marketing using folklore has become a kind of permanent boozy haze, King Falloppa, Meo Patacca and Rungantino, you see them selling everywhere and anywhere, to the young and old in equal measure.

I go down three floors and along a tunnel three metres high

with smaller tunnels leading off it. At the end of the tunnel I can see Emory gesticulating under a water department sign. He is leaning on an elegant walking stick topped with a dragon's head and he is bickering with a food engineer. The bloke in the white coat hands Emory a jar and he dips two fingers in it. Then he sucks them.

"I say it's false... Look at it, it's too red."

His eyes are almost popping out of their sockets in disgust.

"It *is* human."

"If you say so, but it tastes like *dog*. I don't even want to know what veins it came out of or who sent it in. Balkan swine... It's at times like these that I'm ashamed of being born there."

The engineer doesn't insist but it's clear he's annoyed that he can't use this resource. The price of oil is about 110 dollars per barrel, the price of blood can reach 60,000.

Once the red blood cells have been taken for making candy bars, the white blood cells and the platelets are used to strengthen the clotting ability of the blood in patients undergoing chemotherapy. The plasma is valuable for the production of vaccine albumin and antibodies as well as pharmaceutical reactants. Divided into its basic elements the value of the fractionated blood rises to 100,000 dollars per barrel.

"Just get rid of it, please."

There's always someone who tries it on, who thinks the laws don't apply to him. The laws of nature, not human ones. Because the proteins in animal blood are different to ours, when animal blood is put into human veins the body's reaction can be dramatic, unleashing antibodies against the invasion of these alien cells.

Emory turns and I follow. I tail him, he hasn't even seen me yet.

A long time ago, during a stay in hospital when his mother was advised to write her will, Emory and his brothers all went to the hospital to donate blood. While they were waiting for the doctor the older brothers started arguing about their mother's hospital bill, about how badly she had treated them when they were small, and above all about the fact that she was leaving everything she had to Emory, her favourite little monster. Emory donated his blood, but the other brothers refused. When the doctor arrived they had gone, leaving a haemodose with the nurse. The doctor had no choice but to use that blood. When the old lady woke up after the operation to find herself suffering from a strong rejection crisis and allergic reaction she realised, to her great fury, that to punish her for leaving everything to Emory her older sons had swapped the haemodose he had donated with another bag with cow blood in it. These are the kinds of stories Emory used to delight in telling me when I was in convalescence after being wounded on the front.

The moral is you can't mess around with blood. So if one day your piss is black, so black it looks like it has come straight out of a chimney, well, now you know why.

When he finally turns and realises I am there Emory invites me into his office. After looking at me again more carefully he starts with his usual remonstrations about my tramp like air.

"C'mon Alan have you taken a look at yourself recently? It's only by the BloodBuster logo on your uniform that I can tell you apart from a tramp of Termini station."

My trousers need a whirl in the washing machine. I have a week's worth of stubble on my chin that needs cutting and a radical shave. My hair... this is how it is and this is how it's going to stay, Emory will just have to live with that. The most I'm going to about it is tie it back in a ponytail to minimise the fear element.

Whatever, you have to allow the boss to be right sometimes. I've let myself go a bit too much chasing up this Anissa business. The only thing I can say in my defence is that if he gives me a hand I reckon I can tie off the loose ends quite quickly.

"It's a passing phase."

I'm trying to convince him because I'm not really that sure about it myself.

"How long is it since you've been down here in the Cloaca? You not going all haemophobic on me are you?"

Emory's face is pockmarked, his hair is combed back over his skull and shiny with a hair cream that smells so strong the stink of it travels 5 metres ahead of him. I reckon he uses so much on purpose to counter the stink of blood that follows him around like the train of a wedding dress.

"I've had stuff to do. The usual stuff... Tell me, how's business? Are we on target for the month's goals?"

With my best air of nonchalance I flop onto the sofa and let my eyes wander around. Beyond the darkened window behind Emory's desk huge centrifuge plants are simultaneously separating the blood into its components at a rate of three thousand revs per minute, red blood cells, plasma, and white blood cells and platelets, known in the business as the buffy coat. These fractions are then poured into bags connected to the main machinery, all strictly sterile and under control.

The blood runs through a column of chemically impregnated granules which prevent it from coagulating, then through a heat exchanger where it is cooled, and finally, through a series of separation tanks and tubes. The plant is composed of two containers, one inside the other and placed upside down to look like a kind of large cupola. When the centrifuge does its business the heavier red blood cells are pushed to the bottom, forcing the lighter plasma up. The three derivatives cannot be used until they have received approval for a certain line of products. Approval depends on passing serological and viral screening for diseases or infective agents like hepatitis B or C, LUE and HIV.

The blood is then divided – and, let's be honest, sold on,— according to how long it has been stored, to various destinations:

1) less than two weeks and it is good for transfusions. Longer than that and the risk, of blood clots, heart attacks and other complications shoots up.

2) after two weeks it's good for fractionating into its basic components and subsequently used in the production of blood derivatives.

3) after four weeks it's ready for being turned into Haematogen bars.

"Blood runs Alan... We're ramping up production to anticipate the summer peak. This year we're launching Ice-blood, blood lollies to suck on. Even the smallest taxpayer contributes to the final result and is worth more than any number of evaders. With every day that passes we work a miracle, like the miracle of San

Gennaro, but the opposite way around, instead of making blood flow, we solidify it."

When he starts pontificating like this Emory emits a glaring if not exactly philanthropic light, it generally means he can see big profits on the horizon.

I cut to the chase and tell him the reason for my courtesy visit.

"I have to ask you a favour...It's to do with Farid."

He nods and pulls a bag with that bastard's name on it out of the store. He unwraps a disposable syringe and draws up 50ml of liquid which he squirts into a transparent phial.

"I've heard about his treachery. Unfortunately Farid is a Mosquito on a casual labour contract and there's nothing I can do if he's decided to bugger off and leave us."

I often get the feeling that Emory doesn't like my popularity because when one of my colleagues leaves the group he seems to be almost happy about it.

"It's got nothing to do with the contract, I wouldn't take him back for any reason."

He likes hypnotising himself with the phial being filled with the warm plasma of life. For him it is more of an erotic than a morbid moment.

"What do you need then?"

"No one can mete out justice in the name of the BloodBusters or on our behalf without permission or injunctions from the Intravenous Revenue. The bloody bastard had the Robin Blood woman I was after busted. I'd convinced her, that evader Anissa Malesano, to start handing over what she owed within 15 days. I gave her my word and that son of a bitch made it worthless..."

Emory waves the phial under my nose and wants me to sniff at the contents.

"I'm surprised at you... Are you sure you've still got things under control? Can't you smell something bad too?"

I draw back as soon as I catch the rotten smell of the liquid which is almost as blue as Rome's cobbles.

"Fantastic. Now the biggest blood pusher in the capital is acting like my mother!"

"Not at all, I'm simply testing your lucidity. Revenge requires cold blood."

You have to realise that there is something horrendous about Emory Szilagiy, a sense of permanent atrociousness on his jaundice yellow face, which he can never seem to shake off. Ilario says "beauty may only be skin deep but ugliness reaches right into the bone." He must have got inspiration from our boss to spout pearls of wisdom like that. Or perhaps it's a quote from one of those melodic ballads he's always listening to.

I turn to show Emory the little present Farid has left on my face.

"This is his autograph. He told Ilario he didn't have the patience to bother with the whole rigmarole of performing the number of withdrawals necessary to become a Bat.

"Bollocks, you don't need patience to obey. Obedience is easy, that's why it has been practised for so long. Just think about a puppet show: who works harder, the puppet master or the puppet?"

Emory gives the phial a last sniff goodbye and chucks it in the waste bin.

"He's just got the usual delusion of power and importance. I'm not really surprised, I mean he was presented by the Phantom. With his history there was always the risk it'd finish like this."

The Phantom was just another urban legend in the transfusions business. Someone—the sources in these cases can always be traced back to the usual bloke on his deathbed or otherwise unavailable to be contradicted—said that the Phantom had been a prisoner of war. Others, that he was a dirty spy sent by a foreign government to our Belpaese. Whatever, there were always bad things being said about him. Like the rumour that the Phantom was actually an Italian citizen the Secret Services had declared officially dead under enemy fire in Lebanon. The press had been shown a charred corpse as incontrovertible proof. Although actually—according to Emory's contacts—it seems he had an agreement with the Ministry of Foreign Affairs, and not only them.

The voices said that to guarantee his cover the Ministry of Home Affairs had given him a new identity, a passport for foreign travel, and a permit of stay for Italy. Once the dynamics of his disappearance had been suitably covered up, the Phantom reappeared on home soil as a common or garden refugee or political refugee.

The Phantom's task was to open up new trade channels, place large stocks of Haematogen on foreign markets and cash this in with payments in fresh blood and plasma. He had sworn loyalty to the import-export cause. The Italian economy needs people like him, people who know the insidious territory beyond the iron curtain, people with contacts along the Balkan routes and who know the ins and outs of the emerging Middle Eastern markets. The West has no scruples about using blood from outside the EU so long as the amount imported does not exceed a certain limit—considered by many as merely symbolic—above which the intrinsic identity of the European Community would be threatened. Yellow and black blood will never be allowed to colonise the continent.

The Phantom knew he was playing with fire. In his defence he had, over the course of his trade dealings, come into possession of a number of hot documents that might not create the fuss he threatened they would, but were insurance for the moment when he decided to leave the mission.

He is paid for his very useful services and he occasionally presents Emory with hooligans and untiring grafters like Hee-Ho-Fook with the goal of having them taken on in the ranks of the BloodBusters.

Some people turn up their noses at this, convinced the Phantom is getting his finger into too many pies, in places he has no business to be. Emory is one of these. It is clear he is swallowing a bitter pill solely because of the benefits it might bring.

"Farid is rubbish. Formidable organised rubbish. Loyalty, my dear Alan, in this day and age, is not just something to sell, its price has to be renegotiated every day..."

"If I bring you that bastard's head on a plate will you help me pay Malesano's caution?"

Emory's eyes shine with a ruthless light. He stands in front of the mirror and stares at his reflection. Small tufts of beard with metallic flashes run from his ears to his bellicose jaw.

"Oh I agree with you, the BloodBusters' reputation will suffer if something like this goes unpunished."

He has caught the whiff of a deal. He has glowing coals instead of eyes.

"It's not just that... We don't get people thrown into jail without being sure a crime has actually been committed."

Emory just shrugs.

"But as far as I know Ms Malesano's account with the Intravenous Revenue has been unpaid for years, Farid simply executed an act that you postponed on your own initiative."

"That simply, as you put it, was a misuse of power, no question. Any lawyer would get us in trouble with that, even with a jury only slightly sympathetic towards the taxpayer."

"Justice will out, Alan."

Emory goes back to his desk and sits in front of the computer. He probably wants to work on the figures regarding the sum I've asked him to hand me.

"Unfortunately it's rather a delicate matter. In these economically tormented times our taxpayers are like pigeons, as soon as the cage comes apart they fly away through even the tiniest of cracks."

I let him bleat on with his blood tax philosophy preaching like the externalisation of an interior monologue without interrupting. Emory moves the computer's mouse left and right and leans forward till his nose is almost touching the screen, checking and double-checking the data.

I wonder how much usury yields these days.

In the end he pulls a face, just to make the favour seem like a big one.

"You're asking me for a big sum... I wouldn't like us to be making a colossal cock up. There was a capture warrant for Malesano issued by the courts for the crimes committed with the Robin Bloods. It won't be simple to get around this. It's a big sum, Alan, I have to think about it."

Balls! All this pantomime just to end up saying no.

I jump up, about to start swearing. No one does anything for anyone else any more. Ain't that the fucking truth.

"Wait, there's something I've got to tell you... Next Saturday, in five days exactly, Catapano is having his son christened."

Aha! This is what he has to think about: part of the pact is missing.

"You know how long we have been after him. I want you to take him a message from me."

"To Catapano? What message?"

Emory is like the moon, he only ever shows you the same unchanging face. It makes you think there must be something on the dark side that is much much worse. "We have debts to call in. You go to the party. He'll understand."

Regina Sanguinis

*Rule number eleven: blood is produced by bone marrow and the
liver, so don't let things get in too far under your skin.*

"Kick it! Go on Nicola!"

It's evening and Nicola has dragged me too the Romulea pitch
to watch him train. To tell the truth he only really asked me to
take him because Silos Aureliano isn't close and public transport
doesn't go there directly like it does from the EUR.

I know a fair bit about football, even though for Ilario sitting
next to me enjoying watching the action, what I know is just
about the basic minimum. It's easy, you just have to score more
goals than your opponents and get the ball into the net at all
costs in any way you can without using your hands. Whatever,
for me it is and will always be a sport for people who think with
their feet.

"These kids are good. I haven't been to one of these training
pitches for years. Look how well your little friend got rid of the
guy marking him."

I stretch my neck to see past the crowd of parents squashed
up against the fence around the pitch. Nicola is speeding towards
the opponent's goal and instead of shooting, he hesitates, feints,
and twirls around, almost pirouetting.

"Man... what a dancer. The boy really knows how to use his
feet."

His direct opponent, a lean lanky bloke, probably with a
size 45 football boot, launches a determined tackle, sliding into
Nicola in the penalty area. Lanky got the ball, but threw Nicola
to the ground in the process.

"No! Foul!"

"Ref!? That was a bloody foul!"

A tight shout rises from my left. A knot of furious parents have a go at the poor sod dressed in black shaking his head with his opens arms wide.

When I see these kids sweat and feel bad about a tackle that ends in a shitty foul in the penalty area that doesn't get any kind of admonition, I have to track back and admit that at this level at least football can be an excellent place to learn about life. It has no relation to the mess that the premium league has become with its compromised passion and hot bed of illicit betting, high-def shows and all the doping shit, which in addition to making Ilario mad helps him lose loads of money.

A minute later Nicola gets the ball again in the midfield, and after an exchange with a team-mate he shoots off up the right flank.

"Wow, great ball control your kid's got.

If he says so, I can trust his judgement. When he was an active member of Rome's extreme fans he got knifed by the Turin Drughi at the Olimpico stadium and a couple of slashed tyres at a motorway service station on his way back from another away game at San Paolo.

Lanky is loping after Nicola again, but Nicola has a good stride too, fast and tense, and he swoops past him with a couple of changes of direction. Only the centre back is now between him and the goal, a big kid with a vivacious face and a threatening expression, as if to say, no one's getting past me.

Nicola's hair is dancing in the wind, following his dance with the ball. Feint and counter-feint; a double pass, agile and precise and the ball disappears. No, there it is, the Nicky Potter of football! The centre back retreats, and succumbing to confusion tries to play for time, unable to deal with Nicola's inexorable advance.

"Go for it! Go for it!"

The crowd's shouts of encouragement seem to push Nicola on, first he slips past the defender, showing him the ball and then hiding it from him again with a quick touch of his football boot. In the meantime, not far ahead, the goal keeper gets into position.

Surprise surprise, Nicola doesn't face his opponent this time. He slows down for a second knowing that he's not going to be able to inebriate him enough with feints to get him out of the way. Instead, he looks up, takes aim, and shoots a hard right, hard and fast the ball brushes the torso of the centre back and beats the goalie to the net. The ball whams into the top corner, just behind the crossbar.

"Gooaaal! Fuckin' hell what a goooaal! That's one to remember!"

Ilario has jumped to his feet and is yelling in my ear. Nicola is jubilant and the whole team are hugging him. The ref confirms the victory of the boys with the yellow tabards and the training session comes to an end. Handshakes and all the rest.

As soon as I stand up to go and congratulate the kid I notice a woman trotting across the pitch towards him.

"Are you Nicola Malesano?"

He doesn't answer. He looks at her with a surprised expression and doesn't know what to do. He manages a kind of yes with his lips while his eyes hunt for me in the stands. I race down to join him.

"I've been looking for you for three days. There was no one at your house. Where have you been?"

The woman, plain, about forty, large nose, and her hair scraped back like a granny, grabs Nicola by the arm and despite his resistance drags him with her towards the exit.

"Hey! Hold it there a minute...What do you think you are doing? Who are you anyway?"

I shout form a distance. The woman scowls at me, almost as if I'd insulted her.

"I'm doing my duty. Social services. I have to bring in Nicola Malesano and hand him over to the people who are going to look after him while his m-mother is in j-j-jail."

The colour drains from my face. As well as being plain she starts stuttering as soon as things get a little complicated.

"Look, Nicola is staying with me. There's no need to take him to any kind of care home." She splutters and laughs in my face.

"What do you mean c-care home? Nicola will be assigned a

foster family. Excuse me, who are y-y-you? Are y-y-you a relative?"

"What me? No, not a relative. My name's Alan Costa. Withdrawals Agency."

"So? Do you have proof of any right to t-take Nicola into your c-care?"

Time to improvise. But not too much. I have my own reasons for doing what I'm doing.

"Me? ... Of course I do. I am the agent responsible for the amount owed to the Intravenous Revenue by his mother."

The woman shakes her head in irritation, as if to say ... "oh you don't say so."

"What do you mean? You're keeping him hostage and you'll squeeze the blood out of him if his mother defaults?"

It takes him a while to understand, but then Nicola goes white too. His eyes widen like a terrified puppy.

"Hostage? Rubbish! You just ask him if I'm maltreating him."

The kid panics. He looks from me to her and can't get a handle on what exactly is going on.

He can't work out who is hiding the frying pan and who the fire.

"You do realise you are responsible for k-k-kidnapping? I could report you to the authorities for illicit detention of a minor."

"Listen... Just stop right there."

With a yank I pull Nicola back under my wing.

"What are you doing? Perhaps I haven't made the situation clear."

She is furious. She digs in her bag for a piece of paper which she waves in my face.

"I have a warrant countersigned by the social services to bring in Nicola, wherever he happens to be."

Nicola lets go of me and takes a step backwards.

"What, do you want a paper war? Fine! I've got an injunction issued by the Withdrawals Agency. So how's that?"

"What do you mean how's that... You are obstructing the law."

I grab Nicola by his collar again.

"And you are obstructing me. Now go, or I'll stop being nice."

Her mouth hangs open, finally putting a stop to her stutter. I want to end the match in a blaze of glory.

"I was forgetting..."

From my uniform I pull out a visiting card and slide it into the front of her blouse.

"Here's my address. You're perfectly welcome to come and check up on us and see the fun Nicola and me are having, if you feel the need. Maybe if you come wearing a shorter skirt, higher heels, I dunno, but you'd look much more appealing."

She blinks in amazement, and looks at herself from her feet up to her legs. She reddens in embarrassment and we scarper without giving her the time to think up her retaliation.

I keep my arm around the kid, he's still a little shaken up by the whole thing.

"Hit them where they're most vulnerable. You gave me the idea with that goal just under the crossbar."

Nicola says nothing. I'm not sure if he has understood the compliment.

"Well? Cat got your tongue?"

"Is that thing about defaulting true? If Anissa doesn't pay, then I have to?"

I don't want to lie but I don't want to scare him either.

"It's true, but I'll make sure it doesn't come to that."

So we've come to promises. I haven't got myself into trouble like this with my own hands since I was with Ceci. Ilario has been watching the whole scene from where he is sprawled out on the terraces. He is shaking his head with an air of superiority and showing his wry amusement.

The next morning, in spite of what is considered good form, I turn up at the gates to Regina Coeli jail with a bunch of flowers. Personally I've never done this for anyone before. Ceci wasn't keen anyway, she preferred pumpkin flowers for cooking.

I admit this might seem strange, but in my humble opinion flowers should stay with their roots in the ground. Whatever, I know when it's time to make an exception to the rules.

The gate opens. Someone sniggers, others talk quietly to each other. I knew this was a bad move. It's not the flowers, it's me being here that is causing all this confusion. The appearance of a

BloodBuster in scarlet uniform around here has the same effect as the shadow of a vulture circling in the sky.

The warders get nervous. Permission to visit for reasons of revenue assessment is only valid for fifteen minutes, from 12.30 to 12.45.

They make me give the flowers to a women's section warden, a big woman who sniffs them as deeply as if she were snorting a line of coke. Then she makes sheep's eyes at me and tells me to drop my trousers for the obligatory search.

"Don't give me that look boy. These are my rules. First I come in, then you come in..."

And she even gives a crass laugh.

When she has finished unblocking every orifice I possess the matron pulls off her gloves and escorts me at a smart pace to the visiting area. She winks at me, opens the door politely, offers me a chair and says goodbye with another wink.

"Have fun then. With what's left of her..."

There is no one on the other side of the glass partition. I wait for a good two minutes and I'm about to get up and go when from a small door opposite the weary silhouette of Brunhilde appears.

Her hair is loose and she looks as though she hasn't an ounce of strength left in her body.

Close up she is very different to the Brunhilde of better times. Perhaps Regina Coeli has imposed this change of tone in her.

"Anissa has sent me to tell you that she has nothing to say to you."

Her lips shape the same resentful phrases as before, with the same arrogance. Pity though that an amazing number of tics have appeared on her face and she is even a bit cross-eyed. Maybe she always has been. I'm not overly interested.

"You tell her I'm not here for her, I'm here for Nicola."

At this, Brunhilde puts on a disgusted expression and retreats to her cell. After another couple of minutes the door opens again and this time it is Anissa, leaning heavily on a walking frame. Her face is long, there are puffy bags under her eyes and she has the air of someone who died a thousand years ago and has been exhumed. Her skin is the colour of ashes and she looks much worse than when she came in here, if that's possible.

"You again?"

She attempts a scornful half-smile, slightly sweetened by dimples.

The coldness and disgust towards me have not changed. Her over bright eyes on the other hand cut into me like a knife. She has the pull of a black hole, a seductive aura that despite the threat it exudes continues to exert a strong attraction.

"You've been no good for anything. First, when you should have taken my blood you didn't, then when you had the chance you didn't stop that syringe happy madman sending me here with a ridiculous charge that hasn't got a leg to stand on... Unlawful blood donation indeed!"

I roll with the blows as she deals them. Despite the amount of blood she has deposited by forced transfusion since she's been in here, she still manages to get her blood up to throw unfair recriminations at me.

"What a lovely way you have of saying thank you... Haven't you realised yet that I'm plugging the dam for you."

"What the bloody hell are you talking about you idiot?! Can't you see the state I'm in? And you blather on about plugging the dam?"

She is beautiful as she gets angry and bangs her fists on the table. Bandaged up like a mummy, half stoned by sedatives and kept awake by the burning of the valves stuck in her flesh, Anissa needs to believe in someone. You know who I'm talking about.

"Nicola sends his love."

I can see it on her face. I disgust her. Even worse, Anissa looks dejectedly down at the tubes and drips sticking out of her body. She breathes in a sigh impotently; it's as if she would threaten me if only she could get free of that external and extraneous circulatory apparatus, that mess of plastic and metal keeping her blood hostage.

"You haven't...don't tell me you've dared make up the difference with him?"

Her lip curls and she growls in the prey of a hate grown so

much stronger during three days of jail and convalescence.

"I haven't touched him, he's fine. I've taken him to stay with me in Silos Aureliano. I go and get him every day from the school gates and we take Lucy home. In the evening we watch science fiction films, did you know that was his favourite genre? We play on the PlayStation a bit and on Wednesday afternoon I took him to the Romulea grounds for football practice."

Now it's Anissa's turn to bow her head. As I roll off the things we've been doing over the past few days her jaw drops, surprise then happiness flicker across her face. I can see she is drinking in my words like a thirsty plant draws up water. Her expression changes and she realises that I am her only way out, her only hope of seeing Nicola again.

"Why are you doing all this? What's it got to do with you?"

I sigh pull myself straight and shake off any qualms. I might not technically have anything to do with it, but I want to make it my business.

"Anissa, think about it for a moment. There is no one else you know who can take him in..."

I let her realise I've done my homework and continue.

"All the people you know have something to do with the Robin Bloods, and Nicola isn't particularly fond of them, and that's putting it mildly."

She lowers her eyes and gets off her high horse. Her fingers go to the wound at her neck where there is a drip that sucks blood directly from her jugular, drop by drop as her bone marrow does its job.

She feels guilty, as if she has remembered a bit too late how to be a good mother.

"Well, thank you...This is the second time it seems."

She just needs a bit of coaxing.

"The kid's a blast. You should see him playing football, he's a champion. I reckon he's got a great talent for punching the ball into the net."

My choice of words makes her smile wryly. This visit is beginning to have some sense. I have got her attention. Unfortunately for her not all the news I have for her is so good.

"Listen, there's something you need to know. This woman from social services came looking for Nicola yesterday when we were at football practice. She had a signed and stamped warrant with all the trappings. I managed to stop her this time but I'm sure she'll be back on the warpath. If she manages to take Nicola away for one reason or another it'll give her the right to do it again whenever she feels like it. Once you've been declared unfit there'll be nothing you can do to get your boy back."

"When will that happen?"

One of the reasons I like this Anissa is because she's not young and she doesn't react like a new mum. She doesn't whine and then beg someone to help her. Every moment spent in her company is a challenge. Now time is against us too.

"I haven't got the faintest idea. Maybe the social services aren't as efficient in actions as they make out in words. I don't know if I'll be able to block her again with some other Intravenous Revenue technicality. Whatever, I've got a plan for getting you out of here."

Her mouth droops. As well as losing blood, Anissa is losing a substantial amount of liquid as tears. She lifts a bony hand and rests it against the glass partition separating us. I do the same thing and our palms meet. It is as if the glass vanishes and there is nothing left separating her from me. I can imagine her warmth, just above 35 degrees, through the screen. Despite everything Anissa burns with a fire that, it seems, to be appreciated needs first to be tamed.

Our gazes lock for a long instant. Her pupils are pinheads. I know, it's an occupational quirk. But the context is different. She might have a sweet exterior and be deadly inside, but I'm worried I've become the exact opposite. Between ourselves, as it were.

We take our hands down without having touched.

If you had asked me a few years ago what I wanted out of life, I would have answered confidently and without thinking about it more than a few seconds: a mountain of money, a mansion in Circeo and the right number of women by turn. With the passing of time my range of possibilities has shrunk and my ambitions with it. Yes, I'm not ashamed to admit it, I want less, but more intensely.

This time it isn't Farid who interrupts this loaded moment but the fat warden spying on the height of romanticism possible between the walls of Regina Coeli.

There are two hand prints on the glass. Anissa's disappears quickly, mine stays put, a greasy smudge.

Some gestures stay with you as if they are lumps of rotten hope going round in your blood, flowing through your whole body, damaging every single organ. Your ears can't hear any more, your eyes can't see, and no one else interests you.

You've had it, you're in love.

Burned Blood

*Rule number twelve: the haematic flow must be
constant in order to make sure there are enough
Haematogen bars to meet demand.*

It's 4.15 am. The time when people are most vulnerable, the time
when if you are an insomniac or agitated you lie there staring
wide eyed at the ceiling or rolling over in bed for the millionth
time, the time when you are so tired that finally in the end you
drop even if only for an hour or two. It is the time when you are
even weaker than weariness.

The night in Silos is humid. I have only just managed to digest
the sweet and sour chicken from the Chinese take-away "Sky
mountain", when a vibration wakes me. It's a video-message from
Emory. It comes through loud and clear.

"Calling all units. Repeat, calling all units. Emergency call to
Prenestina Station. A goods train carrying Haematogen has just
been attacked and set fire to on its way from Palombara Sabina
to Guidonia. We suspect it is a Robin Blood attack. Top priority.
Save the goods. I repeat, save the goods".

I leave Nicola to sleep in my bedroom, pull on the red jacket
of my uniform, and go.

*

When I am level with Casal Bertone and already driving along
Strada dei Parchi I can hear a friendly siren echoing in the
distance. Soon afterwards I join up with that wreck on wheels
that is Ilario's taxbulance. Ilario and car maintenance are sworn
enemies. Emory leases us the vehicles and Ilario always drives

them right into the ground before asking Emory for another one.

He falls in to drive alongside me on the right. He is murdering the Beatles' *Hey Jude* in his broken English, then suddenly he opens the window and yells.

"Oh... I didn't sleep a wink last night!"

"Perfect, because this call out is going to keep us up until the morning. It's almost here anyway."

The awaited day, the day when Catapano's son is going to be christened is only two days away, the day when we will finally be able to stick a needle in the meaty arm of his father, the *defrauder maximus*. Ilario and me are getting everything ready. We want to leave a mark to be remembered by. Our reputations as BloodBusters depend on it. We are planning on making an entrance worthy of the VIPs who are going to be at the small hereditary evader's party.

Concita will be there too. She got an invitation for the ceremony that's going to be held on Torvajanica beach; the exact location is top secret, a surprise villa, the address won't be texted until three hours before the start. Whatever, she, in her role as escort, has access to lots of exclusive places like this. Who knows how many of her colleagues will also be draped around the event...However, business before pleasure.

Just like white blood cells race to fight the spread of an infection the BloodBuster teams are converging on the road leading to Prenestina station where according to the sightings and reports from concerned citizens alarmed by the pillar of smoke and stink of burning, the flaming 3.42 goods train is about to pass.

In the area in front of the station the North Rome team is already waiting. The Viking, Moffa and Lionheart. Lionheart ha! That's BloodBuster irony that is, Andrea Spaventa was the only BloodBuster to faint on his first blood withdrawal. The West Rome team with Sawn-off, Hee-Ho-Fook and Orko are cutting through the fence to get to the tracks.

Other sirens are coming closer. Only the East Rome team is missing, they're always a bit slow, and Rome Central.

The first thing Ilario and me, the only two left representing South Rome do is to check the time and distance until the train comes through. My comrade grabs a megaphone and starts barking out orders.

"Come on boys! Get moving...We have six minutes to impact. Luckily it was running late. Like Freddy used to say, "Another one bites the dust".

Nearly everyone gets the idea, except Orko who is staring at Hee-Ho-Fook who is even more lost than he is. On the records the Chinese BloodBuster's name is Li-An-Wu, (pronounced Woo) but no one ever calls him that. Ever since they caught him in the toilets with a ninja band tied around his head doing his morning Tai-Chi exercises Sawn-off, roughneck that he is, gave him this new vulgar nickname and began an obscene parody of those ancient, serious and precise movements.

The North and West Rome teams start to unscrew the bolts on the first stretch of tracks. As soon as Marzio and Pino Goodman get here, the heads of the East Rome and Rome Central teams respectively, they set to work removing the second parallel stretch. Ilario and me are coordinating the whole operation and every so often we get busy moving-on the night owls and people staring from their cars who slow down or even stop to see what we are doing.

"C'mon boys! Five minutes to impact."

The first bolts start coming away at 4.32. The Viking loosens them while Moffa and Lionheart finish unscrewing them. Lazybones, on the other side of the tracks is swearing from the effort. He's never worked so hard in his life. Spending the night dismantling railway tracks isn't exactly what he expected from becoming a BloodBuster. His nickname suits him perfectly and I wonder how Marzio convinced him to come out tonight.

Once they've moved the tracks, the teams string out in single file along the banks. One at a time they pick up and pass blocks of cement weighing twenty kilos along the line and dump them to form a rough mound where the tracks were.

"C'mon! Less than a minute."

The night air is ripped open by a whistle. From the direction of Viale della Serenissima a bright light advances on us. The nose of the engine is dark, but all around it is surrounded by a crown of flames licking about two metres high up into the night.

We wait for the train two hundred metres beyond the trap. Nibbles II is nervous.

"You sure it ain't gonna smash into us too, right?"

"Shut it Nibbles. You'll jinx us."

I avoid his gaze and turn to face the oncoming train. If I looked at him I'd feel jinxed by him.

Nibbles is famous for his ability to predict oncoming doom. Almost five years ago he and his brother took part in the Blood Lottery withdrawals while they were both in hospital after crashing their car. He was sure the accident was a sign. He was sure their lane jumping was a sign of a change in their lives.

Well, you can guess what happened, his brother's blood won the Lottery prize. Three million euros, a nice round sum. It's been annoying Giuliano Conti ever since, gnawing at his soul. It gives me goose bumps just thinking about it and not even really so much for the money, but for the importance the Blood Lottery has gained in hospitals and care homes. Rumour has it that patients are so terrorised by the idea of missing the results of the lottery that while they are confined to their beds on the point of death, as it were, they have persuaded the various health authorities to install screens in the operating theatres.

It works like this: each person participates by blood group (if yours is drawn you get a consolation prize) and by specific blood characteristics (entered for the big prize). If you lose, peace, if you win you have to prove that your blood composition is the exact match of that extracted within a month from the draw. This is why ill people fear they might be drawn while they are in hospital, this is why hospital stays create so much anxiety, and wear down the lucky winners more than anything else. Visitors are frequently used as informers to work out the best strategy to follow according to haematic availability and the level of production by haematopoietic organs.

What blood won last week?

How long since a certain "group" was drawn?

Is it better to play with a number of small withdrawals over a period of time, or one big one?

For your information, the world record for transfusions is held by the French Raymond Briez, who in 459 instalments donated 125 litres of blood.

That's not the end of it. The more cunning participants use statistics, like gamblers. They record the sequences withdrawn from other wards and calculate the probabilities of winning at the next draw. Some people have even gone so far as to organise illegal betting on the weekly quotas.

Whatever, everyone is anxious to have their blood taken, sure that winning will change their lives. This is true for any kind of patient, man or woman, old or young. Hope is a treacherous virus, it manages to infiltrate every pore, contaminating every vein. Patients' blood pressure rises dangerously after the withdrawals for the lottery, the mortality rate tends to rise after every withdrawal, but it's not clear whether this is because of excitement or being sure that their blood was not going to win this time either.

It sounds farfetched and is hard to believe... People who are barely able to give 10ml of blood give 100 a pop for the Blood Lottery. The poorer they are the more they squeeze out of themselves, it counts for so little at their level of intoxication.

The nurses who swear blind to the truth of these stories are the ones who Emory passes a certain amount of Haematogen bars to every month, a kind of incentive to make sure he gets a call before the henchman of the various funerary services get there. According to these nurses the patients are high on hope, a sensation pushing them to give a lot in return for nothing. They can't wait until the next withdrawal, to give away blood for free, intent on discussing, arguing and even fighting with those who think differently... It might sound pathetic but have you never, never ever thought you might have a chance, get a stroke of luck, pennies from heaven, an unexpected windfall? I for one bet you have.

Clearly Nibbles I left his BloodBuster job, making room for his younger brother, and as a sign of thanks to the Blindfolded Goddess he renovated an entire wing of a shabby clinic. Now he runs the Blood Lottery (Bloottery) in Sant'Eugenio hospital.

"Everbody ready!"

The Robin Bloods aren't expecting a move like this. Sending a flaming goods train around the Eternal City certainly makes an impression. A brilliant idea that'll definitely leave its mark on the sleep ridden early morning population. But, Ilario's counter-attack has an air of the diabolical. The boy is showing his mettle and a certain kind of class. Like Emory says "Only the devil knows God's private address."

The fire extinguisher valves are all popped off in unison. The Viking tucks the hosepipe under his arm in an iron grip.

The goods train smashes through the barricade of stones and cement blocks almost as if it weren't there. The barrier deviates it a little, hardly perceptible to begin with but soon, without tracks to guide it, it proves enough to make the train lean and run into the embankment.

Safely crouched in our hideaway we see in a few terrifying seconds the approach of the fire sweeping through the central carriages, the smell of burned blood filling the air, and the screeching of metal sheeting crumpling with the impact.

The driver, threatened by a Robin Blood standing next to him, grimaces at me fearfully through the window, then both disappear inside seeking safety.

Fifty metres. We flatten ourselves against the fence.

Swamp Bird jumps up onto an electricity pylon from where he clambers onto the ticket office hut. From up there he is ready to hit the train with the fire hose. A number of figures throw themselves from the rear carriages into the dark. Most likely they are Robin Bloods fleeing to safety.

Ilario has noticed that I'm standing there staring like an idiot so he starts ordering the others around. I just supervise what he is doing.

"Sawn-off! That lot are all yours...Get them back here!"

The train comes past us slowly. Sparks are flying from it like mad and it is shrouded in a thick blinding cloud of smoke that is almost bringing us to tears and soon obscures the night sky. Hysterical dogs are barking their hearts out and at this point I'm hoping they'll be ignored otherwise we'll find ourselves with the whole neighbourhood on the streets protesting.

As the train scrapes across the stone chippings, jets of water from the fire hoses start hitting the carriages. The din shows no diminishing until the engine hits its nose against the separating wall and the only noise left is the crackling of the flames in the background.

Finally the train comes to a stop, immobile along the earth banks. Like a beached whale made of metal, almost like an image from one of those documentaries on Discovery Channel. To be totally honest, those are much sadder.

"That's it! More water there... The first carriage is almost out."

Another two or three minutes pass before the professionals arrive. Well, I say professionals... Two blokes all uniformed up in flame proof overalls full of pockets and reflective strips get out of their fire engine and greet us with as much affection as possible.

"What the fuck's happened here? What in the name of buggery have you been up to...?"

The firemen advance on us, armed with helmets and water guns.

I leave this for Ilario to deal with and take advantage of the few moments of peace to look up at the colours of Rome, an intense golden dawn.

"Left to you lot where would the train be now, eh?"

One of the two lifts his helmet in amazement. In the middle of that chaos of iron and burned blood, he can't get his head around it. He scratches his head, and though I don't think he has my same doubts he comes to the same conclusion as me.

"What a bloody mess!... All this for a few vitamin bars?"

Threads of smoke are rising into the sky from the train's carcass. People in the blocks of flats are staring out of their windows enjoying a good view of the accident over their cups of morning coffee. OK so technically it isn't an accident, I mean, we caused it, whatever, and it really is a breathtaking spectacle, and all for free.

Above the Eternal City my dawn is followed, quickly and brightly, by a thick cloud of humid airlessness, exhaust fumes, and asphyxiating smoke.

"We were only doing our duty."

The bloke with the helmet pulls a face, if that wasn't a direct insult to his work, it was close. "Tell me who had the bright idea of causing a 'controlled derailment'?"

The BloodBusters all turn towards me. Ilario stamps in the gravel to get everyone's attention. "It was my idea. I sacrificed the vehicle to save part of its load."

"Yeah, right, I got that. You looked after your own interests. Who's going to pay the damages though?"

"The load is insured. Who do you think you're talking to eh? Oh, perhaps you missed it, that's our stuff, so try not to give us any more grief or I won't be answerable for my boys' actions..."

Then Ilario turns and carries on running the recovery operation.

From about half way along the train Marzio gestures with his arms and gives us a shout. Jajo and Lazybones are already at the tail end of the train.

"From here onwards everything is OK. At least four wagons are in good condition, the fire never got this far."

The fireman shake their heads incredulously. As far as I'm concerned I'm just there to assess the damage done. Ilario moves towards me, half surprised I didn't stand up for him just now. "What's up with you mate? Where's your head got to?"

"I'm tired. I haven't slept for days and I'm a bit run down."

He's noticed that I've been keeping out of the chaos. It's not like me. It's usually me in the thick of things leading the dance with him tagging along. This time I wanted to let him deal with the hot potato on his own. It'll do him good to learn how to cope with a bit of pressure on his back. To be perfectly honest, not that I want payback or anything for what happened the other day with Farid, but it didn't seem right to get in the way of a salvage operation which was all wrong from the offset.

This isn't even burned blood, it's burned Haematogen bars, and the difference is not a small one.

Sawn-off, Hee-Ho-Fook, and Orko come back towards us dragging another bloke by the collar of his shirt. They are taking turns to kick his arse and are finding the whole thing hilarious.

"Who does this go to now? Just think of all the things that he'll blub about the Robin Bloods if we squeeze him a bit "

Marzio advances on us at a trot, rocking on his false legs.

"He's mine, ours Leave him to Alan and me."

He gives me a slap on the back with a knowing smile. I would watch my back if it were anybody else with that smug expression on their face, but Glad is the Gladiator, not any old bastard. "Do you remember on the front? How many pigeons did we get to sing eh?"

He was the specialist really. I played the part of the good cop. In the end I always managed to make him mad because I would lose my patience and we had to change roles. Whatever, Glad is right, before we became bloodsuckers that was another thing we did, sucking information out of throats.

We stick the prisoner in the taxbulance's boot and finish our job. After about half an hour we have counted 332 burned crates and 215 untouched ones.

I call Emory to give him the good news. Ilario looks a bit put out, the corners of his mouth turned down like a disappointed puppy, as if I was stealing his bone.

"OK, you call the old Goblin. You deserve it after how you dealt with this situation." Emory wasn't going to hold this against me.

Blood and Tears

Rule number thirteen: blood is thicker than water.

We stop for breakfast in a place which isn't even for the night owls, it's for insomniacs, early birds, dawn birds like me. The entrance has a typical carved wooden English pub sign with a unicorn and a union jack. Inside Marzio takes a look at the menu written with chalk on the wall and sits on a bench. The Robin Blood prisoner Piero Savelli follows him with me closing the line-up.

"Like what, you mean you really eat this stuff?"

Glad looks disconsolate. I made him stop here by pretending I had hunger cramps.

"Who me? 'Course... Everything gets mixed up in your stomach anyway when you eat."

This pub is mostly a place for English people, Scandinavians, and foreigners with a north European air: they serve an excellent bitter (beer not lager) and the menu is strictly Anglo-Saxon, this is why there aren't many Italians. It only takes sausage and mash, or baked potatoes with cheese for breakfast, salt 'n' vinegar or onion crisps, or bacon sandwiches and baked beans for lunch to keep the Roman masses at bay.

I order a full monty, two fried eggs, three rashers of crispy bacon, a fried tomato and handful of mushrooms and a ladle of baked beans under the disgusted eyes of Marzio, who is sticking to a simple piece of toast and strawberry jam.

Once the pints arrive we stare at our hostage interrogatively.

"Well then Pié, start talking, we're all ears..."

"What d'you want to know?"

Marzio pretends to give him a backhander while I tuck into

my breakfast hungrily. "Tell us about your little friends. Where do you meet?"

Marzio and me wet our vocal cords.

Piero on the other hand plays for time. He sips his pint and looks emptily at the wall. The screens on the walls are showing two different images. One shows technicians in silvery overalls inspecting the area around Prenestina station with most of the goods train wrapped in grey plastic sheeting. The railway company's official spokesman, half asleep and with a long horse-like face, is handing out reassurances.

"There are no interruptions to service. The line will be ready again before evening."

On the other screen there is a Premier league football match which is well capable of attracting a crowd of spectators when the Italian Serie A is resting. Chelsea scores a penalty goal taking them to two-zero against Tottenham causing Piero to bounce in his chair.

"Goooaaal! I lived in Chelsea Bridge for a year. These hands have fried so many chips they've still got the scars."

He shows us the backs of his hands covered in red marks.

"OK, solidarity with the chip friers of the world. Now sing. Otherwise we'll turn those marks blue with syringe holes."

"How do I know you're not going to turn me over to the police anyway?"

I'm playing the good guy, like we planned. I don't want to exaggerate but you could say that I have acting in my blood, in continuous circulation.

"So, Pié, who do you think we are then mate? If you talk we won't do nothing. Evasion leads straight to jail, truth sets man free. That is our creed."

"Let's say I believe you. We usually meet in the abandoned Peroni factory. On Via dell'Imbrecciato, under the Roma-Fiumicino flyover."

"When do you meet up?"

The music in the background is great, only and exclusively Brit-pop and indie. Groups like Blur, Skunk Anansie, Stone Roses, Radiohead, and Moorcheeba. At the moment we've got

Talk Talk's prehistoric *Life's what you make it.*

"Only during the day. Between about 10 and 6. So as not to make the neighbours suspicious. We don't use electric light inside the factory."

"So right now there'll be no one there?"

Piero downs half a pint and wipes his mouth with the back of his hand.

"No, it'll be empty right now, but it's always shut up, you can't get in. The whole area has been under property seizure for years. Neglected and deteriorating."

"So how do you lot get in?"

"First I need to take a leak. If you don't mind..."

"We mind. We'll come with you."

We all three stand up together. Like the stooges. We all need to go anyway after a pint of bitter each. In the men's room a photo of Thatcher has been stuck in every urinal, with all the uric acid she's been getting the Iron Lady is looking a little rusty.

"We go underneath to get in. Through the sewers. No one has ever seen us."

Instead of a soap dispenser there is a Lady Di soap. What a place for political comment... I love it. Stomachs filled and bladders emptied we get back in the taxbulance headed towards southwest Rome.

*

"The attack on the train was a bit lame really. Don't you think, Alan?"

Marzio, Piero and me slide down into a manhole marked with a red R for Robin Blood. There isn't much light. Whatever, a few rays of sunshine manage to follow us underground and light our footsteps.

The Eternal City's sewers aren't like those of any other city. They are historic sewers. Archaeological sewers. I mean down here even a walk through the murky water and stink of the emptying drains is of inestimable artistic value. There are shards of amphoras wedged into the walls and the remains of pre-Christian mosaics, all that is left of those clandestine meetings of mysterious initiates and members of forgotten religions that never reached the level of a temple, or even an officially recognised altar.

Perhaps the Robin Bloods want to give themselves an air of importance as self-acclaimed heretics, when generally they are seen as simple blusterers, the worst kind of blood tax evaders. Something doesn't add up. Talking it over with Glad might help.

"Yeah, lame. I mean it was only a load of Haematogen bars. You know what? I just don't know... I thought we were doing it because it was the right thing to do. I thought we had to stop the Robin Bloods. But y'know what? When you think about it they don't evade taxes to keep blood for themselves, they do the opposite, they put it back into circulation by transfusion."

I don't want to tell Marzio about what I saw in the grounds of Villa Pamphili. Fuck knows what he'd think if I told him I saw all those people writhing on the ground in the grip of a kind of group haematic orgasm. When it comes right down to it, I don't give a shit what people think. Marzio isn't people though. He and I were brothers in arms, we shared food and a hospital bed when we were sent back home. Whatever, I prefer to keep some kinds of worries to myself.

"You've been looking pensive recently Alan. I reckon that Anissa has got right under your skin and into your blood."

Glad doesn't open up on the subject. Maybe he has his own problems. I shake some of the filth off my jeans.

"I dunno, I'm not sure about anything anymore. Or maybe after any length of time in this job you end up developing a certain instinct that warns you when your luck is about to turn. Whether for good or bad."

I realise I'm being ambiguous and a little evasive. Marzio puts his arm around my shoulders. He's trying to cheer me up, or maybe he's just leaning on me to make walking in the sewers easier.

"Did I ever tell you how I met Sara?"

"You mentioned something about it when we were convalescing..."

"No, I didn't know her then. I met her later, when we came

back from the Middle East."

I don't know why the Gladiator was reserved about the Ematogen thing but is now opening up and confiding in me about this more personal subject. Piero, a few steps ahead of us, says nothing, so we all listen to Glad.

"You remember depleted uranium, right?"

"Like I'd be able to forget about it. Emory washed our blood twice."

Despite the fact that the worst, militarily speaking, had passed, the desert air maintained a good dose of cardiovascular radioactivity. Although the levels were low there were fragments and remains of the API (Armour Piercing Incendiary) ammunition with depleted uranium in our respiratory systems and from there they sneaked into our blood producing systems. Then they attacked and gradually destroyed the bone marrow producing our red blood cells, white blood cells and platelets. Talk about infected blood, that blood was rotten from the moment it was made.

We might have survived conflicts under fire, the ambushes and the mines, but our blood functions had been compromised dramatically and almost definitively. The only way out was a complete blood transfusion. Two, to be completely sure.

"Did you ever wonder who's blood it was?"

"Artificial blood, Arteriocyte 0."

"The first bag, but not the ones that came afterwards."

I say nothing. My thoughts have never wondered so far as to want to know the identity of the donors during our missions.

After another two hundred metres of taking care not to step into the deeper pools Piero shines his torch on a manhole cover about three metres above us. We help him to push it open and slide it sideways, and that's us in the Peroni factory.

I give Glad a hand up, because of his legs.

"And do you know what I found out? That my haemodoses all came from one donor, a woman. You're not supposed to be able to find out, because of the privacy laws, but I stuck my heels in. I had to know her. It was a bit like discovering who gave birth to you for a second time..."

The old factory might look like a ruin of rust and corroded metal from the outside, but inside it is clean. Various pieces of machinery stand on the green linoleum floor. Going by their identification plates they were manufactured ten years ago.

The beer refrigeration systems are still in working order: they are used to refrigerate blood and plasma. On each side there are two, four-metre long tanks, the I-D plates on these show they used to belong to the old rival company, Moretti, bought by Vietnamese Saigon. The Robin Bloods must have bought them at some bankruptcy auction.

Stacked against the far wall are two pillars of plastic crates. Disguised with Peroni labels, the 66cl glass bottles inside must hold blood and plasma ready to be distributed.

The noise of the traffic from the flyover is deafening, so Marzio has to raise his voice, almost shouting to be heard.

"I met Sara by the lake at Villa Borghese. At the start I just wanted to meet her, to thank her for her generosity. When I met her though, I burst into tears... That girl donated almost six litres of blood in a year, hers was the only blood compatible with mine. There aren't many of us who are AB negative. I know it sounds sugary and sentimental, but that's what happened. Emory had just recently taken me on as a BloodBuster even though I was a cripple in a wheelchair without these State handout legs. She was an anonymous donor. I can imagine what you're thinking, I know it sounds pathetic... Anyway, long story short, we got married eight months later. So it isn't really that strange if you've lost your head a bit over Anissa. There's even a saying for it: blood is thicker than water."

"I haven't lost my head. And she hasn't given me anything. It's just everything got a bit complicated and is getting even more intricate. I mean it wouldn't be so bad if that bastard Farid hadn't had her thrown in prison, if her son Nicola wasn't a kid and alone in the world, if social services weren't threatening to separate them for ever...And above all if only I didn't feel responsible for the situation."

"Stop worrying at it, Alan."

"First I have to get Catapano and then Farid. It's the only way to convince Emory to give me a hand with Anissa's bail."

"Well, good luck with that. In the meantime let's see if we can work out what this lot are planning. Oh, Pié, a complete tour, if you please."

Piero takes him literally and starts from the beginning.

"For the ancient Greeks blood was a reflection of the Universal Order, one of the four human humours reflecting the balance of nature. If there was too much or too little it caused illness and insanity. The Christians steeped blood with the spirit and attributed to it the qualities of the beings it circulated in, from human nobility of spirit to the goodness of the sheep, to the fury of the bull. It wasn't until the 19th century that medicine moved on from the theory of humours to that of germs. However, despite the practical applications, blood remained an almost mystical substance. The Soviets saw it as an expression of collectivism; the Nazi's, in their perverse way, saw it as an instrument for justifying racial purity. The Americans bent it to economic demands and rather than lingering over any magical or superior powers, they made it a commercial resource. Blood was removed from the human body, separated, frozen, packaged, and sold for injection into another human being, in another form, on the other side of the planet."

Heaven help us! This business is much more serious than I thought.

"OK Pié. Save us the history lesson and tell us about the Robin Bloods."

Our guide tells us how over the years the Italian Red Cross has been dismantled by all the cuts to resources. The little left of that philosophy that saw blood as a free resource to distribute to anyone, without weighing on the receiver, was reviewed and re-adapted in an illegal clandestine form by the Robin Bloods and their phantom organisation.

The printers' trays are full of their latest publicity campaign, a poster of Jesus Christ, arms open and bleeding. Underneath it says:

HE GAVE HIS BLOOD, HAVE YOU?

When they blanket the streets of the Eternal City with this image the Church will not look kindly on certain juxtapositions which are, to put it mildly, profane.

"Doctors and health professionals," continues Piero, "subscribe to a contrary idea, they say that systems like that run by the Red Cross founded on free and voluntary donations are not sustainable in the long run, especially in periods of peace when people aren't pushed by patriotic motives into donating out of a feeling of solidarity for the soldiers, as happened during the last world wars. This is why the private clinics follow a policy based on the responsibility of the individual, where the person receiving blood must contribute to the blood supply being used.

"It's a pity that anyone who can't bring their blood from home in the form of friends and relatives is taxed 40 Euro per bag. It's a pity that if you can't afford a haemodose, you're left out in the cold."

Piero stops talking for a moment and stands under a painting of a man in green stockings, the movement's source of inspiration, his arms are depicted bare too. A chubby girl is piercing his arm and ruby red drops of blood are forming.

We are all standing there with our faces pointing upwards.

"In the legend as told by Alexander Dumas, Robin Hood died bleeding to death from a severed vein, a wound inflicted by his cousin Sir Guy of Gisborne."

That fanatic Robin Hood reminds me of Sergio, Anissa's husband, the man who set up this whole circus.

Piero carries on with his *idiotology* about the blood trade. It's almost like listening to Emory, though this bell rings with a different tone.

"The government has transformed blood into a commercial commodity, something that can be bought, processed and sold like any other goods. It's wrong, but at least this way it is subjected to the rules of commerce, including guarantees. So the seller is responsible for the safety of the product. So, for example, just as Coca Cola has to be edible, blood has to be clean. If the recipient of the blood falls ill he can start legal action for violation of the guarantee. He doesn't have to prove the negligence of the producer, the producer has to be sure beforehand."

Half way down one side of the factory we are half-way through our tour.

"In response to the government's actions we have our own definition of blood, it is not a trade commodity but living connective tissue, a human organ. A transfusion is not a commercial transaction but a medical service, a bit like an operation. Some people reckon it's more of a transplant. They put an end to the argument by saying that despite the fact that blood can be considered as living tissue, as soon as it is taken from the veins its nature changes because of the addition of the anticoagulant. This chemical alteration makes blood something other than virgin tissue. It becomes a product, more specifically it becomes a resource."

Piero stops in front of the organisation's most precious jewel. A machine, assembled on location, for manufacturing the notorious weresquito bots.

"And if they can consider it as a resource to exploit, well, we started to extract it. It is not only in death that rich and poor are the same, they are when they sleep too. Our mosquitoes have been *taught* this. That is, programmed... We manufacture about a hundred per week. All in tupperware plastic and other biodegradable materials. With solar panels they live for a couple years and then they decompose on their own. They are fantastic, a Brazilian Robin Blood group designed them, they have an open source operating system. In one night they can gather an entire bag's worth of haemodoses each."

Marzio picks one up.

"Who finances you? Where do you get your money from?"

Crossing his arms Piero stares at us with a challenge in his eyes.

"Right now, thanks to people like you, donating blood has become an act of civil resistance."

"Stop beating about the bush, answer me."

"Has it never even occurred to you that people might want to donate their money? Our projects are funded by anonymous donations. It's not easy here in Rome but we make our way."

I make an attempt at easing the tension.

"What's that down there?"

A red cube a couple of metres high is standing in the corner at the back. Each side has a stool in front of a central round opening.

"That's the blood room, where the anonymous donations take place. The donors sit on the outside with their arms poking through the holes. Inside a couple of volunteers make the blood withdrawals in strictly sterile conditions."

Marzio moves closer to the crates. With all that blood, we could meet our yearly quota and party until December.

"OK, enough of this rubbish. Tell us who you've recruited."

"We don't recruit. We are all volunteers."

"So tell us what you are planning to organise."

"I don't know. I'm not in the decisional group. The operations are explained to us verbally on the day they're supposed to take place...to avoid interception and detection."

"Shit Piero, at least tell us who the other members are."

The Gladiator is about to lose his cool. These aren't your regular evaders, convinced it'll never be their turn. Generally, following ancient common belief, the risk of being caught is potentially divided equally between every tax payer and therefore almost zero, once one is caught the others are safe. Given the widespread nature of the evasion phenomenon it would be impossible for us BloodBusters to pinch every possible evader. So no one ever believes they might be the next victim.

This mini but widespread evasion is incalculable, there is always more of it around than you can possibly imagine. It's a battle the BloodBusters have to handle with force, facing ranks of tiny enemies.

"I don't know who they are. When we become Robin Bloods we lose our civil identity and we take on another."

From what Piero is saying the Robin Bloods are different: they have method, they are not stupid, and they don't extort money or let themselves be screwed over.

"Are you taking the piss, Piè? Like priests and nuns?"

"More or less. That's basically the idea."

"Who would you be then?"

"I am Pan."

"Pan who?"

"Just Pan. The god Pan."

"Oh, well... So you know nothing about a certain Anissa Malesano?"

"Only that you lot have thrown her into jail for no good reason."

I pull Marzio by his shirt.

"Let's leave it. Piero is clean. Those stacks of crates too, they're fine where they are. I don't want to dirty my hands receiving stolen goods."

Sunset Torvajanica

Rule number fourteen: he who bends it breaks it.

The next day is a Saturday. D-day. The day of mission "Clean Blood".

Ilario is sitting there silently watching the bumpy roads pass by below us, country lanes full of holes and choked with weeds. I imitate him and look at the bare brick houses below with metal rods sticking up from the flat roofs, rotten teeth scattered across the Agro Pontino plain.

As we get further away from the ring-road the cultivated fields become less and less barren, the hills are coloured with chicory and endives, the wild meadows are home to herds of sheep grazing in the midst of the man-made filth and rubbish surrounding the Eternal City. On the horizon, we can make out Capo Cotta beach, a sandy marsh with scrubby oak trees doing their best to stick their heads up. Another blink and we are right above it.

There are some kite surfers out at sea, and on the beach there are some dads winding in kites that have flown out of their kids' hands and ended up behind the dunes.

*

We land on a large white H marked out on a perfectly manicured lawn. The helicopter blades stop rotating above us. This is a good sign, both because we have reached the ground safe and sound, and because of what we are about to do.

If you have never gone to one of these parties then you have no idea how Ilario and me are feeling, or what a rush a transgression like this gives you. Don't worry, I'm not empathising too much with the evader mentality. This is a personal victory.

As a kid I was never allowed in. Anywhere. You know about these places, right? Acropolis? Executive? Hysteria? Piper? Jackie'O? Veleno? Goa? Well, maybe you've seen them from the inside, but not me, not ever. Because I was never on the guest lists. Because I didn't know the bouncers or the PR ready to say the right names at the door. Because they wouldn't have let me in even if I'd had a mouthful of money.

I've never understood what was wrong with me. Maybe I was a part of a "fixed quota" of undesirables who served to feed the myth about the exclusiveness of the venues. Perhaps I looked like a loser, one of those people who already feel "excluded" rather than "exclusive".

The hopes of so many Friday and Saturday nights were always dashed against some muscle-bound mountain, some fat bald-headed bloke claiming the right to make me step to one side, week after week after week, *ad infinitum*.

In the end, all those refusals made me give up, and though I've had surgery on my nose it wasn't for beauty, but because I had it broken for me during a fight *outside* a disco.

Maybe it has happened to everyone a bit... Except the people on the guest list. I don't want to get boring but even they don't know what it means to cross the threshold of a venue after being ignored with such irritating frequency.

When you are a kid these things burn you up inside. With a name like mine, I wouldn't have looked bad alongside the various Dominiques, Chantals, Audreys and Sebastians, children of the Parioli district, the better-class Romans, from the good neighbourhoods Corso Trieste, Camilluccia, Prati and so on.

This time things are going down our way. We are in the right place and we are the right people. Even better, we are the ones bringing a handful of rules to this lot who look like they are at best intermittent taxpayers.

Emory hired a helicopter for us from the emergency services, it leaves us in the small heliport in front of the building rented by Catapano in Torvajanica.

Misuse of a state vehicle in such a barefaced way gives the

perpetrator the status of a powerful person, whatever his name, something that many, perhaps most, Italians aspire to. Including those who feign disdain when you're looking and eat their hearts out behind your back. Including those who with the right hand show indignation and with the left carry on evading.

At a party like this one, held in honour of the entrance into the Catholic community of the young Catapano, the least we could do was come in politely by the front gate.

As soon as we show our invitations to the security gorillas, the two brutes look at me and my colleague questioningly. Ilario has given the box with the white mice in it to the second bloke, just like it said on the invitation. We have also told them our real names, Alan Costa and Ilario Ventura, proudly printed there on the invitation in elegant letters, but something isn't right.

The gorillas answer to the same kind of hierarchy as the BloodBusters, they aren't soldiers, like Marzio would say, but it is something they aspire to and this is enough for them to count obedience as a value. The same goes for caution though. Unhappy with their inspection Gorilla One turns on his walkie-talkie.

"Gino, can you check these names for me please?"

After all my experience queuing outside posh venues, I know the best thing is not to interfere or attempt to argue our case. Gorilla One has to believe he is the Alpha male and you have to make yourself really really small and accept his magnanimity. At this point it's got nothing to do with an invitation, a card, rights or similar, it is simply the wielding of power that's keeping the show rolling.

While we wait for Gino to confirm our cover story, I sneak a look at the guest list and find the usual high falutin' sounding names.

Ciro Rummolo, otherwise known as "Love on the trot" for the speed with which he falls in love with one political orientation and then changes allegiance during the parliamentary season. A little below this is Tommaso Castagna, originally from the Rione Monti district, a judge who has been recorded in the press as having "decapitated" numerous criminal organisations. The people who respect him call him "Mastro Titta".

Time passes and there is no word from Gino. We are led to one side to allow people without credibility or identification problems to enter the villa. I don't want to show my irritation. They might not know it, but I'm working.

I'm wondering if it's our clothes making Gorilla One suspicious, but I even got Concita's seal of approval. We went to the Diesel store together to throw ourselves into shopping. OK, it's true, she advised a shop for smart types like David Saddler or Cenci, but I've never like checked or striped shirts. The world is diagonal, curved, full of strange things and varying forms. What is the point of reducing all clothes to a couple of designs and variations thereof? Keep your eyes open, you'll see what I mean, go into any shirt shop in Rome and try asking for something that isn't:

1) one colour
2) striped (as thick as you like, in any colour, but stripes)
3) checked (see above)

They will look at you as if you are asking for a suit made of human skin.

"It's all fine Gaetano. The guests can go in. Their invitation has been approved by Lucio in person."

We have the long arm of Emory to thank for not being kicked out onto the roadside along Via Pontina. Gaetano stares at us for a minute frowning as he gives us back our invites, finally moving aside to let us in.

Here we are then. The belly of the Catapano dragon. We move around a bit, to get our bearings and stretch our legs, mingling with the nobs. The first thing we notice are two big military looking amphibious vehicles, Humvee style, and off-road SUVs with dark windows snoozing in the car port in front of the villa. I can smell a bad smell, the one I'm most allergic to, the smell of politicians.

"So, Alan, what d'ya reckon. Shall we have a drink or what?"

Ilario is wound up like a spring. I don't know whether his excitement is down to the party or the surprise we have ready for Catapano.

"Agreed, good idea. Let's stick together though."

There are people playing golf on velvety greens. For me golfers are no different to kids who instead of playing marbles on the street walk across the greens with clubs of all shapes and prices, the sense is the same, they play under the sun with smart caps on their heads. I mean, if they wanted to go for a walk they wouldn't use those ridiculous invalid cars.

My colleague blocks a waiter and grabs two Manhattans.

"Starting off easy?"

"Start as you mean to go on I say, mate."

Ilario downs his drink as if it were a big gulp from Fast Blood, grabs the waiter again by the sleeve of his jacket, and gets another one, his big perennial grin plastered all over his face. Two green eyes and a handful of crooked teeth in an enormous mouth.

Opposite us, on the stage set up above the swimming pool an all-girl group are playing banal covers of banal tracks, from pop to rock and back again. The VIPs are getting excited as they bid for songs in the musical auction. It works like this: each table has a list of songs, like a menu, and the VIPs choose a song to bid for. The highest offer decides what the band plays next.

At the moment they are wading through an excellent vintage Cocciante song.

A little more attention on my part shows me the group Catapano, the crafty old dog, has hired to keep his son happy is the Vampirettes. They are a band of provocative adolescent airheads who wiggle and strut their stuff as if possessed by the devil even when they are playing a tear jerking ballad, or a slow smoochy tune.

We decide to move up to the raised patio. The sun is drowning in the waves of the Torvajanica sea. My Manhattan disappears with the dusk light.

"I'm going for a top up, wait for me here."

It's already 2-1 for Ilario, and he has absolutely no intention of holding back.

Dozens of flaming torches light the party as the sun goes down.

Not far below me, only a few metres away, in the luxury open-air restaurant next to the bio-swimming pool, a pond with papyrus plants and mail order animals, I recognise the faces of actors and singers, journalists and footballers, all talking to each other over plates of *bucatini alla amatriciana, rigatoni alla carbonara* or *pajata*, beans with pork rinds and chicory, as they wait, full and sated, to go to the dance floor to show-off their moves in the marquee on the right where the stage has been set for a blockbuster disco scene. Salvatore Paoletti, the building entrepreneur responsible for the construction of the residential area Castel Malnome, raises his glass to me. Holy fuck, the disguise is working. Here everyone toasts everyone else just to make sure they don't miss out anyone important and to make themselves feel they are amongst friends.

"Here I am... Hey, have you seen those two?"

Ilario jerks his chin in the direction of a couple of models in an obvious state of paranoia, the two bored hot chicks are shamelessly pretending to laugh at the bad jokes of a red-faced Russian who is already drunk.

"Leave that well alone. We're here for a different kind of fun."

"Yeah, but if I manage to get a phone number... I mean for later..."

"Leave later till later mate... It's time to find our host, I can't see him anywhere."

As we focus we discover some interesting details, like Giulio Piovan minister without portfolio who is fondling a busty waitress wearing a miniskirt and fishnet stockings.

The point is, after a while in this job your heart hardens. It's a natural process originating, inevitably and unoriginally, with the equally hard heads of haematax evaders. If they can avoid paying what they owe it is because they see it as a duty that doesn't concern them, an irritation they can eradicate by moving an account, reinterpreting a decree and acting creatively to salve their consciences. They take this liberty in the sincere belief that it is their right, because they are cut-off from the real world. We, on the other hand, to get by have to pay the price of their evasion, in order for these rich people, stuffed with vices and spoiled rotten, to carry on as they are without being held to account.

Well. Today things are going to be different.

I light up a filterless roll of happiness. Some fat man-cubs are hanging around the side of the pool, completely unselfconscious. They have no shame in externalising their future crimes. On the other hand you can hardly blame them, I mean look at their role models; their fathers' drooping paunches bounce around under linen shirts and the same goes for their mothers wearing wide dresses. Those are matrons from a time when size was a sign of affluence, not of barefaced egoism bordering on misanthropy.

All those rolls of fat, of blood yielding adipose, of flesh fed by years and years of tax evasion get me down. I pity them as a dangerous blast of hate rises in me. My nose itches, that feeling of being a shark in a fishmonger's is back.

"What do you reckon, shall we get moving?"

"Wait...hang on a tic. I'm having fun."

After three Manhattans Ilario is tipsy. To hit a vein he'll have to use a large calibre needle, a Needler or maybe a Slayer.

"That's enough. I'll go and get our kit. You give the alcohol a rest."

At the back of the villa a waiter pulls me to one side and opens a cupboard. Inside are the two MT67Fs and the tools of our trade plus the documents Emory has given us authorising the CLEAN BLOOD operation. In order not to create panic amongst the guests the bags have been carefully camouflaged as ordinary ice boxes.

"Thanks Mario, great work. Cool stickers."

"They're from the Diotallevi restaurant, the initiative's sponsor. He couldn't wait to finance us. Catapano has a big debt with him, meals and meals and meals. He's never once paid a bill."

"You don't say..."

I wink at him and I'm off. The waiter goes back to preparing open sandwiches and spiking olives on cocktail sticks. The other face of the "Aperitif" generation.

As I turn the corner a noise grates on my ears. Instead of the strutting Vampirettes I find them reduced to singing syncopated backing vocals for Ilario, microphone in hand singing *Ma il cielo è sempre più blu*. Singing it? I mean murdering it! I run, leaving the bags under a table.

CHI SOGNA I MILIONI, CHI GIOCA D'AZZARDO
CHI GIOCA COI FILI, CHI HA FATTO L'INDIANO
CHI FA IL CONTADINO, CHI SPAZZA I CORTILI CHI
RUBA, CHI LOTTA, CHI HA FATTO LA SPIA
NA NA NA NA NA NA NA NA NA
MA IL CIELO È SEMPRE PIÙ BLU UH UH, UH UH,
MA IL CIELO È SEMPRE PIÙ BLU UH UH, UH UH,
UH UH...

Ilario yells out the "ooooo" of blue. Everyone turns to look at the patio, mouths open in surprise. At the end of the spectacle he strikes a theatrical puppet like pose. He looks like Scialpi or Renato Zero at their best.

After a moment's tense pause, another of disbelief, a smattering of applause ends Ilario's sorry exhibition. Ha! They know how to play along. But not me. Music should be respected. If you hear Jimi Hendrix's solo in *Born Under A Bad Sign*, you can't just sit back untouched and indifferent.

Whatever, I drag him off the stage flashing an all-purpose smile at everyone. Yeah OK, my colleague is an undiscovered talent... In the sense that he'll never be discovered because I'm about to kill him.

"What the hell were you thinking of Ilà!? This is the most important day of our career and you start making an arse of yourself in front of everyone..."

"Rino, Alan... Rino has always been my weak spot. A genius!"

Thank fuck the party atmosphere helps us not stand out too much or catch the eye of the security guards circulating amongst the guests with their earpieces and dark glasses.

Then I see an arm waving at me, it's that hot Concita. I wonder how she managed to recognise me after this morning's shave. It must be the suit, after all she hemmed the trousers and turned up the sleeves. At the Diesel store they quoted us 85 euros for the tailoring at which Concita snatched the suit and stuffed it in her bag.

"Usted está loco." That's what my sex bomb housewife said.

At last we are getting to the heart of the matter. On the right-hand side of the villa the density of VIPs per square metre rises sharply. It might be the concentration of the escorts, it might be the magnetic pull of Catapano himself.

I give my "chica" a hug and introduce her to Ilario. He smiles foolishly, she grimaces back. They ignore each other, as is only right. Then Concita turns and rests her head on my chest, disgusted.

"Ahi, Alan... que no puedo ver."

The scene being played out before our eyes does indeed need a strong stomach. People raised on tripe, garlic, olive oil and chilli pepper and oxtail stew and chicken with bell peppers. Now I understand why we had to bring mice with us.

Catapano's intimate friends are standing around a cage. The inner circle, the most loyal, the most trusted. A kid is standing on a yellow pouf, he is Valerio Massimo, Catapano's son, and he is feeding mice straight into the wide open mouth of an enormous boa. The snake is coiled on itself and occupies a space more or less the size of my living room, including the kitchen area. The ten mice disappear one after the other.

"Well done Valewio. Feed the hungwy. Now you can be chwistened."

The woman muttering Christian maxims is old Lucrezia Luisa Catapano, an embalmed harpy who it is rumoured went to a speech therapist to unlearn how to say her "r"s properly, and not happy with the result or the effort necessary to sound like blue blood, she had surgery done to weaken her mouth muscles and speak with an aristocratic pronunciation "naturally".

The group of the elect move slowly towards the chapel where a priest is preparing the host and a Castelli nouveau red for the religious function. It's not any old priest, it's our old friend Cardinal Pezzi! A little wan but even more sprightly than when we made our withdrawals from him at the Gemelli hospital.

In the midst of the crowd, or rather, between a curvaceous redhead and an anorexic brunette I spot him. Our haematax target of the year. Lucio Sergio Catapano.

Over recent months we have carried out numerous cross-checks concerning the ambiguous "nature" of his haematax evasion and in the end we built a model. From this simple representation, a flood of outgoings left behind him, we were able to reconstruct his cash-letting down to the smallest detail and gathered enough elements to establish the size of the damage to the Intravenous Revenue and consequentially the amount to be collected. Needless to say Catapano should be hooked up to the suckers at Rebibbia jail instead of partying in Torvajanica. Not like Anissa whose missing payments had already gone back to circulate in the veins of the blood beggars adding to their taxable level, here we are talking about total evasion that has been going on for at least five years.

I have been following the case personally. I know what Catapano consumes and how much he consumes. I unleashed the gypsies to sift through every dustbin near his house. I have analysed what goes in and I have analysed what comes out. Week after week. The best way to catch someone is to learn about their habits, and I am now in a position to say without a doubt that Catapano's blood is in need of a good washing.

"Entro a oír misa, Alan."

"We'll catch up later back here somewhere."

Conci goes back to her friends. We loiter outside the chapel, waiting.

To take part in the function you have to be on another list, even more restricted than the previous one. Before being allowed in the chapel the guests have to leave an offering in a large urn with *charity* written on it, beneath which it says:

FOR OUR BROTHERS ON THEIR MISSION

It's not clear whether the brothers in question are missionaries or mercenaries.

It would be so good to stick a 13 gauge needle, the much feared Spritz, in the virgin veins of Catapano and see the blood spray over the waiters. *That* would be charity.

Whatever, the Mass is coming over the PA system loud and clear.

Valerio Massimo is nearly eleven. A bit big to be christened, and during his sermon Cardinal Pezzi never misses a chance to underline how it is never too late to become part of God's flock.

In fact, it appears Lucio Sergio had confessed to him that he wanted to wait until Valerio Massimo was fully aware of the choice he was making and able to embrace the Catholic faith with his mind as well as his heart.

After these wonderful words I almost want to get myself unchristened. I wonder if the Church offers a service for terminating contracts of faith, maybe there's a shaman somewhere ready to grab the opportunity of entering into the business of certain innovative practices.

On the other side of the villa, the Vampirettes are playing again, this time the song is *Roma nun fa' la stupida stasera*. The atmosphere is more languid. This is the height of Roman folk. The VIPs stand up and sway in couples, smooching, they gaze into each other's eyes with affection, on the crest of warm emotions.

No one can resist the song of the Tyrrhenian sirens. If I had anything to do with it I'd give them the sound of another kind of siren.

Before Ilario starts chasing another waiter I grab him by an arm.

"Where do you think you're going? It's nearly time."

He staggers, pushed off balance.

"I mean have you seen this lot? The spitting image of the others, just on a bigger scale. Same tastes, same poses, same mentality. I reckon you couldn't even change them with a syringing. Evasion is a weeping sore we end up having to live with."

Ilario suffers from a kind of verbal diarrhoea, a flow of idiotic words come out of his mouth at regular intervals, and when he drinks he gets worse.

"You live with it. I'd rather get rid of it."

*

The waiters are all in position. The cake is about to be served accompanied by the deafening sound of knives and forks being crossed.

Ilario and me tackle Catapano with a clever pincer action. From either side of the immense ceremonial table we converge on the centre. Along the way we think up a wisecrack, greet a VIP in need of attention, and find ourselves on either side of Lucio Sergio at the head of the table. He is a man with a paunch and a receding hairline with curls reaching down to his neck, a caricature of Nero, or if you think that's too grand, Gianni De Michelis.

I lean down to ask him if he hasn't by chance received a text or e-mail from the Withdrawals Agency recently. One of those formal messages usually followed up with a courtesy visit, or better still a haematorial check-up.

His "I don't give a shit" air is not a good start. He tries waving me away with one hand, as if I were just some pesky unauthorised lighter or droopy rose seller. Catapano goes back to stuffing his face so fast he hardly leaves himself the time to breathe. Every now and then he holds his belly with both hands. He's stuffed... the crafty sod is totally full of himself, just like the gang of greedy guzzlers who gravitate around him.

"We are here are on behalf of Emory Sziliagy, remember him?"

I wouldn't like to be forced to search the villa. His deals are not at all obvious. With the contacts he has developed over the course of three terms of government Catapano is protected by a network of so many omissions and quantities of silence that we might end up being here all summer.

From the looks of him, legs wide so as not to sway too much, Ilario wouldn't be too fussed about this option.

"I let you in... Do you really think I'm stupid? Emory is an old friend. I though he was going to come in person actually, it's all the same to me though. But he sent you, so just enjoy the party in his place."

I wonder if he'll still be making wisecracks when I stick a purple *Spritz* in his jugular and pull back the plunger?

"Perhaps I haven't made myself clear. Emory sent us with a message for you."

At this he starts. Strips of green and yellow fettuccine pasta fall from his mouth. His confidence clouds with anger.

"That filthy son of a bitch...!

He has finally realised we're not here as guests or with our tongues hanging out begging for patronage.

"There's no need to get all worked up."

We always knew Catapano was going to put up a fight. We always knew he was going to try to wrong foot us and throw broken glass in our path.

"We are trying to settle this peacefully. We are tax collectors, civil servants, answerable to the state just like you."

At this point he gets up and faces me with bravado. He wants to answer me face to face; he wants my face burned into his memory. To do this better he has to stand on tiptoes. I motion him to follow me, to settle this alone, one on one.

He fishes a cigarette out of his pocket and lights up, blowing a stream of smoke out from the side of his mouth. He makes a sign to the lackey at his side, a certain Alessandro Masia who has also been in our black book for years, to say he has everything under control.

"You lot are nothing... Why didn't Emory come himself, eh? Is he scared to show his face outside in the daytime? I'm as clean as the driven snow and he knows that. It's you who know nothing, you bloody little leeches."

Right, so the fact that Catapano feels as clean as the driven snow, in Rome of all places, smells fishy. Whatever, it's down to me to justify myself and explain things to him, y'know just to keep out of trouble. It's not like we've come here to beg.

"Listen, your face has been plastered all over the city's billboards. I know for sure that you have never, not even once, come, when you were supposed to, to the Withdrawals Agency for your haematax returns. That's what I know, and it's more than enough."

A few metres away Ilario is busy keeping the guests at bay. He is asking them politely to kindly stay sitting down and not move or cause trouble. People are working for them, whether they like it or not.

I take out the documents and stick them under Catapano's nose. He dodges them with another gesture of annoyance. He grabs me by the shirt, thinks better of it and rests a hand on my arm, as if we were lunch buddies.

"Do you want to know something? You're a dickhead. Emory and me thought up those posters together and I paid for them. You'd be better off leaving before I really get angry. You and you gang of *hole punchers* are ruining my party."

Oh for fuck's sake! The ways of economy and politics are neither infinite, nor mysterious, however their ramifications are invisible.

The two dishonest bastards have made a pact. Who knows how long they have been secret allies. For some reason Emory must have decided to go back on his deal with Catapano and without suspecting a thing this is the message we have brought.

So, now what?

The Call of blood/Blood Calls Blood

Rule number fifteen: in a perfect world taxes should be paid without coercion.

I don't care what people think.

The heart is an organ that we need for earning a living, not for spreading useless sentiments. I've nothing to apologise to Catapano about. He is a haematax evader, I am his worst nightmare.

"I have a warrant for your capture issued by the Withdrawals Agency and I'm here to collect what you owe. At this point you'd be better off confessing. You've been smart, managing to keep out of the way for all this time, throwing up smokescreen after smokescreen in front of everyone. Even now, with Emory's latest scam. I send whole packs of people like you down to Rebibbia jail, compared to you they have a good excuse. They have families to feed, they are people who have lost their jobs and work their hands to the bone to make ends meet..."

Catapano takes out his phone and flicks through the address book. Our moral ranting slides right off him. He finds the number of his salvation and mutters, "I'll show you what'll happen to Emory's scam."

What would happen to the BloodBusters if we allowed sentiments to influence our decision making abilities? Or if we allowed our feelings to interfere with our jobs? A human disaster, a social catastrophe, the unravelling of every haematax rapport; long story short, the collapse of this Belpaese. It is this lack of cooperation, this typical Italian trait, that is so frustrating.

I motion to Ilario that the long awaited moment has come. The moment to draw and cross syringes. He gives the order to the other waiters scattered through the villa.

On the fourth unanswered ring I snatch the palmtop from Catapano's hands.

"I represent the government. You are a criminal. I don't give a shit whether you know my boss or not."

He is not fazed. On the contrary, he jabs at me with a finger and hurls another threat at me. "Your boss won't be at all happy to know how little respect you have for him. And when he finds out he won't pretend he doesn't know it was him who sent you..."

I mean, obviously he wants to widen the diameter of the no-man's land around me, so I, losing my patience, throw the smartphone into his plate still full of sauce.

"If he sent me, it's because I'm the best man for the job."

There is no point trying to negotiate with him. Catapano would only ignore me from the height of his domineering position: he will only listen to me if I demonstrate strength and determination, otherwise he will send me away with a flea in my ear like he has all the other BloodBusters who have tried to collect from him before me.

"So... What are you gonna do? Pay or Not Pay?"

"I'm not going to pay anything. Nothing. You can bugger off now. Security!"

Pity Security can't come to help him. Each and every one of them has a syringe with a Penetrator 23g needle pointing at his neck.

The guests start trying to get away. Like a bunch of terrified rats they get up one after the other only to be made to sit down again by the waiter serving at their table.

I glance at the seating plan of the tables and the VIP list.

I wouldn't mind checking them all, one by one, to see who is really spotless. A haemoscopic investigation to shine a light on what has passed through their veins.

It's the moment of truth. Our heamatic truth.

I am electrified by the idea of having run into a place like this, on the war path and dressed up to the nines, ready and willing to terrorise the guests.

Give me a microphone. I'll be the soloist.

"Ladies and gentlemen..."

Opening the case I show my host my dear old nickel Pravaz. If I were him I would feel honoured to be treated this way. People of Catapano's calibre have to be handled with kid gloves. In theory people like him should give a good example. People like him should be the first to deposit blood in the name of solidarity and social justice. Instead it's people like him who moan the loudest and find thousands of loopholes to escape from executive injunctions. They are hardened criminals, re-offenders who must be followed, smoked out, caught, and made to face the evidence of their crimes and forced to cooperate.

"Please stay sitting down where you are. This brief interruption will only last the time necessary to complete the blood withdrawal operation concerning Mr Lucio Sergio Catapano."

Now they know. They also now know that if they dare move we have *carte blanche* on how we react to their actions: at the thought of having their blood drawn out the VIPs sit there horrified, the hair on the back of their necks standing on end. They hear the clatter of syringes, the rattle of handcuffs, and they would like to scarper... Knowing the kind of people we were going to be dealing with our lot have deployed about thirty Mozzies on call up contracts who were in the Torvajanica area with nothing better to do. The catering agency received an appreciation not to check their credentials too thoroughly. You can take my word for it when I say that the last thing you want is to have one of this bunch using a syringe on you.

Another piece of good advice: the simplest way of provoking a man and make him lose his temper is to use his things, sit in his chair, eat from his plate and generally take over the objects he considers to be his without asking for permission. So that's what I do, and indicate another place for him.

"Sit there, this'll take less time than you think..."

He slumps, realises he has no choice and obeys against his will. Frustration and anger, bordering on hate flash in Catapano's eyes. I help him take off his jacket. He unbuttons both shirt sleeves and just sits there, palms facing upwards. He cannot believe his eyes, he cannot believe we have pinned him down at last.

The music has stopped and you can't even hear anyone breathing. No one else knows, but we are only warming up.

"I'm a haemophiliac. You can't withdraw blood from me."

Here he goes, trying it on again, the filthy git. He seems sincere, and who wouldn't be, finding themselves at syringe point with bare arms.

But the surprises aren't over. My Pravaz is a luxury, but it's still a syringe you can mount standard issue needles on. In fact our kit also provides us with special needles with hooks because in some—how shall I put it—excitable situations, it's difficult to hit a vein, easier to hit the sternum.

I undo his shirt to the waist. He is horrified by the sight of the needle I am mounting on the Pravaz's ridged cylinder. It is the notorious Cannolo, 10 gauge and capable of making 3.7mm holes, inserted in a toothed chamber to prevent recoil. I place my hand on Catapano's sweating forehead and gently push him back so his head is resting against the chair back. I aim the Cannolo at right angles to his chest, right at the centre of his sternum. Then with a flourish worthy of a magician, voilà, I change my grip. I am no longer holding a syringe in my hand, but brandishing a dagger.

"A little fear in your eyes at last."

I breathe in.

"Do you have anything to say?"

He shakes his head again and again and again.

I hit. And draw, pulling the piston out as far as it will go, until the cylinder is full and Catapano's face is not pulsing at its regular pace. Then I remove the Pravaz's cylinder from Catapano's chest. He screams like a stuck pig, but the needle hasn't actually moved, it is still in his chest. It's all a bit of show, because I haven't finished yet.

I throw the water from a finger bowl on the ground, and let a drop of blood ooze into it. I watch how it moves and can only admire the fluidity of how it runs. Catapano really looks after himself. I wonder who his blood pusher is. He says he can't pay what he owes because he is a haemophiliac. In truth not even the blood running through his veins belongs to him, having come via some private clinic or other. Judging by his breathing his body is about to move up to red alert.

"I've got a weak heart. And I'm getting agitated, if you carry on like this you'll kill me." Another bag, another excuse.

It's obvious really, seeing as in parliament Catapano has always been ready to lie about corruption or a contract managed in a dodgy way, he's going to have no qualms about telling lies concerning something as unimportant as taxes. The lie, in his case as in many others, is a symptom of something much worse: it's a tendency to parasitism, a claw reaching out to the state's purse strings.

This sly slimeball is a weight on society.

"Dearest Catapano, if your heart is unhealthy, I'm sure it's because of the vices you indulge in... And then you try to tell us that it doesn't pump as well as it's supposed to? Well, my answer has to be, like that of my colleague here, "do you think we fucking care?" Do you expect us to pay for your heart's weakness? I can see that it is a sad thing, but you should have known better..."

All of a sudden I am overtaken by a madman's whim. A breath of air blows over my face, cool and fresh from the sea, it's a light westerly, bringing the fragrance of sea-spray and tar with a classic dash of rotten salt.

"You see, to tell the truth blood is the last thing I want from you."

"What the fuck are you doing then?"

It's down to us lot to face up to the worst politics, industry, and trade have to offer. Day after day it is becoming a thankless task, the way we are treated borders on the disgraceful.

"You know what, *Mr Cataclysm*. We all have something to be ashamed of in our veins. The difference is you pretend not to be like us, you think you are above the law."

So I do what I have to but get distracted, I look to one side at a scared hot chic, unknown VIPs, the showy spread of food and the English style lawn. Bloody hell, where do I get these mad ideas from? If the present state of raging evasion is a result of bad habits, of a culture spoon fed since the beginning of time, and around here that means roughly two thousand seven hundred years... We are old from birth and this atavistic disease of evasion, of finding loopholes has been transmitted down the generations and runs in our blood. You can take as much blood as you want, there's no escaping the fact that it re-forms the same as before, maybe even worse. Nothing changes.

No, I won't get to the point of thinking the same way as Ilario. It's better to throw yourself into something rather than shilly-shallying around it.

"Repent, Catapano. Evasion reduces us to silence, speaking out and honesty make us free men."

It's obvious I'm not saying this for show only. Tax evasion is to sin what tax returns are to confession. If you take the trouble to check them out, the two institutions have a lot in common: self-respect and respect for the community you live in. Emory's word.

The second bag is swelling now too. Ilario can't keep still and passes me the third bag, excitedly coming closer.

"What a lot of whining, Catapano. Come on, you tell us, what do you think we should do, eh?"

Catapano starts mumbling things at random. Senseless sentences, a flood of accusations and recriminations. His voice comes out small and squeaky, damaged, the falsetto of a cornered animal.

"You little shits. I'll ruin you... You won't live long enough to tell anyone about this."

Something inside me snaps. As soon as my hands are free of the third bag, I land him a heavy blow to the neck. This takes me another rung down into the drama. Ilario can hardly contain himself any longer either and brandishes an armed syringe hooked up to a fourth bag.

"A lot of people would like to see you spend the rest of your life in prison. Some of us on the other hand would like the big evaders to end up on the end of the hangman's rope or with a lethal injection in their arm, like in America."

The guests start to mutter. Some napkins are blown away by the same breeze that is messing up the ladies' ornate hair-dos. I can smell sea spray and hair spray, the fragrance of Mediterranean pines and patchouli. Whatever, it's not clearing the air.

"Leave him alone you bwutes. How dare you come here and do these tewwible things!"

The old Gorgon makes a pale job of defending her son while the security blokes, under threat of forced withdrawals, daren't react. But Ilario over reacts as usual and fuelled by alcohol and the grotesque turn the situation is taking, exaggerates. He is heavy handed and draws so much liqueur from Catapano's body the bastard starts to turn blue.

"D'you know that sonnet by Belli? The one called "È 'ggnisempre un pangrattato"? I want to recite it to you. Listen up, are you ready?"

Ilario has lost his head.

PE NNOI, RUBBI SIMONE O RRUBBI GGIUDA, MAGGNI
BBARTOLOMEO, MAGGNI TADDEO, SEMPR'È TTUTT'UNO, E
NNUN CE MUTA UN GNEO: ER RICCO GODE E 'R POVERELLO
SUDA.

NOI MOSTREREMO SEMPRE ER CULISEO
E MMORIREMO CO LA PANZA IGGNUDA.
IO NUN CAPISCO DUNCUE A CCHE CCONCRUDA D'AVÈ
DDA SEGUITÀ STO PIAGGNISTEO.
LO SO, LO SO CCHE TTUTTI LI CUADRINI C'ARRUBBENO
STI LADRI, È SANGUE NOSTRO
E DDE LI FIJJI NOSTRI PICCININI.

CHE SSERVENO PERÒ TTANTE CAGNARE?
UN PEZZACCIO DE CARTA, UN PO' D'INCHIOSTRO,
E TTUTT'*ORA-PRO-ME*: LL'ACQUA VA AR MARE.

***

FOR US, WHETHER SIMONE STEALS, OR GIUDA STEALS,
WHETHER BARTOLOMEO EATS OR TADDEO EATS,
IT'S ALL THE SAME, IT DOESN'T CHANGE ONE JOT FOR US:
THE RICH MAN GETS AND THE POOR MAN SWEATS.

WE WILL ALWAYS DISPLAY THE COLISEUM
AND DIE WITH BARE BELLIES
BUT I DON'T UNDERSTAND THE REASON FOR CARRYING
ON WITH ALL THIS SNIVELLING.
I KNOW , I KNOW THAT ALL THE MONEY THESE THIEVES
STEAL FROM US IS OUR BLOOD
AND OUR KIDDIES' BLOOD.

WHAT USE IS ALL THIS NOISE AND FUSS
A SLIP OF PAPER A DROP OF INK AND YOU WILL SEE
IT'S THE SAME NOW AS IT EVER WAS:
ALL THE WATER ENDS UP IN THE SEA.

No one applauds this piece of poetic bravura or my colleague's vibrant heartfelt rendition.

Not that he cares a hoot about a contemptuous audience.

"Do you see? Now make sure you tighten those fists nicely. The tighter you squeeze them the more you reduce your debt with the Intravenous Revenue. C'mon, show us how strong you are..." But Catapano can't. He has slumped and his vision appears to be blurred. When Ilario realises the mess he is getting in to he turns to me, almost begging.

"Oh! This one's about to leave us Alan. Gimme a hand getting some soup back in his veins.

That'll sort him out."

I shove him out of the way and take out the needle taking care not to twist the hooks in the hole or rip the tissues. They say the side effect of using the Cannolo is bone ache. I've never had the pleasure of being in a position to confirm this.

"You reckon that'll be enough do you? There's a third option, the Costa treatment. Do you have any idea how much our friend here has kept hidden behind those decrees concerning the "haematax shield" and the "tomb tax amnesty?"

So we have come to this. To the point of having to spike Catapano with a syringe to make him collaborate. To give us what we are due. Blinded by a totally foul pleasure I feel the desire to torture him.

"D'you want to hide some more? Fine, here you are. Open your mouth."

I grab the first haemodose and squirt it down his throat.

He swallows and chokes and tries to spit it out so I hold his nose closed with two fingers. "You disgusting little parliamentary piranha. That's it, a nice big swallow. Let's see how much you can swallow. Let's see how much you can swallow in one sitting."

It is said that in ancient Rome the gladiators drank the blood of their defeated opponents, believing the drinker would absorb the strength of the defeated. In the Eternal City I have decided to do the opposite: defeat my opponent with his own blood.

"No... I... can't..."

"Don't talk with your mouth full."

Ilario guesses at what my perverse actions are leading to. With a malignant sneer he copies me and sticks a needle into Catapano's flunky, Alessandro Masia, the skinny arse licker who evades his taxes by staying in the protection of his boss's shadow.

He makes a great effort and manages to miss an uncooperative vein three times in a row. It would obviously be better to try the other arm, but Ilario continues, and pretending he doesn't have much experience he sticks doggedly to one flap of swollen red skin.

When he has finished filling the bag he pours the red gold into Masia's mouth.

Catapano blinks in disbelief. He is showing signs of failing, beginning to shake and judder. Nothing tragic, it's just a hiccup of fear. His head is thrown back, mouth wide open with blood running down his neck and shoulders, dripping onto his taut swollen paunch, like a man drowning in the Tiber.

The sound of gushing blood is only disturbed by a movement above us, a plane coming into land at Ciampino airport, its vapour trail drawn over a background of clouds. It makes me remember that when a plane crashes the first class passengers have the same probability of dying as the other passengers.

"OK... OK. I'll tell you everything."

I let go of the bag a little.

"But first please help me..."

Before his veins collapse and block, I open a dose of plasma and pump it into him. He picks up instantly and sits up against the chair back. Then he spits it all out, every single tiny detail of the whole affair. The whole list of names, from A to Z, comes out of Catapano's bloody mouth. We even get the secret identity of the Phantom, and this gives me a shock because it turns out I know the man.

He continues to spill the beans about every dubious deal past, present, and future. False tax returns using the names of figureheads, receiving blood derivatives from the morgue, unlawful removal of blood from Transfusion Centres.

In the end, exhausted, he droops in his chair.

"I need an ambulance..."

No one moves. Catapano's mobile rings and Emory's name comes up on the screen, answering Catapano's earlier call. I let it ring until Gloria Gaynor's *I will survive* comes to an end. While I'm thinking about this, I waste too much time.

This is when we are overpowered.

A bottle flies from the left, I don't duck quickly enough and it hits my head. Ilario is hit on the leg by a golf club wielded by little Valerio Massimo who has been hiding under the tablecloth.

The security guards disarm our army of waiters, unarmed and precarious, and rush us. Fists and kicks fly and we are their punch-bags for a while.

We have achieved the best we could have done, we have humiliated Catapano, and full of pride as we are, neither me or my colleague put up any resistance. They beat us blindly, and we are too happy to react. We lie there face down laughing like a couple of idiots, arms tight around ourselves to protect our bodies as best as we can. They try to make us shut up by hitting us even more but it doesn't work. They spit in our faces but we don't give a shit. They stamp on us with their combat boots but we feel nothing, they insult us but we hear nothing. Actually that's not quite true, we can hear the welcome sound of an ambulance siren coming this way. We don't care about that either because we know it isn't coming for us.

Four of the security gorillas throw us into an SUV. They aren't going to stop hitting us, they just want to do it in peace and quiet without being watched by the impressionable eyes of the VIPs. As the vehicle is about to leave through the back gate it screeches to a stop and we slam against the sides of the car.

I raise my head to see out of the window. In front of us three half-naked girls are blocking the service exit standing in provocative poses. I don't know who they are. Angels of salvation. Masked avengers.

With a broken nose, split lips and a few loose teeth I can't quite get my head together. Then a voice almost brings me to tears.

"Usted no van a ninguna parte. Que te pagan bien. Adelante niñas!"

The back hatch of the SUV opens and we are thrown out of the villa's grounds. Only now do I notice it is called "Sunset Torvajanica".

Concita's friends stay inside to pay the balance for our liberation while she drags Ilario and me to the roadside. She rummages in her handbag for the first aid kit she always keeps there, a must in her line of business, and starts tending our wounds.

"No te preocupes, Concita está aquí. Yo sé cómo curar las heridas."

Compassion in this day and age is so hard to come by you hold on to it tight. It's hard to tell if Ilario is more drunk or happy. Whatever, he still has the strength to shout.

"Sing sing out! I so like how you sing."

On the other side of the gate the band starts playing again, this time the song is *Arrivederci Roma*.

A terrible realisation is growing inside me: this has really happened. I lost control. Even though I was following the rules, I broke every limit to do so. I look at my blood covered hands.

I'm finished.

Sometimes there is bad blood

*Rule number sixteen: where there are numerous evaders,
others follow suit.*

"Take us back to Rome."

It took us a while to limp back to the field where the helicopter was waiting for us. There was no chance that we were going to be able to climb up any kind of ladder they could throw down to us while the helicopter was in the air. Even just getting in normally was a real torture.

We take off and from above the lighted roads are beginning to look like giant worms of phosphorous, nocturnal maggots feeding on layers and layers of tarmac, fattened on the blood shed by road accidents.

The city passing by underneath us is not the same one.

From the dark lumps that are the Alban Hills, a large red moon is rising to light up the night. Then that amazing vision changes and the maze that spreads from the Pontina and Laurentina highways seems to form coils like those of a snake suffocating the buildings and strangling the inhabitants.

The kicking I got has left me with a dislocated shoulder. Concita had to re-sew the five stitches over my right eyebrow. My mouth is swollen and full of congealing blood. Two teeth are loose, and as if that wasn't enough, I'm almost sure I have a couple of cracked ribs. Last but not least I'm covered by a leopard skin pattern of bruises.

But when I swallow I swallow satisfaction mixed with the blood from my sore gums.

Concita sitting in the front seat doesn't take her eyes, full of tenderness, off me for a second while she looks after my colleague's wounds. Ilario is still under the anaesthetising effect of alcohol and he is singing Rino Gaetano songs under his breath.

I MINISTRI PULITI I BUFFONI DI CORTE
LADRI DI POLLI
SUPER PENSIONI
LADRI DI STATO E STUPRATORI
IL GRASSO VENTRE DEI COMMENDATORI
DIETE POLITICIZZATE
EVASORI LEGALIZZATI
AUTO BLU
SANGUE BLU
CIELI BLU
AMORE BLU
ROCK AND BLUES
NUNTEREGGAEPIU'

He's in an even worse mess than me, eyes reduced to slits, his nose bleeding and purple like an aubergine, and he has a broken arm.

He stops singing and starts talking, it sounds like a load of reminiscences.

"I don't get attached to people who are going to hurt me. I left home when I was eighteen...and d'ya know why?"

Judging by his muttered tone Ilario isn't expecting a reply, and he doesn't even appear to be really talking to me.

"Because my dad used to beat me. He used to hit me with his camera tripod. That's why... So I said to him: go on, hit me again and it'll be the last time you see me. No sooner said than done, that's all he was waiting for, an invitation, so I vanished. I was sorry about my leaving my mum. She was a victim too, poor darling. Since then I have no father. Actually no, I am my own father. I don't need someone like him to teach me how to be a father. And y'know what? He taught me what not to be."

Luckily Ilario hadn't been listening when Catapano talked about the relationship binding him to Emory, and I'm not going to enlighten him. Not so much for him, but his sister Mirna. If my colleague were to take it badly, if he couldn't accept being made a fool of and manipulated like a puppet, it would be easy for him to be blackmailed. The hydrant providing blood and the Haematogen bars which Mirna needs to live would be closed instantly, and if Ilario couldn't find an alternative supply in time she would die within a short period, suffering atrocious pain. The pains of anaemia caused by breaking capillaries in her hands and feet followed by sudden spasms all over her body, and her bone marrow would swell.

I find myself contemplating the abyss of truth while staring at the Pravaz's cylinder covered in dried blood. The truth is always down in the depths, where you can't get at it unless you have been through all the rest. It doesn't much matter whether it is love, hate, politics or friendship.

In addition to its sentimental value this syringe has the charisma of an antique object, an object of prestige suited to the work of a BloodBuster. For me the Pravaz was important even before Emory hired me because my mum gave it to me on my eighth birthday.

At the time I couldn't see the point of that gift. It was beautiful, seductive, full of a mysterious elegance increased by the fact that it could contain a liquid as precious as blood. But as a birthday present it was a little out of place. The first time I had an illness that required injections, my mum sat by my bed.

"Alan it doesn't matter what you do so long as you do it well. This is the secret of everything. When you have learned to use this syringe you will understand what I mean. You'll have to use it on yourself when I'm gone."

I'm not the kind of person who believes in fate. Whatever, with time you learn to accept the fact that certain roles are prearranged by life. What we fail to see is that we can refuse them.

I have twice been entrusted with certain responsibilities while I was sick in bed.

Now, from a number of small details that might seem insignificant and following the best traditions of urban legends, I realise that the first person to start spreading strange rumours and insinuations about Lucio Sergio Catapano was Emory. It was

Emory who raised extra doubts about Catapano's tax situation and suspected repeated evasion. It was Emory who instigated us with ironic little laughs and remarks that made us imagine thousands of different things every time his name came up.

It's as clear as plasma in a bag now.

Think of the Devil and the smartphone rings. The ring tone has the same effect as someone snapping their fingers, rousing Ilario from his alcoholic stupor.

"Don't answer Alan. We're gonna have to play this with care."

"Don't worry mate. No way am I going to answer now."

When my smartphone stops ringing Ilario's starts.

It's time to work things out: Catapano is in the Ministry of Home Affairs. He is Emory's contact. He must be the one who smoothed the way for the licenses when the Withdrawals Agency was starting up. So that was the trick. A license to sell Haematogen bars in exchange for a license to evade haemataxes. And that's not the end of it. The two of them both falsely publicly claim to be enemies. Catapano played the part of the baddie so he could complain about being persecuted, to play the part of being the victim of injustice. But behind it all he had his own reward in image. There's nothing better for increasing your number of followers than a bit of negative publicity. In the Eternal City it appears to be a moral obligation to defend ancient legal rights, juridical principles buried under a pile of books and written in Latin. The presumption of innocence... I'm not even kidding you, there are flocks of nit-picking hair splitters ready to rip themselves to shreds to defend the criminal entrusted to their hands.

There's not much left to wonder about, this is how things must have gone.

With time the Sziliagy-Catapano relationship, founded on a gentlemen's agreement, must have degenerated into an agreement between vultures. In order to continue his expansion over the length and breadth of the blood derivative market, Emory must have asked his contact for a never ending string of favours. Thinking about it, now I can see how come the ambulances from San Camillo hospital stop round the back of the Withdrawals

Agency for a withdrawal on the run before going on to the Verano and Prima Porta cemeteries. That definitely has the mark of the politician all over it, and in exchange he will have demanded something more than his already guaranteed haematax immunity, a piece of the pie for example. And so on and on, year after year, until the slice became too high a percentage of Ematogen's balance. Call it extortion if you want, but with Emory it's like stealing from Peter to give to Paul.

It's a fact, you only need to corrupt a man once, then it is merely a question of setting the terms for your silence. Whatever, with Emory and Catapano it's hard to tell who is blackmailing who.

Ilario is sitting hunched in on himself in silence like a wounded animal.

"Can you drive with your arm like that?"

"I can try. I can move it at least."

"Thank fuck it's Sunday tomorrow. It'll do us no good to be seen in this condition."

The H on top of San Camillo hospital is getting closer. There is no welcoming committee out there to greet us. No colleagues to welcome us back and congratulate us for having nailed Catapano at last. When it comes down to it this is a good sign. A sign that Emory has not yet found out how we executed the task. A sign that the beating we received will pass unobserved at least for tonight.

*

The windows are rattling. It's Monday morning and I have woken up on the sofa. Since Nico took up residence in my bedroom, my bed consists of two cushions. The wind can't get inside the house, but, whatever, the grains of sand are scratching against the windows with enough force to scrape the plaster from the walls.

The same old African storm.

Next to me Concita rubs her leg against me mischievously. My blood is circulating again, except down there. She is sweaty and a bit sticky too.

"I'm going to have a bath."

Concita half opens one eye then sticks her head under the pillow.

In the bathroom I turn on the taps. Three parts cold water to one part hot. A cocktail for a nice slow reawakening.

I sink in, my cuts and scrapes sting, and my skin pulls and complains.

Then I hear footsteps. Small fast steps. Concita, covered by a thread of a thong around her waist, slips into the bathroom.

"Es lo suficientemente grande para dos?"

A rhetorical question. Of course it's not big enough for two unless we lie one on top of the other, and since I didn't say no she slides out of her thong, leans her two soft pert breasts close to my face and lowers herself in on top of me.

My blood continues to avoid my lower regions. It has rushed in a completely different direction.

Concita whispers dirty thoughts in my ear then kisses my neck. "Duele aqui?"

"I shake my head, and she slides down to my chest.

"Y aqui?"

Another no. She ends up kissing my belly with her tongue flicking lasciviously. She scratches her nails down my sides.

"En este caso?"

"Oh yes, there..."

I grab her hands, and lift her chin with a finger.

"Nicola is sleeping next door..."

"Con esta tormenta? Y entonces poco a poco. El niño no se oye nada."

"C'mon Conci. I'm sorry but I've only just got it back together. I have to go to Emory soon." She lifts her top half and snorts, worse, a flash of anger passes across her eyes.

"Alan! Es verdad entonces... Ceci tiene razón. Tú tiene siempre la cabeza en otro lugar. Sólo piensas en el trabajo."

If she knew the truth about Anissa, Concita would respect me more. If she knew the whole truth about Anissa that same respect would convince her to stay even further away from me.

Irritated, Concita gets out of the tub and pulls her thong back on. Dripping water everywhere she pads down the corridor and Nicola sees her walk by half naked. I stick my head out over the edge of the tub. I would like to have his dreamy expression still when faced with those two magnificent posterior melons.

"Come here a minute you..."

He yawns and rubs the sleep from his eyes.

"What, is there a storm coming?"

"Ah so you can hear without headphones...Yeah, it really looks like it. Nicola, I'm going out soon. If you need a lift hurry up and get dressed, I'll take you to the Metro and you can get yourself to school."

"And after, are we gonna hook up again at the Metro?"

I heave myself out of the tub and Nico hands me my bathrobe.

"No, afterwards you have to come home on your own and behave like a good boy with Concita. She looks after you better than she does me anyway. Believe me."

A smug little smile curves his lips. He's about to turn and leave when he remembers something.

"Listen Alan... I got an e-mail form the social worker yesterday. D'you remember her? That woman down at the pitch."

Of course I do. She must still be fuming about how I treated her.

"So what did the ugly sister say?"

"She says she's going to my mum in jail tomorrow with a load of signed papers about his and that, and then on to the tribunal."

Oh crap. I've only got 24 hours.

After getting dressed I turn on my smartphone. I have accumulated eight missed calls. All from just one caller.

To the slaughter

Rule number seventeen: the largest contributions are in the last place you would think of looking for them.

I waited for evening to come before going to the Cloaca Nova.

Not least because the dentist fixed my appointment at 4 o'clock on the dot. One of my canine teeth is cracked and has to be replaced, the incisor has been through a bad time but he's going to be able to save it.

Even though it's Monday they told me that Emory is pacing up and down in his office. No one knows how long he has been there. It doesn't take a genius to know he must have worn a trench in the floor in front of his desk by now. His back and forth pacing makes it look as though he's mounting the guard over his own anger. Worse, he has absolutely no intention of trying to calm down. At least not before having dumped a fair share of the blame on my head.

"Ah! There you are! Found the courage to show your face at last have you?... I've been trying to call you for two days."

I carry on walking towards him limping and holding my arm.

"I've not been well. I had to get my mouth sorted out. Your friend Catapano's security detail really had fun with me."

"So shut that fucking sewer of a mouth! You're in an even worse state than a week ago. The more time passes the more you look like a badly cooked black pudding."

I do as he says and can't work out whether this is just another of his sadistic tests to see if I am worthy of being given a loan for Anissa's caution or not. By the tone of voice this doesn't seem like the best moment to bring up the topic. Mind you, with Emory, any time is a bad time.

Emory looks at me through half closed eyes. He'd have no qualms about asphalting roads and fertilising the land with my blood to maintain a position of power.

"How is it possible that you lot didn't understand the drill? I send you to Catapano's party, I get you an official helicopter, which is like getting blood from a stone, to make you look good and this is how you repay me."

"There was a misunderstanding. The message didn't-"

"That wasn't the message I wanted delivered you idiot! You were supposed to intimidate him, not risk killing him."

Even though my apologies are implicit, I'm not really sure I should be apologising. Emory dragged me into his shady business without even bothering to warn me what was going on. Actually he kept me in the dark on purpose with the intention of taking advantage of our blessed ignorance.

"How was I supposed to know? You didn't explain any-"

"Shut up! Thank the good God you don't believe in that Catapano is still alive. And that you two are still alive."

He rummages around in his pockets and finds nothing, then opens and shuts a number of drawers in his desk and pulls out a packet of cigarettes. As far as I remember he never smokes. It must be a real emergency. Emory's cigarettes are an unknown brand, they are dark and the filters look like they are made of blood they are so red. He lights one with a Zippo, draws deeply, and lets the smoke out like a dragon, through his nose.

"Isn't that what you wanted?"

He glares at me furiously.

"Like fuck it was! Witness after witness saw what you did to him. In case it wasn't already clear, I'm a business man and this affair involving you, one of my best men, one of Ematogen's Top Vampires, is more than a little irritating."

I agree with him about the fact that serious things are happening. And not just concerning his business.

"I'm guessing your irritation stems from the fact that after having trained me and helped me rise through the hierarchy of Ematogen I have been irresponsible and heavy handed with a persistent and evident evader? Or is it because I misinterpreted an order?"

I know he won't be able to resist the temptation of laying into me. I can see it written all over his face. This is his plan:

1) spit a certain amount of poison at me;

2) unwillingly accept every wild excuse I make for having let the situation get out of hand;

3) take advantage of the momentary superiority he has gained and make me pay in the very near future.

"I told you to shut it!"

Emory surprises me by opting for a silence loaded with meaning as the instrument for dragging me back into line and making me think about my unforgivable mistakes.

The Emory I know wouldn't let himself be screwed over by clumsy excuses. The Emory I know is treacherously and cruelly ferocious. He is capable of crushing you without even having to touch you, like those chess computers that can predict your every move, from the first to the last stupid decision you make. Then he takes advantage of every error and uncertainty to always come out the winner. One way or another. Catapano is the same, he is made of the exact same stuff. It follows that those two aren't conducting a real war. Their fighting is a sham. They devise strategic plans, for fun, drafting bogus tactics. At most they might play tricks on each other, using us as their pawns.

Emory looks at me sullenly. He sighs suddenly and stubs out his cigarette butt in an ashtray shaped like a red blood cell.

He doesn't look convinced by what he can see in me.

His mobile vibrates and he checks the incoming number before answering. "Hello?"

His calm makes me realise there must be a tip-off in the air, or, as he says, business.

He lights another cigarette. Behind him, in orderly rows on the shelves, there is a collection of phials of blood in various stages of separation. Our old sample set. He gets up and looks them over one by one. It's as if he's trying to suggest that, willing or unwilling, sooner or later this is how we will all end up, so in the meantime we might as well do the best we can.

He puts the phone down.

"Alan, your luck has held out again."

He is talking in a softer voice but it doesn't make me feel better at all. When he says things like this my blood starts to run cold.

"I'm giving you the chance to make up for messing up so fucking badly. There's massacre going on at Sant'Andrea hospital. Those crazy food integralists have turned up again... They've been off the Roman radar for a while, another sign of how the veins are loosening. However, a large quantity of blood is becoming available. They are interested in the fat in this situation not the blood. I wouldn't be surprised if all the BloodBusters in the area turn up there, authorised or not. I bet your friend Farid, as the greedy traitor he now is, won't let such a rich opportunity slip through his fingers."

Emory stops for breath. The Sant'Andrea hospital is in north Rome, on the Viking's territory. As far as I'm concerned it's almost a foreign country.

"You know I've been thinking about what you said last week. Farid's head in exchange for the caution you need for that evader you are so fond of. Well, add five crates of blood and you can call it a deal."

All this news does nothing to cheer me up. On the contrary, it throws me into a state of serious agitation. The most I can do to show Emory my gratitude is grunt. As I stand up he speaks again, this is it, the usual cherry on top of the cake.

"Ah, yes, another thing. For that terrible mess you made with Catapano I need you to bring me an extra ten crates of blood to make us even, and if I can I'll see to cleaning up your reputation a bit."

I'll have to work my arse off to deliver on a deal like this. It's not even a deal, it's extortion, pure and simple. I send a text to Ilario telling him to meet me at the exit for Grottarossa in 40 minutes. I get the impression that Emory is saving me by shoving me to the bottom of a deep dark chasm.

*

The noise is deafening. A force four sandstorm, the side winds on the ring road make cars rock and push scooters off course, even the heavier ones, as if they were leaves on a tree. It could be worse, at least it's not raining. Yet.

I park the taxbulance in the hospital's dirt track. The sky is dark with elongated mustard coloured clouds. I can hardly see as far as I can spit.

Ilario warns me of his arrival with a signal, blasting his horn as he comes to a stop. He jumps out of his car and into mine. The orthopaedic collar round his neck keeps him looking directly in front of him.

"Don't say a word. Agreed? I know I look ridiculous, so let's just leave it right?"

"Yeah right, 'cos you think I'm any better off?"

I lean towards him opening my mouth wide to show him my battered mouth. We laugh painfully.

"You do you realise, don't you, that you have narrowly escaped death not once but twice already this week?"

"And it's only Monday... C'mon or we'll be late."

We grab an Ematogen beach towel from the boot of the taxbulance and throw it over our heads for protection and fight our way through the elements with difficulty. The radio news has just confirmed that, counting both patients and the medical staff, at the moment of the massacre there were 560 people present in the hospital.

We stop for a moment in the security guard's cabin and take a rest from the squalls of wind. I call the other Vampires, team work always gives its results.

"If you see Farid give me his position."

They all confirm. No one has seen him.

"That bloody Emory makes me feel no better than a beggar."

Ilario mimes a pair of martial art moves.

"I'd like to give him a couple of kicks in the right places. I swear Alan... Does he have the same effect on you, yeah, Alan?"

It's a pity he has only learned a kind of sham kung-fu from watching Jackie Chan films on the telly. When Ilario tries a roundhouse kick in the air he slips mid-pirouette and lands on his arse on the floor.

"No, I reckon I'd have had to spend twenty years in therapy

if it hadn't been for him. What do you want me to say, at best I'd have found a better way to kill myself before this."

I hold out my hand to him and pull him up so we can carry on. The air smells of flesh, human flesh. I make a gesture against bad luck, so does Ilario standing next to me.

The mission Emory has sent us on entails drawing blood from hundreds of corpses. There are few enough people left in the Eternal City who respect the living, so you can imagine the situation when it comes to the dead.

The approach ramp is cluttered with bodies. Some have been quartered, some are still writhing and implore us for help with their hands. They moan and beg and spit out silent profanities which rise from the ground like curses. I'm so glad we're not nurses.

At the entrance we cross the "curious onlooker" cordon made up of the boys in blue who on seeing our scarlet uniforms split open like a watermelon to let us through.

"Are you really really sure about it then Alan? I mean d'you have any idea how much a year in prison will take out of you?"

"Stop it right there with your whining... It might not be a year. Everybody knows how things are run down at Regina Coeli. Do you really think they are as efficient as us down there? And like I told you, it's a question of principle. Have you got any honour left in you at all?"

I make a rollie and light up. The first draw whets my appetite and the rest tastes even better.

"Understood. D'you reckon we can hit that bastard Farid with the old laughing gas. I mean it...and then Anissa would be out in a flash. Just like that."

Ilario clicks his fingers.

"A year...just like that. *Tempus fugit*, that's what they say, isn't it? Are you following me, bro'?"

I ignore him as we cross the entrance lobby. Blood spatters like red shooting stars move slowly on the hall's befouled ceiling. Next to hit us is the stink of piss, roasted liver, and burned fat. It fills our lungs and there's no escaping it.

The wheelchairs have all been piled up to one side.

If you ever end up in a situation like this here's a tip: you can get blood off walls by sprinkling the affected area with semolina and then wiping with a sponge soaked in cold water. This works on sofas and mattresses too.

The blood spilt on the floor is so slippery that it's like walking on thick jelly or worse, pats of butter.

"How many corpses do you reckon there are?"

"Half a thousand... Watch it though, they aren't corpses yet. Have you even ever read the manual, eh, Ilario?"

"OK, if you insist *still-hearted-donors*. As far as I'm concerned they're stone dead."

"Whatever, they're going to be in cold ischaemia soon."

All these mangled obese bodies tell a pitiful story: they come to the Sant'Andrea hospital to lose weight, full of illusions and ballast, convinced that by having large slices of fat removed they will solve the problems of their lives, but the more they have removed the hungrier they get and so they produce more fat: a vicious circle that goes from the mouth to the wallet and ends up bloating the treasury of the Intravenous Revenue.

There is a sound not far away.

"Shhh, can you hear it too?"

Ilario confirms my suspicions. It's almost as though our imaginations are giving us a hand. From the floor above we can hear creaking, like the sound of rubber boots walking, stopping, and walking again.

"There, there and there."

I whisper indicating the various points with my hand.

Now I understand why Emory has sent me here. In this neighbourhood whose name I don't even know on the northern borders of the city, practically the opposite side of the city to where my beat is, I have no sway over anyone, I'm just one of the many, a nobody. An old saying comes to mind, "cross this line at your own risk".

The area by the Big&Fat ward is scattered with corpses dumped on sofas soaked in thickening blood and others that have been hooked to withdrawal tubes directly where they passed away. The cracking sound of bones under our feet risks giving our position away. Luckily the wind outside whipping the windows is covering the sound of our advance and the singing of the sand deadens any noise we might make.

"Oh, tell me something Alan, what would you have liked to have done before dying?"

As I check whether there is any blood left, if any veins have been overlooked by the competition, I notice the smell of gas, an intestinal gas leak. Yeah I know, stomach turning.

"I wish I had left this job a long time ago."

"I want to live in Forte Garbatella... You know, those old council land lots, a spectacle of yesteryear."

There are old people here too, I can tell by the stale smell my nose membranes are picking up from a long way off. We don't even think about taking their blood, it would be like trying to sell a quantity of cheap watered down wine to a Rotary Club event. Whatever, Farid won't have had any scruples and will have sucked even them dry in this new stage of his career that I so want to crush before it gets properly started.

We make our way around other obstacles, human shaped figures, and then it hits me: Anissa and me share the same pathological fixation even though we come at it from opposite ends of the spectrum. Call it "haemaempathy" if that helps. I remove blood from future corpses to help them on their way (I'm talking about those ten hours during which the blood retains its composition), and Anissa prefers, as a hobby, to donate her blood to the dying in an attempt to prevent death. Now try telling me we are not compatible.

At the end of the Cardiology ward we turn towards General Plastic Surgery. Someone lifts an arm in greeting. It's that horse-faced Marzio. He motions us to come forward. With a series of arm and hand signals he tells us the ground floor has been sucked dry. That makes sense: as soon as the food integralists ran off the BloodBusters must have swooped in to leach the flesh.

Whatever, Glad lets us know that he and his team are going up to the first floor.

"Ilario, this way. Let's take the other stairs..."

The first floor has been thoroughly "dried up" too, vein by

vein. The bodies here have been scarified though, and deprived of those five or six litres that each of us carries around with us from birth, our intravenous credit. By the style of the cuts I recognise this as that sodding Farid's work, him and his ex-tattooist's touch.

On the second floor things get complicated.

The Viking, a smug smile on his face precedes Moffa and Lionheart who are pushing a gurney jam packed full of haemodoses with great enthusiasm.

The North Rome team have filled up. There's nothing left for us to do but hoover up the leftovers.

The walkie-talkie in the Viking's belt comes to life, it's the indecisive voice of Sawn-off: "The bastard's turned up on the fourth floor. I repeat, the bastard's turned up."

With a hand on his helmet the Viking salutes us. He got this nickname because when he was a kid he always came to fancy dress parties dressed as Thor, with winged shoes and a winged helmet.

Well, it's not exactly a normal helmet anyway, it's part of the gear the riot police use, with wings drawn on it.

There is a strong smell of decomposition as we climb to the next floor. It's the smell of well-hung meat to be exact. And I don't think I am far wrong if I say that this wasn't simply a massacre, but a mass *fatticide*.

"Ilario, put your mask on."

"I just did..."

Bodies are hanging from the hall lights, immense viscid deformed human carcasses. Skinned patients, some still have the strength to twitch, the reaction of a bared nerve. The integralists have stuffed lemon halves in their mouths, and from their flaccid feet an oily liquid is leaking, melted adipose dripping plentifully, flowing in rivulets along the floor.

That isn't all. The air is thick with vaporised blood and the stench of people who have lost control of their bladders. There is no sound except our own heavy breathing trapped in our masks.

We climb over a parapet near Oncology. Ilario has my back, and like a good Bat stays crouched up on the walkway while I drop down to the ground. The only thing is I land badly, slip in a pool of blood and end up lying on the floor. When I get up I can feel a syringe pricking my throat, suddenly I can hardly breathe.

"Put the bag down Alan. Slowly. On the ground, man." There is bad blood between me and Farid.

Truth Injections

Rule number eighteen: if evasion reduces us to silence,
speaking out and honesty make us free men.

"I want to get out of here! D'you hear me?"

Farid, in keeping with his reputation as a coward, has jumped me from behind. I can't see him, but we are so close we are practically hugging and I can hear and recognise a certain sound, a sound that is totally wonderful for us BloodBusters. The greedy freeloader has filled a ton of blood bags and is carrying them about his person, he is like a terrorist about to explode.

"So where have you left your fried noodle Chinese friends, eh? Did they leave you here all on your own? Didn't have the courage to come with you, eh?"

He whispers in my ear.

"I don't need them. I'm more than enough on my own."

The next thing he says shows how pissed off he is because no one has answered his question. "If you don't want me to bleed him dry here in front of you all, let me go. Understood?"

A wheeze gurgles in my windpipe. Farid saws at my throat, Arab style. I can hear him invoking his God through gritted teeth. "*Staghfir' Allah...*"

Under my chin a reddish spurt stretches from side to side giving me a second, macabre grin. "Work it out, bloodsuckers... How much time has he got left?"

Farid bares my torn throat and exposes the rip by pulling my head backwards.

He is opening the wound, and my platelets will already be moving *en masse*. I know the process is unstoppable. A gluey clot is hurrying to prevent the blood oozing out but the barrier thrown up by my body's defence mechanisms for retaining blood is not strong enough. Despite being a bloodfucker Farid has had a lot of practice. At this rate I'll bleed to death within twenty minutes. My immune system is not what it used to be.

Farid digs in his pocket. He hasn't got twenty minutes of patience.

"No wait. This will hurry things up."

He rips open a bag of anticoagulant with his teeth and pours it over my throat. Like throwing petrol on a fire.

"*Subhana Allah...*"

Then he recites his incomprehensible evening prayers.

The platelets are washed away, dissolved and broken down, and the blood speeds up on its way out now there is nothing to slow down its separation from my body. I am awake and alert, soon though the adrenalin rush is going to slip away with the rest of my vital fluids. Then I will lose consciousness.

In the shadow of the parapet I can just make out Ilario's comical tuft of hair. I blink at him three times in the hope that he will understand what I mean. My colleague nods. Luckily my captor doesn't notice this exchange.

Farid is using me as a human shield so Ilario opens a bag of blood, works out the trajectory and pours it all right over that son of a bitch's head. Then with a catlike leap he flings himself on Farid and I seize the moment to extricate myself. Using my hands and feet I scrabble back along the floor as far as I can until I come up against the metal trunks of old Glad, another new arrival on this floor.

From here, I can finally see what Farid has done. The hotheaded puppet. He is wearing a *pakul* on his head, a typical Pakistani headdress, and army style combat trousers. His torso is bare, showing his many prison tats. Above them all it says *ALLAH AKBAR* in Arab writing incised across his chest.

The red on his face fades, diluted by the sweat on his hands transferred there by his vain attempts to clean himself up. He looks like one of those big flies who are always rubbing their heads with their legs.

Whatever, now Ilario and Farid are really laying into each

other, syringes flashing, pure BloodBuster fighting style. They have mounted fighting needles, Straws, pointed 7 gauge weapons used for ear piercing, and just to make sure they do enough damage, they have sharpened the tips by dragging them along the rough walls.

Marzio hands me a bottle of water so I can clean myself up a little. I take a sip, but instead of going down my throat, it dribbles out of my new smile.

Farid waves both arms in time with his delusion of power. The swaggering bastard advances on Ilario with such force it's as if he is recharging his blood. Ilario doesn't even flinch, hands by his sides in a position of readiness. He challenges Farid by staying on the defensive.

It feels like watching the main scene of *High Blood*, a "dark-haemo" reinterpretation of the celebrated western *High Noon*.

Farid lunges and misses, but with the second blow on the way back he hits his opponent in the ribs. Ilario manages to hit Farid in the leg as he falls back, they both yell out in triumph and pain.

"Shut that fuckin' mouth!"

Farid yells, drops the syringe and grabs the end of Ilario's long tongue. He is so quick I hardly realise what he has done. If Ilario dares bite he will slice his tongue off, so he is stuck, trapped between the fingers of the traitor dragging him towards the flight of stairs.

"Finally! At last you gonna have to shut up. I couldn't stand you and your stupid chatter." Ilario might be in an awkward situation, but my throat is no better off.

I dab at the dripping red half-moon as best I can with the lapel of my coat, at the same time I watch Marzio who is doing nothing to help. Fuck it all, he's standing there motionless, enjoying watching the duel between those two syringe happy maniacs.

Then my bloodsucking colleague does an amazing crazy thing, far beyond his usual reach, almost at the level of a confirmed Vampire. Something even Farid would never have expected. Ilario bites down hard on his tongue and cuts it right off. First the tongue goes limp and then falls from his mouth like a wriggling maggot. Then he lands a sharp kick on Farid's shin making him tumble down the stairs. Blood and spit dripping from his lips Ilario launches himself after him, all cocky like.

"I halk wheng I wang coo...."

One nil for Ilario, a dearly bought point.

Farid, shoulders on the ground, throws his syringe at his opponent to slow him down and earn time to get back into position. He is off target though and is hit by Ilario's counter attack.

Second round: a tremendous bone cracking blow followed by the clatter of needles bouncing one by one across the floor.

Ilario pounds Farid with a barrage of right and left jabs. His brain is clouded by pain and he is trying to get as much of it out as he can. As angry as he is he's not doing too bad a job of it.

With a push Farid rolls across the ground. He does a kind of break dance spin and goes for Ilarios's bare calf muscle with his teeth. He bites so hard that my colleague staggers and is forced to shift his weight onto the other foot to prevent himself from falling.

Ilario starts waving his arms wildly like a windmill, performing a ridiculously expressive pantomime of a ferocious Bruce Lee pastiche: he waves his legs in Farid's face and this time he doesn't fall because he is holding on tight to the bannisters. He does all this despite the orthopaedic collar he is wearing which sends his blood pressure up and with it the force of his release.

When he has finished his charge, Ilario drags Farid out of the mire of liquids, dirt and smeared blood by his jacket, hauling him back up the stairs, and offers him to me like a sacrificial Easter lamb.

He unbuttons his shirt and pulls out the tupperware lid from his chest. That is what softened the blow Farid landed in his ribs, and permitted him to gain that precious initial advantage.

Limp and filthy with blood, Farid Sedef falls to the floor on his back. Behind him he has left a trail of coagulating blood. Very symbolic.

However much they do and undo, people like him, hypocrites and go-getters, will never get the better of people like me. Not even by cheating, playing dirty, playing with superior numbers, jumping us from behind or any other way that comes to mind. Organisation trumps every time. He has ended up alone and I have the Vampires on my side. Someone like him is a disgrace for our profession. Couldn't give a shit if he's Arab, Italian or Chinese. Someone who preaches rubbish and practises worse deserves no better than to flounder in his own crap.

Standing and swaying with syringe in hand, the needle glinting with red, Ilario is panting worse than a Labrador in a hot car; his face is swollen and darkened by a barrage of bruises.

"Zere'sh nufiing coo be gun for zish shit."

It is only now that Marzio bends down to help me. His legs creak and he hands me a gauze pad.

"Have you finished with the water?"

I hand back the bottle, but it slips from my hand and lands standing up straight.

"You're a phenomenon Alan. You always manage to end up in the same trouble!"

"What are you talking about?"

He picks up the bottle and an awful scene enters my head. A terrible *deja vù*.

"I've always liked you. You're one of those people who are capable of pulling their destiny apart day after day. Your destiny is a strange one, you lose, you are overcome, beaten, wounded, and stamped on.... You fall and fall again but you always get up. I have to hand it to you. You are a fighter, in your own peculiar way..."

"Instead of standing there doing fuck all why didn't you give us a hand?"

Marzio is immobile as if he hasn't heard me. He goes back to what he was saying, a monologue with no real start nor finish.

"On the verge of bleeding to death for some stupid action... Have you forgotten the Middle East?"

Yeah, that was my *deja vù*. The water, the girl soldier, and the bullets. Those are my fuckups. All paid for. Debts extinguished if not with tears, then with blood.

"What do you know about it?"

192

Marzio's long beard was there, though not full of white like it is now. I never said anything about that fuckup to anyone. But it's a well-known fact that fuckups, like lies, travel like wild fire.

"Alan, Alan... In all these years I've never managed to work out whether you're more of a cynic or an idealist. I reckon you must be an ingenuous dunderhead who prefers to only believe what you understand. Have you never wondered why we were never given water in our kit? Have you never asked yourself why we were all always so thirsty during missions?"

Me and my stupid head. Now I see. It wasn't the facts that fooled me, it was how I interpreted them.

Marzio looks at the time. Actually that's not quite right, a countdown clock has appeared on the screen of his smartphone. He started it the moment Farid cut my throat, the figures measure out the time I have left. Practice and my familiarity with self-withdrawal help me to stay lucid, they help me not to lose consciousness.

"We have all been trained to play the idiot, my friend..."

The bottle of water was the bait for recruiting us. The wounding, the method for creating a blood debt with Emory, to make us happy to be transformed into BloodBusters. At the end of our convalescence Emory wanted us to feel morally indebted to him. A team of loyal bloody bloodhounds in his service.

"I'm supposed to make sure you don't get out of here alive."

Another piece of the puzzle falls into place. Obvious, right? Dog eats dog. Each one of us is below someone else on the food chain, pity you never know who the link above you is.

"But we can sort things out a different way. Without anyone having to suffer too much."

"Shoot."

"Drop him."

"Who?"

"What do you mean, who? Can't you see? He's a fucking parasite. He holds us by the throat with invisible talons, and when he wants to he tightens his grip. As long as you do his bidding and show balls, he keeps you by his side, but as soon as you make a mistake he wrings you out..."

"Crystal clear. Excellent system. I know the mechanism. You are another one of his messages."

"Shit Alan, we've been through a lot together me and you. You don't need me to explain these things to you."

The Gladiator looks at Farid with contempt; the man is still unconscious. He was one of Glad's recommendations. Not exactly a pupil but almost.

"Right, and you don't have to. It's Catapano's fault. I knew he was going to get me into trouble."

"I'll say it one more time Alan, for the last time, drop him."

The Gladiator pulls on a pair of gloves and opens a phial of Cryo, a coagulant compound a hundred times more potent than plasma. He bends over me and tightens a tourniquet around my arm. After loading the serum in a disposable syringe he pumps it into my veins.

"Excellent advice, thanks..."

The Cryo is a true delicacy in my comatose state.

I'm not sure if this gesture can be considered as desertion or an act of pity. The fact is that this is finally an injection of something good.

To avoid misunderstandings Marzio dumps the syringe and gloves.

I stay leaning against the wall for a good minute longer. If I had told Marzio that Catapano had blown the whistle on his double dealings he probably wouldn't have let me live. I mean, he hasn't confided in me about his secret identity, he hasn't revealed where he disappears to when he doesn't turn up in the Agency for days on end. As long as the Phantom exists it means there is someone on the other side of the barricade, and I'm not the kind of person to blow on the flame that would burn the cover and arse off old Glad.

In this case, the weight of the things left unsaid is greater than that of those actually voiced.

Finally I regain enough strength to stand up again. The effect of the Cryo is unbelievable, an instantaneous and near miraculous effect.

Ilario is checking the piece of tongue he still has in his mouth.

"Grab what you can and let's get out of here. I've swallowed enough crap for one day."

"Yeah but firsht I wanna find za poingt. I shaw it over zere."

When the last obese body has been exsanguinated, the stink of offal will stick around the Sant'Andrea hospital for years.

At the end of the day

*Rule number nineteen: blood glitters even
when the stars are shining.*

Behind everything that I took as real, behind everything that persuaded me to carry on, a terrible lie has been growing and now, standing in front of Emory's villa and contemplating all he has meant to me, it is as if my circulation, pushed by one burning desire, is going to liberate me of all this venom accumulated over the years.

After 5134 days of haematic taxation, if I have to vanish from the scene, I don't want to leave any debts lying around. I am clean as far as Marzio goes, because I could have sold him out to Emory to save my own arse, or I could have told everything to one of those serialised pseudo-news programmes and milked the story for loads of money. I'm clean with Emory too, even though I used to think I owed him still.

It's late at night when Ilario and me come to the gate of the Sziliagy residence.

The storm shows no signs of abating. It is sitting over the Eternal City like a lid speeding up the boiling process. Yellowish dust and bits of rubbish twirl here and there in small vortexes along the Via Appia Antica. Gusts of wind, rustling through the electric cables strung between pylons play grim spectral melodies. The fronts of the villas next to Emory's are beginning to turn brown and grey from all the sand that has spattered against them.

The dogs in the garden howl, their muzzles as pointed as those of jackals. Only dragons in the moat and vultures on the window ledges are missing for the Haemogoblin to feel perfectly at home in his natural habitat.

Neither of us is fit to be seen, more blood out than in, but the gate opens anyway as soon as we are recognised by the video camera.

Emory's house flaunts his Czechoslovakian origins. It has been built full of spires, protuberances and metal globes made green by the rain. Depending on the weather it swings from anthracite grey to the off-white of Roman tuff. At the moment it looks brick red.

The dogs run at us barking loudly, then stop and growl, intimidated. We smell of death, so much of it is dripping off us that they don't dare attack or come too close. Like Ilario would say if he still had his tongue: "Not even the dogs..."

Our hands are loaded with the haemodoses we have managed to gather together, our footsteps crunch over the gravel making a sound like glass being crushed. Emory looks neither sober nor pleased to see me. He's a good actor and manages to show no surprise that I am still alive after having assigned the Gladiator with the task disposing of me.

"First of all please tell me you have a very good reason for coming here during a sandstorm. Secondly, you look disgusting. Thirdly, I'll give you thirty seconds to tell me what you have to tell me and then I want you to vanish."

We have probably interrupted him in the middle of *syringing* some anaemic nymph.

I advance on him, staining the entrance's terracotta floor. The madman inside me is throbbing under my skin. I would so like to headbutt him right on the nose. Just to straighten it up a bit, y'know? Instead I thrust my face just a metre away from his and jab my index finger into his chest.

"No, you tell me, why did you choose me?"

At first Emory stares at my second mouth, the red scab matches my uniform, then he bares his fangs and sneers. On a normal human face this would be a crooked smile.

"Do you want to tempt fortune too? The best BloodBuster south of the Colosseum feels hard done by?"

He starts with the blarney but I'm not falling for it. Whenever Emory is sarcastic an alarm bell screams inside me.

"It's got nothing to do with luck. I've already used up any of that I had left."

From the doorway a panther-lady looks in, she is statuesque with a splendid physique and two melons on her that could feed a whole neighbourhood of the Eternal City.

"Emory babe, what's going on? Come back inside, there's a storm out there..."

He doesn't even turn around, instead he waves her away with a nervous hand behind his back. "Go back inside you! When I've finished with these two I'll make you wish you hadn't come out here."

The panther deflates, pouts and disappears.

"Alan, listen...This is some advice from me to you, as a friend. Don't try to go against the flow, especially when the river is mine. Do you remember BloodBuster rule number one? The heart is an organ that pumps blood, not emotions."

Ilario says nothing; Emory is the only person I know who has this "mute" effect on him. Whatever, even if my colleague wants to add something to the conversation he wouldn't exactly be much help at the moment seeing the state his mouth is in.

"What did you think then? That I'd come back from the massacre at Sant'Andrea clean and spruce, all dedicated to the Ematogen cause as if nothing had happened?"

He crosses his arms, looks at us threateningly and forces us to take a step backwards into the gusts of sand.

"Do you want to be a hero? Trust me, you're better off holding onto your place as a soldier for the Intravenous Revenue, you'll have much less trouble. Chasing after some brilliant ideal is really not worth the heartache. You kicked up a big fuss with that Malesano, then that revenge business with Farid, and last but not least the scene in front of Catapano's guests. Listen to me Alan... you're better off enjoying the same values and routines as everybody else. Rome is generous with those who doff their caps.

"With arse-lickers you mean..."

"Yours is a subjective point of view. I am convinced that blood means life and its abundance or scarcity have always decided the future of any country, and Italy is no exception."

This is where he always ends up. But this time I haven't come to his house with a mutilated colleague and my own throat cut to lap up his low empire morality.

"Italy is always an exception. We are a country founded on exceptions: exceptions to the rules, exceptions to work, exceptions to rights, exceptions to duties. The house speciality is exceptions to the exceptions."

"How many stories we make up to justify our failures... I bet you're going to pretend you don't know how come you got wounded now. Why you ended up crying and begging someone to save you."

I let him blather on, for me the strongest desire at the moment is to dive into the pool lined with grey granite and clean myself up. When Emory had a fountain sculpted for his garden, he had an exact copy of the fountain in Piazza Farnese made. Anyway, I was expecting some of his psycho-mental bullshit. I've got used to it, I've become *bullshitrepellent*, guilt proof.

"Just drop it, Emory. I know how you recruited us. The Gladiator told me about the bottle of water trick."

I have to be careful because talking to Emory is like walking through a minefield, on the other hand I don't give a shit any more about causes or consequences. When you come to look at it, it's as if things in the Eternal City move with their own brand of bizarre logic, like a horror ride, a merry-go-round of low down acts and atrocities from which, one day, we must all get off.

I wonder in what other ways Emory is going to unleash his revengeful fury on me. After the failure of the first attempt to get rid of me, how is he going to make me pay? Is he going to set all the BloodBuster teams on me to get even? After all, in his mind I have betrayed the gratitude he expected me to show him for ever. Or will he make it impossible for me to work in any Withdrawals Agency in Italy? A word from him to the managers and I would be blacklisted forever, damned, *urbi et orbi*.

Emory stares at me indignantly. He clenches his jaw and when he reopens his mouth he looks like an insect, an evil spider hiding behind a web of complicated but perfectly balanced arguments.

"Marzio? The Gladiator Poleni? You're out of your tiny...

It's better to cash in a withdrawal, even if it hurts, than live in a world without blood. People who don't give blood to their country contribute to its ruination. Use your head Alan ... That butcher Marzio just wants to get rid of some of the competition. Do you really think he gives a flying fuck about you? Do you really think he is being honest in the name of some kind of ideal of brotherhood? Don't you believe it, he's doing it for himself, to earn more and get the chance to stick his needles in the veins of your taxpayers."

I know, he's on a roll. In the moment I realise that I know more than Emory, I grin on the inside. A low joy, deep in my bowels, the best kind there is. My thoughts turn to Anissa and the fact that you need a pinch of awareness and mania to guide the direction your fate is going to take. Even if it isn't the fate you want. Perhaps there are also intermediate fates where you have to make a stopover before you can go on to the final one. Something like that, anyway, this is not the end.

Ilario and me each put our MT67F containers on the ground. The dogs circle them, sniffing excitedly.

"This is what we managed to get."

"You must be mad. Do you think you can cover the cost of the caution with four *miserly* crates? Where is the blood for Catapano? I haven't got time for this. Go and sell it on your own if you're so clever."

"We worked our arses off to get these four miserly crates. Ilario lost a piece of his tongue for these."

Emory says nothing. This stuff isn't going to work anymore. Too many plans have gone up in smoke: mine, for scraping together the caution for Anissa and redeem myself in the eyes of my boss, his for eliminating me and appeasing Catapano for the blood taken from him so heavy handedly.

"OK then. No caution money. But I don't owe you fuck all. Not now not ever. No hard feelings...In fact, I'll leave you Ilario in my place. He deserves it, he collected 48 bags in a single night. He's an excellent Bat. I can sincerely say that the pupil has surpassed the master. Considering he even saved my hide from Farid I'm presenting him as a candidate to take my place as Vampire."

It might seem absurd, but I have often had the feeling that by staying in one place for too long, doing the same things with the same people over and over again, I was going to come to a bad end. As if stagnating blood could transform into a filthy but fertile pool where bacteria start to reproduce and proliferate.

Instead of sinking roots I would just sink. Instead of making headway, I would simply lose my head.

At the moment the aim of what I am doing here is to throw a number of things back into circulation, so that others, hopefully, will fall back into place on their own.

"So? Do you accept my resignation?"

Emory does not like this decision I have made. Oh no, he is annoyed he can't "liquidate" me in the way he thinks would be best. Nor can he forgive me for standing here in front of him taxing him with irrelevant things in the middle of the night when he would rather being doing something completely different.

It's obvious that nothing is going to be resolved so easily. Running away is no solution, at best it could be seen as a manoeuvre. Sometimes this is how life goes. I remember my first time with a tart. I was sixteen, it was my birthday, and my present to myself was a woman. A madam who received visitors at home in Via Tuscolana, to become a man with. I was too timid to approach the ladies of the night, especially because it would mean asking one to jump on the back of my moped, a patched up Honda SH, the survivor of many accidents. Too uncomfortable, too exposed. Whereas the small ads in the paper made everything easier and more discreet. When it came to it I wanted to show I knew what I was doing, but when she saw the track marks on my arms she thought I was a junky, and it all ended badly. Well would you have liked to explain to her that my mother and father, to instil a sense of responsibility in me, allowed me to make self-withdrawals before I had reached the age of 18? Would you have liked to explain to her that my exhaustion and droopiness were only a temporary impediment? She slid me into a rubber and got off with a beggar's blow job. I mean it's not like I haven't had sex since then, it's just I've never paid for it again.

Now I am consoled by knowing how this mess came to happen. Without further useless details I'll just say that I *want* Anissa. From the day I first saw her half dead in an armchair in her friend's house. Then at her own home at death's door down in Torrino, and later, sad and angry in WOK, the sushi bar. Then there was that mess at the Shroom and again behind glass in Regina Coeli.

Since then, it's as if a part of me feels the need to go to Anissa, to be close to her, more intimately than making out, or rubbing against each other, or a push or a meeting of organs. I want to flow through her veins, wherever she is.

I know it sounds pathetic, what with her hooked up day and night to a drip and me not knowing where to turn or what to do to get her away from that legalised vein draining transfusion system.

Whatever, I don't want to share this stuff with Emory. I'm not going to tell him what I think about his way of running his business. The whole "trial by water" lark which he used to initiate me and who knows how many other poor sods into their roles as BloodBusters, is nothing more than an enormous pile of shit. A more exact definition would be: a low down and shameful way of choosing personnel.

I turn on my heels and leave.

Emory is not the type of man to kill me in cold blood. Ordering Glad to eliminate me and failing is somehow proof of this.

"Oh, and when you see *that* Anissa, send her my love."

Whatever happens, my ex-boss never misses an opportunity to rub salt on a wound. Part of me would like to scream out everything sticking in my throat, another part doesn't want to give him the satisfaction. I force myself not to turn around to see the sneer he must have on his face.

I motion to Ilario to get a move on, we're off, and before getting back into the taxbulance I remember the second reason we are here.

"Oh yeah, we dumped Farid outside. Keep the dogs on their leashes, or set them on him, whatever, it's up to you..."

With each step I strip off a piece of my uniform. It's as if my life has lost all its importance. Off with the scarlet coat. Am I important to Emory? Not even a little bit. I am one of the few survivors of his little personnel selection tricks. Now I am leaving the world of the BloodBusters. Off with the scarlet shirt.

At this point what is actually important? Haematax policies? That pile of crap forcing us to hunt our peers right down into their veins? Off with the trousers too. And money? In the name of which every other thing is pushed into second place, disputable, justifiable? I am down to my boxers so I pull my boots back on, the Pravaz in its case clutched tightly in my hand.

Given the turn things have taken, I don't care who lowers the curtains, the show is well and truly over. Maybe this is neither a courageous nor heroic way to act, but whatever, it is another way of surviving.

Tomorrow will be the start of a new ending.

I get back in the taxbulance and turn on the radio. They are playing *Wrong* by Depeche Mode.

Heart-o-matic

*Rule number twenty: tax yourself as you would
tax your neighbour.*

I give Nicola, sitting in the seat next to me, a friendly punch on
the shoulder. He is, as usual, snacking on a Haematogen bar, this
time it is a *grilled albumin* one.

"Have you really found a way of getting her let out?"

I've spent the last eight hours squeezing my brain and in the
end I came up with something.

"It wasn't easy but I managed to convince them."

"How did you do that?"

I'm almost scared to tell him the truth. Knowing about what
goes inside Regina Coeli isn't the greatest thing for a kid who
scoffs Em&Emos, Bloodshakes and Bloodae. "All you need to
know is I made them an offer they couldn't refuse."

"What kind of offer?"

I swear I never thought it was going to end like this.

I have no idea when the next bus will come along Via della
Lungara. Punctuality is not a Roman virtue. Looking behind me
there is nothing yet, that's a good sign, no social worker come to
exercise her crazy rights to be seen through the back window.

"C'mon, get out and I'll show you."

I pull the pneumatic trolley out of the taxbulance and start
unloading a stack of ten MT67F containers. My life savings.
Blood of my blood. Withdrawn from the Haematic Bank in Via
XX Settembre this morning.

The NEE-NAW racket of a siren is advancing on us rapidly. I
recognise it, Ilario's souped up siren coming to our appointment.
He pulls up at the junction and double parks, he turns the

siren off but leaves the flashing lights on. He winds down the window and lights up a rollie. He says nothing, jerking his head in greeting. I acknowledge his arrival in the same way and carry on unloading the crates.

So many things have gone wrong over the last few weeks. Only two, to be exact, though the rest wasn't easy either. Things I knew nothing about, like my recruitment on the front, things I couldn't have known anything about, like the illicit dealings between Emory and Catapano, things I would have liked to have avoided, like Anissa's caution, and lastly things that thanks to Ilario and old Glad I had found the way to sort out, bad vibes, like Farid's threats and my brush with bleeding out for a second time.

Now it's my turn. Sometimes the last step has the same flavour as the first. It depends where you decide to start counting from. It depends from which point you decide it really counts.

I wonder if this solution counts as a kind of psychotherapy: sorting something out, anything, whatever it is. The young Arab girl, Nicola, Anissa, my life even.

A flock of pigeons rise in flight from the Gianicolo hill. I think about the significance of this exact moment. Like, get out while you still can. Run and don't let anyone drag you down into the deep well of a life made up of rubbish, greasing palms, and blackmail. But who am I trying to kid, no one believes in this kind of pseudo-symbolism anymore. Reading meanings into the flight of birds, tarot cards, and tea leaves, are like labels, easy to stick on, just as easy to peel off. And underneath in the end you find there is nothing, or worse than nothing.

It's me against the rest of the world. I am awake, even though the anger inside me has not yet subsided.

Nicola is all bright-eyed and helps me push the laden trolley to the prison gates where a pair of guards are waiting for me.

A hundred metres away the door of Ilario's taxbulance opens. He is dressed up and looking good, and I hope he has had a shower too. Instead of coming to my side he goes the other way, towards Via della Lungara, where the sound of high heels on the cobbles is coming closer.

After having given a cursory glance at the haematorial file certifying the quality of my self-withdrawals, these two call another guard. He starts checking everything over again like a good little boy. He goes through every piece of information with a fine toothed comb, every haematic value, he reads through it without saying a word. Then he gets bored and stops keeping us on tenterhooks.

"Go ahead. This is all in order."

I wink at Nicola. He hasn't quite grasped the terms of the agreement. Whatever, when he sees the slender outline of his mother crossing the threshold of Regina Coeli he forgets everything and runs to her.

In the meantime, Ilario slows down the social worker with a street pick up line worthy of a great kerb crawler. If I know anything about him at all, with the tongue he's got on him, cut-off or not, he'll get straight to the point, hitting home with a few well aimed lines.

I'd even bet on the favourable outcome of the operation. Not least because she looks different. What I said to her the other time must have hit a nerve. Taking a look at her, I see they are chatting, better still, she is talking and he is nodding. Ilario, crafty lad that he is, is unfurling his cleverest most subtle cunning, a vocabulary of body language, non-verbal communication.

She lowers her gaze and runs a hand through her hair which is no longer trapped in a bun but loose on her shoulders. Her white skirt with blue flowers stops just above her knees, it bears no relation to the severe uniform she had on before. They might even end up getting sweaty in my colleague's taxbulance in the back lane by the Gianicolo hill. I bet when she's excited the social worker is as fast as she talks.

My head is full of fantasies.

Silhouetted against the gates of Regina Coeli, Anissa is pale, almost spiritual. I wonder if prison has the power to pull out the true nature of the people who end up in it. There are people who repent and those who don't; people who lose their way and people who find it again.

My arms feel swollen, my legs too, as though they've been

turned into sieves. The Pravaz is safe in my pocket, its barrel full.

Once, when I was a kid, while I was shaving, I cut my finger. Why am I remembering all these things right now? It was a clean but deep cut, just above a joint calloused by the strange way I had of holding my pen. The surprising thing was that it didn't bleed. Even though it was deep it wasn't enough to reach through the layer of dead skin. I was stupid to be surprised, because everyone knows callouses don't bleed. And that's why there are no tears on my face now.

Anissa hugs her son tightly and lifts her gaze to look daggers at me. She is as rigid as a neon shop sign, and I wonder if she's hiding any coded messages, feelings held in the cage of her bones, which I'm supposed to be able to decipher in some way.

I'll admit I don't know whether what hit me about Anissa was her air of someone ready to fight to the death, or the tragedy of her life, of a love blotted out by disease, of so many haematic errors, not least Nicola who was conceived under the shadow of the crazy idea of producing a Perfect Donor.

Who knows...Maybe I am drawn to her because of something I can't explain. An aura filled with grace despite the coarsening inflicted by her intubated detention. Maybe it is just my fault and it's nothing to do with her, I am attracted by mysteries more than needs.

Mother and son come towards me hand in hand, and when I lift mine to touch the bandages on her face Anissa lets me caress her. Seeing how she has been reduced I can imagine her ready to die for a different humanity at the drop of a hat, maybe even a better one. For me, having worked for the dregs of the human race, this idea sounds crazy.

I have never believed in coincidences, nor chance moving people from X to Y in an irreversible way. I'm not talking about playing dice, chess, or other stuff with probabilities to work out, I'm talking about something dark and chaotic, something similar to our free-will, something that often moves like leaves in the breeze or changes direction suddenly like lightning in a clear blue sky.

When I start thinking like this, well, it's better I stop straight away. Anissa reads my mind. "You know what we Robin Bloods say?"

"No, I don't know. You lot say so much..."

"We say that blood is a gift, and, on the contrary to time and work, it comes straight from a person's heart."

There isn't much to add. At least, not in words. So I pull out the Pravaz, and Nico's eyes widen.

"Wow! Cool! Can I see it? What, will you lend it to me? I'll show it to Lucy."

"No, I won't lend it to you. Syringes are for personal use only. Whatever, this is an exception, it's a loan for your mother."

Anissa shows the syringe to Nicola, looks at the full barrel and hugs it to her.

"I'll inject myself with it with great pleasure Alan."

My skin gets goosebumps. There is a practice, some people say it is erotic, of exchanging blood, like you can exchange other bodily fluids. I have never found the right partner to try it. I mean, can you imagine Ceci? She didn't like fresh blood. But people who have tried it say that every time the effect is revitalising. Because every transfusion of foreign blood makes the immune system more sensitive and increases the production of antibodies. Because high haematic excitability is a kind of high, a blood orgasm.

"I'm sorry, I've not got a drop of blood on me to exchange with you."

We almost laugh. The situation has become grotesque, almost to the point of being ridiculous. "Don't worry. You start, and tell me how it feels."

"I like you, Alan."

Are her words sincere or is it just something to say, like a banal form of thanks? Whatever,

I'm not exactly expecting Anissa to start purring. She looks so worn out I almost wonder if there is anything left in her veins at all. Hugging her would be the most natural thing, but her body looks dried out, as dry as an overworked gold vein. For me her blood has become solid gold, and I'm not talking about nuggets of Haematogen. Unlike gold though, that blood is only of any value if it stays *in* her body.

I pull out the keys to the taxbulance and leave them on the bonnet. "No one will bother you in this."

Nicola is even happier than before, Anissa a little less.

"So where are you going? Aren't you coming with us?"

I don't want you to take me for a completely crazy son of a bitch. The law allows this. I know a load of people who have been fleeced who have had to resort to it. The rest is just hypocritical whining from cowards, or worse, flea ridden penniless evaders.

The truth is that I owe myself something. A clean up, to use Emory's favourite words, if not complete atonement. For what I'm not absolutely certain, but if you dig deep enough you can always find something that needs forgiving. Maybe that's not even it. Maybe it's because nothing in the world can make up for the absence of a mother. I had my mother, but I've seen how devastating it can be not to have one around and I feel I owe Nicola and Anissa something. I know that sounds vague and abstract, I do know that, but seeing them together, side by side, makes it rather solid.

"There were no other available veins. You see the blood on its own wasn't enough..."

"If you go in there Alan, it will never be enough."

"You don't produce much per day, it'll take me less time. Whether you believe it or not, time is money and money is blood, so time is blood too."

I hate moments like this. Logical and inhuman. I hate the bitter wake they leave behind them, afterwards it stays stuck to your thoughts.

Finally the guards get their act together and get all the crates into the prison's depot. I'm handed over to a stocky warder who looks a bit wanting. First thing he does is push me with an excess of intimacy without even pretending to think he is my friend.

"Don't I know you?"

Filthy bastards like him have passed through the ranks of the South Rome team in droves.

"Course you do! We pulled back loads of plungers together..."

Maybe I've got it wrong, maybe he was one of the many who

don't have the balls to be a BloodBuster and end up watching over poor sods counting their steps in the cells. Without dipping into the Withdrawals Agency archive I'll never know. The fact is, right now, I don't know who is the worse off of the two of us.

Before saying goodbye to the Eternal City for an indefinite period of time governed by uncontrollable variables such as the price of blood on the stock market, the whims of the judge presiding over Anissa's appeal, and my own haematopoietic capacity, I see Nicola helping his mother into the taxbulance.

"Mum, are you still going to do holes for other people?"

"No, Nicola. I think it's time to consider our own happiness."

As I face the corridor, I don't know where to place the blame. With Farid. With Emory. With Catapano. With the Eternal City.

I am shown to a cell. I go in and yet another warden, thinner than any of them so far, sneers at me tauntingly.

How often have I unleashed that same sneer on a withdrawal client? It all fits. As soon as I am hooked up to a drip and my blood begins to trickle, I become my own scapegoat.

*

The cell looks towards the Gianicolo hill, or rather at the shadow it casts. My cell mate is Jesus Christ. That's what he says anyway. He says he has already served his time by living in this awful world. He says he has paid the taxes for all the sinning taxpayers. He says that each and every evader deserves a single punishment: eternal haematic damnation. It's not what you'd call fun being shut up with a madman like this. Sometimes he reminds me of Emory. The good thing is Jesus Christ listens to *Rare Tracce* by Rino Gaetano. The bad thing is he listens to it non-stop on loop, all day long.

Today the post came. It was a letter from my mum, answering mine telling her of my holiday here in Regina Coeli. She says I did the right thing. She says she can't help me though, because of her age.

During the first week, as expected, they bled me dry, and then again the week after, and the week after. A rather repetitive experience.

You just have to get used to it. You just have to stay calm. When it comes down to it, it's as if they're squeezing the life out of your veins and pushing it out through every pore.

In the end, you are not your blood.

Whatever, in every season there are whole days when the corner of sky I can see over the Eternal City doesn't clear up completely and stays solid looking, almost flaming red. Quite often from the uneven Gianicolo road and from below where the Lungotevere runs shaded by the lines of plane trees, I can hear wailing taxbulance sirens. Their call moves nothing within me.

In the distorted universe that Rome has become, I wouldn't be surprised if even evil turns out to be capable of performing miracles.

CPSIA information can be obtained
at www.ICGtesting.com
Printed in the USA
LVHW110548200420
654104LV00007B/1922